THE TROUBLE WITH *flirting*

Also by Rochelle Morgan

THE TROUBLE SERIES

The Trouble with Flying

The Trouble with Flirting

The Trouble with Faking

The Trouble with Falling

THE TROUBLE WITH flirting

ROCHELLE MORGAN

The Trouble with Flirting
By Rachel Morgan writing as Rochelle Morgan

First published in 2014. This edition 2017.

Copyright © 2014 Rachel Morgan

ISBN 978-0-9947040-3-0

I HAD EVERYTHING PERFECTLY PLANNED FOR MY FIRST year of university: I would be accepted to study my degree of choice; I would get into one of the best residences; I would secure myself an intelligent and attractive boyfriend; and, most importantly, I would finally ditch my high school nerd status. So eager was I to carry out my perfect plan, that—despite living on the other side of the world playing constant entertainer and caregiver to two German brats for the year leading up to Perfect Freshman Year—I had all my forms filled out and submitted long before any deadlines.

That, apparently, was a mistake.

Perhaps my forms landed at the bottom of the pile. Perhaps they were so early they ended up lost and someone only found them after the deadline had passed. Whatever the case, some grumpy admin lady took a look at my meticulously filled out residence application and came up with one word: rejected. My parents told me I should at least be grateful I was accepted to study my first choice of degree—a BBusSci in Marketing—at my number one university—UCT—but neither of them stayed in res when they were studying, so they have no idea what I'm missing out on.

Nevertheless, I moved onto Plan B. Digs. A room in a flat or a house. Surely I could find a group of people who needed a new housemate this year. After contacting everyone I had even the vaguest sort of friendship with at school, I found the light at the end of my darkened tunnel with Nicky, a fellow violinist from orchestra. "My dad owns a flat in Rondebosch," she told me, "and there's a second bedroom. I've been using it as a study, but I think Dad would appreciate the rent."

Great. Sorted. I was back on track for Almost Perfect Freshman Year. That is, until three minutes ago when Nicky sent me a message that completely annihilated Plan B.

Nicky: I'm SO sorry to do this to you a week before registration, but I can't offer you a place at the flat anymore. With the divorce and everything, my dad decided he has to sell it, so I'm going to stay with my aunt in Kenilworth. I'm so, so sorry. But I'm sure you'll find something.

Panics tightens my chest as I stare at the message. She's *sorry?* She's sure I'll find *something?* One freaking week before registration? THIS IS NOT HAPPENING! And I can't even get mad at her because her parents' divorce has been super messy, so I'll come across as mean and uncaring if I express my intense frustration.

My phone starts playing Dario Marianelli's *Mrs Darcy* from *Pride and Prejudice*. Sarah. Number one best friend, epic storyteller, and recent university dropout—which sounds a lot worse than it actually is. I flop back onto my queen-sized bed and answer the phone.

"Congratulations!" Sarah shouts before I can say anything.

"What?" For a moment I have no idea why she's congratulating me. Then I remember that this day hasn't been completely terrible. "Oh, yeah. Thanks."

"What do you mean, 'What?'?" she demands. "You pass your driver's test on the first go, and an hour later you've forgotten about it?"

"I happen to be having a housing crisis that is currently overshadowing the euphoria of becoming a licensed driver."

"A housing crisis? In that gigantic mansion you call home?"

"Not this house, silly. You know I'm supposed to be moving into a flat in Cape Town with Nicky next week?"

"Oh dear."

"Yeah. Her father's selling the flat."

"What?" Sarah sounds suitably horrified. "Where are you supposed to live then?"

"Well, at this point, I'll be camping in Adam's lounge." Adam. Number two best friend, fellow classic music lover, and UCT freshman this year.

Sarah laughs. "Does Adam know this?"

"Not yet."

"You should tell him. Not just to find out if his couch is available, but because he might know somewhere else you can stay."

"I doubt it." I pull a blanket over my legs, then reach for the aircon's remote control on my bedside table and increase the temperature a few degrees. "I'm pretty sure everyone's made a plan already for this year."

"Well, I guess that leaves Adam's couch then," Sarah says with a sigh. "It shouldn't be too bad. Waking up every morning with three guys walking through your living quarters, one of whom is Adam's Gross Cousin."

"Ew, okay, you're right. I should definitely ask him if he knows somewhere else I can stay."

"Or, you know, your parents could just *buy* a flat for you to live in. Or five flats. Then you can move around when you get bored."

"Ha ha." I inject as much sarcasm into my words as I can. "You know how monumentally stingy my parents are when it comes to their one and only child. I have to learn how to provide for myself, blah, blah, blah."

"Yeah, yeah, I've heard it all before. It's a miracle they're paying for your tuition and rent and not forcing you to use your au pair money for that."

I wind a strand of unruly red hair around my finger. "Don't worry, I'll be using that for all my other expenses."

"Well, let's hope it—oh, hang on." I twist another piece of hair around my finger and listen to the muffled noises coming from Sarah's side of the phone. "I'm sorry," she says a moment later. "I've gotta go. Aiden just arrived."

"Ooh." I make some kissing noises while Sarah tells me to shut up. We both end up giggling, and then I let her go so she can make out with the newfound love of her life.

I slide my phone into my shorts pocket, then roll off the bed and cross the room. I open the French sliding doors that lead onto my balcony and step outside to warm up in the baking sun. In a few minutes I'll be wilting, at which point it'll be time to go back into my air-conditioned room. I lean on the railing and look out across the golf course. Beyond it, the sea is flat like blue glass. A perfect day to be on the beach.

I wonder if I'll miss this place. The perfectly maintained fairways, the infinity pools, the golf cars zipping around.

Probably not. I'm ready to say goodbye. I'm ready for my next adventure.

I remove my phone from my pocket and search for Adam's number. He was the first person I called after Plan A fell through. Like me, he took a gap year and then decided to head to UCT this year, so he was also looking for accommodation in Cape Town for the first time. I got to him too late, though—he'd already made a plan with Gross Cousin Luke. Luke spent last year in a house with two other guys, one of whom decided to move back home at the end of last year, leaving a room free for Adam. Adam's Plan A worked out perfectly.

I've just found Adam's name under my recent contacts when the main theme from *Pirates of the Caribbean* starts playing and Adam's face appears on the screen. I'm tempted to leave it ringing for a while because I love the music so much, but my housing dilemma is more important.

I answer with, "Sarah told you, didn't she." I'm surprised she removed her lips from her boyfriend's long enough to make contact with anyone else.

"She just sent me a message," Adam says, his voice distorted against a noisy background.

"Where are you?" I ask.

"Home. Sorry, just—" I hear a shout, then a loud bang like the slamming of a door, and then the noise disappears. "Sorry, my brother's got this new habit of blasting his music as loud as possible the moment he gets home from school."

"Annoying."

"Yip. Anyway, I phoned to give you some awesome news."

"Oh yeah?" I head back inside and slide the French doors closed. "What's that?"

"Mike's transferring from UCT to Wits," Adam says, as excited as if he just presented me with a brand new car. Which, incidentally, I could use now that I'm a licensed driver.

"Who's Mike, and why is that good news?"

"It's good news for *you*, because Mike is one of the guys I was going to be sharing a house with this year."

I freeze in the middle of my bedroom. "What? Seriously?"

"Seriously."

"There's a room up for grabs?"

"There is."

"Ohmygosh, ADAM! You are a LIFESAVER!" I jump onto my bed and hug the nearest cushion while squealing with delight. "Oh. Wait. You're a guy."

"I am."

"And so is your cousin."

"I'm pretty sure he is."

"Ugh, my parents wanted me to stay with girls." I punch the cushion. "They were pretty insistent on that, remember? That's why I was so happy when I discovered Nicky had a spare room. Quiet, hardworking, *female* student. My parents thought it was perfect."

"Well, your parents have to realise that you don't have many options at this point. And they know me, which will probably help."

"Maybe."

"Play up the whole safety aspect. It's safer to stay with guys because they can beat up any criminals who break in."

"Yeah, I'm not sure mentioning criminals is gonna help."

"Well, remind them how amazing I am, and then say it's either this or they buy a flat for you."

I consider his suggestion for a moment. "That could actually work."

"It will work."

"Okay, I'll let you know tonight."

"You'd better." I hear the squeak of Adam's desk chair as he spins around on it. "The news is already out there that we have a free room now, so it's bound to go quickly."

"Eeek! Okay, chat later."

I put the phone down and start praying. "Please, please, please …"

From: Alivia Howard <livi-gem@gmail.com>
Sent: Mon 3 Feb, 7:39 pm
To: Adam Anderson <ADA007@gmail.com>
Subject: I send emails cos I'm old fashioned that way

I'm in!!!

____

"ROAD TRIP!" I JUMP DOWN THE LAST THREE STAIRS INTO the entrance hall and throw my arms around Sarah.

"I wish I could go with you," she wails into my hair.

I step back and gather my wavy mess of hair over one shoulder. "Sorry, didn't mean to choke you. And yes. I wish we were still doing Take One: Livi and Sarah Road-Trip to Cape Town." I peek into our Olympic swimming pool-sized living area, then turn back to Sarah and lower my voice. "Take two of this adventure is going to be super awkward. I've never spent so many hours with my mom in one go. We'll run out of things to talk about before we've left the province."

"Hey, this is a good thing, remember?" Sarah leaves her handbag on the entrance hall table and slides her phone into her pocket. "She wants to, like, bond with you, or whatever."

I let out a dramatic sigh. "Right, because she's spent the past nineteen years choosing her job over me, and now she's suddenly realised I might be leaving home for the last time."

"Exactly." Sarah pokes my arm. "So you'd better make the most of the next few days."

"Fine," I say with a groan, even though I know she's right.

"So, am I too late to help you pack?"

"Too late?" I take her arm and drag her up the stairs. "Sarah, my dear, I've barely begun." We reach my doorway, and Sarah gasps at the clothes, shoes, books, DVDs and other belongings strewn across my bedroom. It's as if every cupboard, drawer and shelf threw up.

"Oh my catastrophe. Livi! You're leaving at 5 am tomorrow morning. How are you going to get everything packed before then?"

"Well, because you're going to help me."

"I can't even see the floor. Where are we supposed to stand?"

"Don't be silly." I nudge shoes, a music stand, and a pile of photo frames out the way with my feet. I reach the bed and perch on top of the Harry Potter Marauder's Map cushion Sarah, Adam and Logan gave me for my fifteenth birthday. "Look, there's a path now," I tell Sarah.

"Uh huh." She doesn't sound convinced.

"Okay, so there's my one suitcase—" I point "—and there's the other. And there are a whole lot of boxes in the bathroom. So we're just going to pack as much stuff as will fit into my car, and then we'll be done."

"Oh, your car! I haven't seen it yet."

"It's hiding in the garage. It feels embarrassed in front of all the fancy Zimbali cars."

Sarah laughs as she climbs over a pile of sheet music and leans into my bathroom. "I know how that feels." She tosses an empty cardboard box to me, then fetches another one for herself.

"You should have seen my parents' faces when I brought it home," I continue. "My dad was like, 'You paid money for this piece of crap?'"

Sarah shakes her head, then points to the sheet music at her feet. "Are you taking all this?"

"Um, yes. So I told him that if he felt like donating a small amount of his obscenely large salary to his one and only daughter, I'd be happy to use it towards a new car."

"I'm guessing that didn't work."

"No." I start hunting my bedroom floor for shoes and packing them into the box. "So then I told them that my car is actually a Transformer in hiding, and if it wanted to, it could transform into a sleek new Ferrari or a Lamborghini or any one of those posh cars whose names I don't know."

Sarah smiles. "I bet they had *no* clue what you were talking about."

"Of course not."

I move on to choosing a selection of my favourite DVDs while Sarah starts folding all the clothes I threw onto the chair in the corner. "You said this was the 'yes' pile, right?"

she asks after a few minutes. "The clothes you *are* taking with?"

"Yes." I tape the box of DVDs closed and look up.

"Are you sure you want to take this?" She holds up a black lacy nightgown.

"Whoa! What the bleep? That isn't mine."

"Okay." Sarah lets out a relieved laugh. "I was about to say you've got some explaining to do about exactly what went on in Germany last year."

"No, definitely not. That must be my mom's." And I do *not* want to think about her wearing it.

Sarah throws the nightgown into the passage. "Well, we definitely don't need Adam or Gross Cousin Luke seeing you in that."

"Ew! No, no, no."

"You know, he might not be gross anymore," Sarah says. "We haven't seen him since … grade nine?"

"I think so. He didn't seem to visit Adam much after that." I sit on the floor beside my sock and underwear drawer and cross my legs. I have way too many socks, so it's time to chuck the old ones. "Anyway, maybe he's not gross anymore, but all I can think of is that last summer holiday and how he used to stare at us every time we visited Adam."

"And he had that dirty blond hair that was actually, like, dirty for real, not just dirty in colour."

"Yes, all greasy and long." I aim for the bin in the corner of my room and send two pairs of socks sailing towards it. "And it would hang in his face."

"And he would suck the ends of it."

"So creepy." My giggle joins Sarah's laughter. I toss a knotted bundle of old socks at her and laugh even harder when it bounces off the side of her head and lands inside one of the handbags hanging on my wall.

"We shouldn't laugh, you know." She reaches up for the sock bundle and throws it back at me. I dodge, and it knocks a tube of hand cream off my bedside table. "I mean, we were hardly the definition of cool back then. The popular crowd at school probably called *us* gross."

That wipes the smile off my face. "Really? They called us *gross?*"

"Yeah, you see? It's not nice being called gross," she teases.

"Hey, you called him Gross Cousin Luke just as much as I did." I'm starting to feel a little guilty, though. Nobody deserves to be called gross, not even if they suck their hair or frequently do the creepy stalker staring thing. Or play in the school orchestra or sing in the choir. "Did they really call us gross?" I ask as I gather up a pile of underwear and add it to my suitcase.

"No idea," Sarah says. "Who cares, anyway? You shouldn't worry about what people think of you, Liv."

"I know," I say, hoping I sound like I mean it. I do worry, though. The nerd label never bothered Sarah and Adam that much, but it bothered me. And clearly it bothered Logan too, since he cut off all communication with his nerd friends after the four of us left high school. "Hey, you haven't heard anything from Logan, have you?" I ask.

"Nothing since that last get-together we had before you and Adam went overseas and Logan left for Cape Town. Oh, hey, I wonder if you'll bump into him." She stands up and carries a neatly folded pile of clothes over to my suitcase. "He's at UCT, isn't he?"

"Yes. He's in second year now, obviously, but we're in the same faculty, so maybe I'll see him. That'll certainly be an awkward conversation."

"And you have to tell me all about it, if it happens." Sarah turns and surveys my room with her hands on her hips. "Can we move the packed things into the passage? There's still barely any room to move in here."

"To the passage," I announce loudly, pointing at my doorway before picking up the nearest box of shoes. Sarah rolls her eyes and mutters something that includes the word 'dramatic.'

We've lined up several boxes, a bag of hangers, my music stand, and my violin case when Dad appears at the top of the stairway in his work suit. He's home earlier than usual. "You'll be done soon, I hope?" he says. "It's our last dinner together tonight. I was hoping we could enjoy it without being rushed."

"Yes, yes, of course." I look at Sarah. "Less chatter, more packing."

She salutes, and I stick my tongue out at her.

It takes us two and a half more hours, but by 7:30 pm we've finished packing everything that will fit into my car. I want to hang out with Sarah for a while longer, but Mom is giving me that look and making comments about how she and I need to get to bed soon so we can be up early to face our full day of driving.

I walk Sarah out to her car. "I'm sorry," I say. "I'd ask you to stay for dinner, but I was told yesterday that tonight is Family Night." Translation: awkward, tense conversation so my workaholic lawyer parents can tick 'bonding with daughter' off their to-do lists.

"Don't worry, I understand," Sarah says. Her car beeps at us as the doors unlock.

"And I'm sure you're desperate to get back to Aiden, anyway," I add.

Her cheeks go pink and she smiles at her feet. As the fair-skinned redhead, I think I'm supposed to have the monopoly on uncontrollable blushing, but I've never been as bad as Sarah. "Yeah, I haven't seen him all day," she says.

Oh, wow, ALL DAY? I want to make fun of her, but I think of a certain dark-eyed German guy and remember what torture it was when I went a whole day without seeing him.

"He was meeting with some professor dude today about studying further here," Sarah says. "He has some options in Joburg, but obviously I'm hoping he'll end up somewhere in Durban. Anyway, no matter where he chooses to study, he still has to go home in two weeks when his holiday ends. Then he has to organise study visas and all that other boring admin stuff."

"But he'll be back—that's the important part." Her blush intensifies, and I laugh at her.

"I hope you find someone equally amazing," she says,

nudging me with her elbow.

"Oh, I am going to find someone *truly awesome*, do not worry."

We hug and squeal and giggle some more, and then I try really hard not to cry. "I'm not saying goodbye," I tell her, "because I'll see you again soon. I'll be home in April for the short holiday, which is actually really soon. So make sure you're in Durban then, not jetting off to some exotic writing retreat or something." After a year of studying courses she hated, Sarah decided to leave university and focus on honing her writing skills so she can publish amazing stories that everyone will love. I have no doubt she'll be famous one day, and then I can tell everyone my best friend is a celebrity.

"I'll be here," she says. "And don't forget to tell me *every* exciting thing that happens to you."

I squeal again. "This is going to be even more exciting than Germany!"

"THERE IT IS," I SAY, POINTING TO THE ROAD SIGN AS MY mother navigates the narrow streets of Rondebosch in the 'piece of crap' I've decided to name The Tin Man. "Toll Road. That's the one."

"Oh, finally," she says with a small laugh. Her relief mirrors my own. An entire day in the car with her yesterday was painful. She took the first driving shift, so I was able to sleep through the early hours of the morning. After I woke up, she insisted on driving further because she didn't feel tired at all. I told her I need to practise, and what better way to get it than the 1600 kilometres between Durban and Cape Town, but she told me to relax a little longer. So that left me in the passenger seat with my legs wrapped around a cooler bag wondering what to talk about and feeling anything but relaxed.

She asked me about random stuff, like what I'm most

looking forward to this year and what societies I plan to join. When she ran out of questions, I tried to think of all the things I hadn't yet told her about Germany—not the dark-eyed guy of noble birth I managed to fall for, of course—and after that, we lapsed into silence. I couldn't handle it, though, so I put on one of my collections of epic movie scores and told her about the game Adam and I used to play. We'd put the music on shuffle and see who could name the movie first each time a new track started. But Mom didn't know any of the movies—and didn't seem to appreciate me yelling out "The Hobbit! Braveheart! Indiana Jones!"—so after a few tracks went by, we simply listened to the music. Three times.

I was so glad when we reached the B&B Mom had booked for last night, I think I climbed out before she'd even brought the car to a complete stop. She suggested we get to bed as soon as possible so we could leave even earlier this morning—and I had no problem agreeing with her.

Now, as we turn into Toll Road, I'm so excited to finally be here it's all I can do to contain the squeal threatening to burst from my lips. "We made it, Mom. We're actually here!" I squeeze her arm, then check my phone for the message from Adam to make sure I've got the right house number. "That one." I point to a gate that was probably painted white once upon a time, but is now more rust than paint. I call Adam.

"Hey," he answers after three rings. "Are you here?"

"Yes! Open up, please."

As we reach the gate, it shudders, then starts rolling open

at the speed of a granny pushing a walking frame.

Mom beams at me while we wait for the gate. "10:17 am," she says. "We made excellent time."

"We did." My smile matches hers. "Well done."

Mom drives through the gate, looking for a spot to park. Adam's car—which belonged to his grandfather until two weeks ago—is taking up most of the short driveway. In front of his car the driveway ends at a single garage, which I'm guessing is where Luke's car is.

"Well, I suppose we'll be parking on the grass," Mom says, turning the steering wheel and aiming for the tangled weeds in front of the house. We unstick ourselves from the car seats, climb out, and Mom places her hands on her hips as she looks around. "Well. The, uh, garden could certainly do with some work."

"Hey, you made it," Adam calls from the open front door.

"Hello!" I wave, then run—or rather, attempt to run— through the weed jungle towards him. "When did you get here?" I ask after I've jumped up the two steps onto the verandah and hugged his skinny frame. "Yesterday, right?"

"Yes. And my mom's been in a cleaning frenzy ever since."

"Livi! You've arrived!" As if to illustrate Adam's point, his mother appears in the doorway behind him, complete with a pair of yellow gloves, a feather duster in one hand, and a bandana keeping her hair out of her face. "It's *wonderful* that you'll be sharing a house with Adam and Luke." I smell Handy Andy when she hugs me. "Oh, hello!"

She waves over my shoulder, and I turn back to see a startled look on my mother's face. I doubt my mother's ever held a feather duster in her life, and the only reason she knows which supermarket aisle to find the rubber gloves in is because she buys them for the two maids who keep our house clean. A second later, the startled look is gone, replaced with the pleasant smile she keeps for acquaintances and strangers.

"Lynda, how lovely to see you," she says, walking up the stairs. "You poor thing, working so hard to clean this house. Livi will be happy to take over now."

I give Adam a look. *See how she doesn't offer her help?*

"Oh, don't be silly," Lynda says with a laugh and a wave of her feather duster. "I'm happy to do it. Cleaning everything out helps me to see all the amazing potential this house has. It was disgustingly dirty after a year with three boys living in it. And it's half-empty because most of the furniture belonged to Mike and he took it with him to Wits, but we found this darling little second-hand furniture shop yesterday afternoon. I'm sure we can find plenty of affordable items there to fill the house."

"Lovely," Mom says. Her smile stays perfectly in place, but Lynda may as well be speaking a different language. 'Affordable' isn't something my mother ever considers when furnishing a room. Lynda heads back into the house, saying, "And we discovered an ancient lawn mower in the garage, so Adam's going to tame the garden later this afternoon."

Adam gives me a look similar to the one I just gave him.

"My mother is a slave driver," he mutters.

"Your mother is awesome."

"You wouldn't say that if you were the one forced to spend an hour scrubbing mould in the shower this morning."

I make a show of sniffing the air around him. "So that's why you smell like chemicals."

"I think I lost a few thousands brain cells inhaling those chemicals." He leans against the doorway and watches my mother following his. "Okay, so my mom is now going to give your mom a tour of all the parts of the house she's already cleaned, she's going to point out the layers of grime the landlord has either ignored or knows nothing about, and then the two of them will comment on how male students, and possibly men in general, are the messiest creatures on the planet."

"I'm guessing you've had to listen to that little speech several times."

"It's a song that's been on repeat since we got here." He sighs. "This house is in pretty bad shape. Doesn't bother me too much—being a messy male student and all that—but it's going to be a definite step down for you, princess."

I punch his arm; he knows I hate that name. "Hey, you have no idea how much I'm looking forward to living here, okay? I'm tired of being alone inside a house large enough to shelter a small village."

"Really?" He looks doubtful. "You're tired of Chateau Zimbali?"

"Yes! I want to be here. Creaky floorboards, old pipes,

rusted window frames, the works. Bring it on, Toll Road."

He smiles. "Well, we'd better unpack The Tin Man and get you moved in, then."

"Wait, I want to see inside first. Give me the tour."

Adam was right about the house being in bad shape, but his mother was also right about it having potential. The cracked window in the bathroom can be covered up with a curtain, the splintered floorboard on one side of the living room can be concealed with a couch, and the fireplace that looks like it was used as a rubbish bin on top of about twenty years of ash will be quite charming once cleaned up. The kitchen, which hasn't yet been tackled by Lynda, is currently a health hazard, but the counter tops are probably a pleasant colour beneath the layer of congealed food. At least, I hope that's a layer of something and not the actual colour of the counters. I put my hand over my mouth and try to keep my stomach from reacting.

Across the passage from the bathroom is a closed door, which is apparently where Luke is hiding. Further along, past a peeling section of paint, is Adam's room. I recognise the grey-and-white striped duvet cover and the computer screen on the desk. Everything else is still in boxes.

"And here's your room," Adam says, gesturing to an open doorway opposite his. The room is empty, aside from the built-in cupboards along the wall opposite the window. Smudges of dirt cover the vomit-coloured paint, and the wooden floorboards are dull and scratched from years of wear. At least the room is a decent size, though. I walk to the window, which is wide and gives me an excellent view of the overgrown back garden. I think I spot a wheelbarrow out there, but it's been taken hostage by a tangle of weeds.

"Well, this will be nice, won't it, Livi?"

I turn as my mother walks into the room. "Yes, this place rocks." I spot a poster of a half-naked woman on the back of the door. I wander over and push the door open completely so Mom won't see it. Unlike her, I actually mean what I'm saying. She's trying to keep her nose from turning up in disgust, whereas I can't wait to get all my things in here and make this space mine. Sure, it's not exactly Chateau Zimbali—as Adam likes to refer to it—but that's the point. Chateau Zimbali is the last thing I want.

"Help me unpack?" I say to Adam.

We navigate back and forth across the weed wilderness while balancing boxes and bags in our arms. Adam's long legs don't have much of a problem, but I trip over hidden garden debris more than once. When I fall into a bush for the third time, spilling hangers out of the packet I was balancing on top of a box of shoes, Adam orders me back inside the house while he carries the last few items across the garden.

"You missed some hangers, Princess Clumsy," he says as he squeezes through my doorway with my puffy winter jacket over his shoulder, a suitcase in one hand, and several hangers in the other.

"Hey, knock it off with the princess names, Mr Dust Bunny." I take the jacket and open one of the cupboards to hang it up.

"Mr Dust Bunny?" Adam peers into the mirror inside

the cupboard door. "What are you talking about?"

"There's, like, a whole family of dust bunnies living behind your right ear," I tell him. "Someone obviously told them your mom was on the loose with a feather duster, so they evacuated whatever cruddy corner they were living in. They're refugees now. You should take care of them."

Adam adjusts his glasses, then swats at the cobwebs in his dark hair and mutters something about my tendency to exaggerate. His hair is longer now than it used to be, and product-free. He did the short, spiky, gelled look in high school, like all the other guys who thought they were awesome, but this more natural look is so much better on him. I stand back and nod approvingly. "You are well on your way to completing Project Ditch the Nerd, Adam. Good job."

He rolls his eyes and heads out of my room without commenting. He bangs on a door. "Hey, Luke, thanks for all your help with unpacking," he shouts. "Livi really appreciates it."

Crap! What the hell is Adam doing? I'm happy for Luke to stay hidden in his cave and never come out. I rush into the passage to tell Adam to shut up and leave Luke alone. The bathroom door opens and my mother emerges looking traumatised. I guess the toilet experience wasn't up to her high standards.

"All right, then," she says, holding her wet hands away from her body as though trying to avoid further contamination. "Shall we, uh, go and find some furniture for your bedroom?"

"Yes. Sounds great." Maybe I can get out of here before Luke surfaces and starts the creepy staring thing. I dash back into my room and find my handbag. "Okay, Mom, let's go." I find her in the lounge watching Lynda kneeling in front of the fireplace giving instructions to Adam. "Thanks for helping me carry stuff," I say to him. "We'll see you later."

He gives me a wide-eyed look that clearly says, *You're leaving me here?*

"Um, hi, everyone."

Crap.

I cringe at the sound of Luke's voice behind me. I suppose I can't avoid him indefinitely, though. I may as well get the awkward greeting over with, then try to stay away from his creepy gaze as much as possible.

I swivel around—and drop my handbag on the floor.

Oh. My. Incredible. Hotness.

It's a universal truth that the majority of people are more attractive at the end of their teenage years than at the beginning. Who hasn't had the urge to burn their pimply-skinned, brace-faced, weird-haired early high school photos? I know I have. Then you get the people who are lucky enough to become not just attractive, but properly beautiful. You look at their pictures on Facebook and wonder where their supermodel genes were in grade eight when no one seemed to fit into their own skin properly. And then you get the people who look so vastly different it's entirely possible they climbed into a new body.

Luke is one of those people.

His skin is perfect, his blue eyes are bright, and his chiseled jaw and artfully tousled bed-head would make any of the top one hundred hottest men in the world jealous. The only thing remaining of the creepy boy who used to stare at me is his hesitant demeanour and the way his eyes dart away when I try to meet his gaze.

After several moments of gaping on my part, Luke looks up briefly, gives me a shy smile, and says, "Welcome to Cape Town, Livi. Um … I hope you enjoy staying here."

Blank. I'm going blank. My knees feel oddly weak, and I think my mouth is still open.

"Thank you, Luke" my mother says, filling in the gap left by my sudden inability to talk. "Livi is so looking forward to living in this … lovely house."

Be cool, Livi. BE COOL. Salivating over hot guys like a groupie at a concert is not part of Project Ditch the Nerd. I suck in a breath of air and clear my throat. "Yeah, um, thanks. Anyway, Mom and I were just heading out to do some shopping." I casually bend down and pick up my handbag, arranging the expression on my face so it says, *No big deal. I drop my handbag all the time. Nothing to do with the hot guy in the room.* I catch Adam's eye, and he sticks a finger in his mouth and mimes puking. I glare at him before straightening.

"Yes, we have lots to do," Mom says. "Lynda, do let me know if you need anything for the house. I'll be happy to pick it up while we're out." After nodding to Adam's mom, she heads past Luke. I follow her, refusing to look at the blue eyes that could potentially freeze me in place.

"This is going to be so much fun," Mom says to me as we climb into my car. "We haven't shopped together in *ages.*" She doesn't ask if I want to drive, and I don't offer. I have messages to send.

Livi: You didn't tell me your cousin is now one of the hottest guys on the planet.

Adam: I don't really think of guys in that way.

Livi: Adam! As one of my best friends, it's your duty to point out attractive potential boyfriend material to me.

Adam: *throwing up* I don't think it is, actually.

Livi: You could have mentioned his hotness when you invited me to live with you guys.

Adam: Perhaps I was waiting to see you become a speechless, handbag-dropping mess.

Livi: *sigh*

Adam: *throwing up again*

My mother is scared of old furniture that's been used by other people—"You never know what might be living in it now"—but after a lengthy argument, I remind her of what she and Dad always say about *not* giving me the best, biggest, and newest of everything because they don't want to raise a spoiled child, and that's how we end up heading to the second-hand shop Lynda mentioned. I breathe a sigh of relief after winning that battle—I can only imagine the princess names Adam would come up with if a delivery van from the most expensive home decor store at the V&A Waterfront showed up in Toll Road to drop off my designer furniture.

After an hour or so of Mom trying to touch as little as possible and me examining every item of furniture in every room of the rundown house in Muizenberg that now serves as a second-hand furniture shop, I've chosen my collection: a desk, bed, bedside table, bookcase, and a comfy old armchair covered in a hideous green-and-brown patterned material that I assure my mother I'll be covering with a throw the moment it's delivered.

"Okay, that's all," I say to Mom after pointing out my chosen items to the guy behind the make-shift counter in the centre room of the house. "Do you, um, want me to pay?" I never know with my parents if I'm going to catch them in a generous mood or a Livi-needs-to-learn-how-to-support-herself mood. On the one hand, they were happy to pay for my ticket to Germany last year, and they've assured me they're fine with paying my rent this year, but on the other hand, they flat-out refused to buy me a car.

Mom heads to the counter without saying a word. She whips out her credit card, gives me her be-grateful-I'm-paying-for-this look, then exclaims in surprise at the low total. "Oh, goodness, Livi. These things cost hardly anything. Are you sure they aren't going to fall apart five minutes after they're delivered?"

The guy behind the counter assures her that all items are thoroughly checked when they come into the shop, and anything broken is fixed before going on display. Mom looks doubtful but pays for everything anyway while I write down our Toll Road address so someone can deliver everything this afternoon.

"Now that you've had your second-hand shop experience, we're going to the Waterfront," Mom says as we climb back into my car and wind the windows down to let some air into the oven-like interior. "There's a hotel there with the most gorgeous views out onto the water, and their sushi is simply superb. Your father and I ate there often the last time we were on holiday in Cape Town. How about we have lunch there? And then we can shop for the rest of your things. Some curtains and bedding and a decent mattress— and something to cover up that awful armchair you seem to like so much. Perhaps I'll even treat you to some Egyptian cotton items."

After the shopping expedition is over, and my furniture has arrived at the house, I spend the remainder of the afternoon helping Adam and Lynda clean. Mom hangs my curtains, makes my bed, and takes her time arranging cushions and other frivolous decorative items around my room so she won't be roped into anything that involves dust, household detergents, or a wet cloth. She even unpacks all my clothes and shoes and arranges them neatly in my cupboard when it becomes clear that the only other task left in the house is cleaning kitchen shelves.

As evening draws closer, Mom goes for a walk and comes back with a selection of gourmet sandwiches from a restaurant she found a few roads away. Mom, Adam, Lynda and I—not Luke, who left the house so quietly no one is sure exactly when it happened—sit on the floor of the empty lounge eating our sandwiches, and Mom and Lynda reminisce about a time long ago when their children were young and the idea of sending them off to university seemed like an eternity away. Even my mother, whose butt probably hasn't touched a floor since she was a teenager, seems to be relaxed and enjoying herself. I suddenly wish Dad were here too. This is what our last dinner together should have been like: laughing about the past and dreaming of the future.

At the end of the evening, when Mom and I have finally unpacked and put away all the stuff I brought with, I collapse onto the mattress on my bedroom floor—a blow-up mattress borrowed from Sarah's family—while Mom climbs into my bed.

My lamp clicks off.

"I enjoyed dinner," I say through the darkness.

After a pause, Mom answers with, "Me too."

I roll onto my side and pull the blanket up over my shoulder; the evenings are cooler here than in Durban. "I kinda wish Dad had come with us."

The pause is longer this time, and my mind is already drifting into that half-awake, half-asleep state when Mom's second answer comes, quieter than her first. "Me too."

Sunday dawns bright, beautiful, and disgustingly hot. I layer sunscreen over every exposed part of my body, and Adam and I head into the garden to battle the weeds while Mom and Lynda drive to the second-hand shop together to find furniture for our living area. I thought Mom would try to find a way out of returning to 'that bug-infested place' and simply offer to pay half of whatever Lynda chose, but, to my surprise, she seemed happy to go with.

The sun climbs higher, Adam fights with the lawnmower, our moms return, the furniture arrives, we spend all afternoon transforming the house into a home, and before I know it, it's time to drive my mother to the airport and say goodbye.

We're quiet in the car. I'm concentrating on the road—having actually been allowed to drive my own car this time—and Mom doesn't seem to have any words to say other than those required to direct me to the airport. It's only when we climb out at the drop-off zone and she's standing in front of me with her small suitcase at her feet that I notice her red eyes and trembling lips. She blinks and presses her lips together, swallowing hard as she tries to remain composed. I've never seen my mother in an emotional state like this before, and suddenly I feel like crying.

"I … I don't think I ever told you how much I missed you when you were in Germany," she says. "It was all arranged in such a rush, and then you were gone, and we'd barely said goodbye to each other." She tucks a stray piece of hair behind her ear. "Now you're leaving again, and this time I want to say goodbye properly. I want to say all the things that should be said."

"Mom, it's … it's okay. You don't *have* to say anything." Deep Meaningful Conversations have never been my mother's strong point. She gets uncomfortable when people start getting too personal. So does my dad, for that matter. It's a miracle I didn't end up with the emotional IQ of a brick wall.

She smiles at me and takes hold of my hand. "I know we haven't always found it … easy … to talk to one another. But I hope you know how much I love you and how excited I am for you embarking on this new journey in your life. Please don't think that I don't want to know about it. I do. I want to know everything. Well," she adds with a laugh, "perhaps not *everything*."

Holy hippogriff, did my mother just make a joke? On top of getting personal? Who is this woman! I wrap my arms around her and laugh to keep myself from crying. "I'll be sure to keep you updated."

After a few more sniffles, she gives me one last smile and turns away. I watch her go, trying to imprint this relaxed, smiling, jeans-and-T-shirt version of her over the suit-and-high-heels image my brain always defaults to when I think the word 'Mom.'

On the drive back to Toll Road, I'm too busy concentrating on the dual task of not getting lost and not crashing into something to focus on my feelings. But after parking my tin oven in the vastly improved front garden and looking out at the tall trees across the road that hide the mountain, I'm aware of an odd mixture of nostalgia and excitement. A kind of mourning for everything I took for granted in the past—passing notes to Logan during Afrikaans class because Mev. Pretorius was always too ditzy to notice; lying on the grass in Our Spot every breaktime at school; sleepovers with Sarah—and a joyful anticipation for tomorrow and every day after that.

It only takes about half a minute for the excitement to begin burying the nostalgia. It rises up like bubbles in a jacuzzi and blots everything else out. I slam the car door shut and bound up the stairs to let myself in—with my very own key. "I'm home!" I shout, just to see what it feels like to say those words.

Home. My home.

It feels good.

"Good to know you're still alive," Adam shouts back from his bedroom.

I dance down the passage, run into his room, and jump onto the bed with a squeal. "This is really happeniiiiing!"

I'VE NEVER BEEN PARTICULARLY GOOD WITH EARLY mornings, but I'm up with the sunrise on Orientation Day Number One. I barely slept all night, even though the linen spray Mom spritzed all over my high thread count sheets is supposed to create 'a mood of peace and tranquillity' with its 'delicate fragrance.' I should be exhausted, but TODAY IS THE DAY my fabulous university life begins, and nothing can keep me in bed a second longer.

Despite our cleaning efforts, an unpleasant damp odour still clings to the bathroom, but I soon manage to mask it with the scent of strawberry body sorbet and grapefruit shampoo. I exit the bathroom in a cloud of steam, waltz into my bedroom, and throw my cupboard doors open dramatically. After almost losing my towel and checking behind me to make sure my bedroom door is closed, I step back to survey my outfit options. I did a complete revamp of my wardrobe during the post-Christmas sales, paying close attention to items considered Fashionable rather than Comfortable.

After far too much consideration, I pick out a tight-fitting, blue-patterned mini dress that shows off plenty of my recently tanned, I-wish-they-were-longer legs and just a hint of cleavage. I have to suck my tummy in and stand up as straight as possible to pull it off, but I'll be wearing heels, so that'll remind me not to slouch.

After shimmying into the dress, I grab my phone and check the numbers on the screen. Hmm. I've got fifty minutes until the time Adam and I agreed we'd leave for Upper Campus, and I've still got to eat breakfast, do make-up, and, of course, tame my hair. Frizzy mess is not part of Project Ditch the Nerd. Deciding to do hair first, I plug in my straightener and drag my desk chair in front of the mirror inside my cupboard.

Half an hour later, I open my door, flick my sleek hair over my shoulder, and sashay down the passage towards the kitchen. This is excellent practise for my high-heeled sexy walk. I should grab a bowl of cereal and do a few laps up and down the passage while eating. I need to know I can pull off the sexy walk without actually thinking about it.

"Good morning," I sing as I enter the kitchen and find Adam in boxers, a wrinkled T-shirt, and hair pointing in a hundred different directions. He's typing a message on his phone—probably to girlfriend Jenna who's stuck on the other side of the country finishing her last year of high school—with one hand while taking a bite of toast from the other. He doesn't look remotely close to being ready. "Hey, you know we're leaving in twenty minutes, right?"

He swallows and carries on typing. "Yeah. I can get ready in—" He looks up, and both his jaw and the piece of toast hit the floor. His eyes travel all the way down to my peep-toe heels and back up again, freezing on my face. He clears his throat. "You … why are you … where are you going?"

"Uh, to campus? Just like you?"

"In that?"

I place my hands on my hips and give him a glare to hide my disappointment. This is not the reaction I was hoping for. "Project Ditch the Nerd, remember? Losing labels like Orchestra Geek, Choir Monkey, and The Ginger."

"And this—" he gestures to my dress "—is supposed to help?"

"Yes. If I have to be a ginger, I will at least be a hot ginger." And with that, I turn and flounce from the kitchen. Who needs breakfast anyway? Not me. Not if I'm planning to fit into dresses like this every day. So instead I take photos of my bedroom and send them to Sarah along with the message, **Remember Gross Cousin Luke? He has been replaced by World's Hottest Hunk Luke! No kidding. Deadly serious. And he is still super shy, which makes him even more adorable. Now I feel bad for always thinking he was creepy when he was just too shy to talk to us. Although there was the hair-sucking thing … which thankfully he doesn't do anymore. Now he has hot-guy hair. Anyway, I'll call you later!**

Adam and I are in his car reversing out the driveway less

than twenty minutes later, because apparently that's all the time you need to get ready when you don't care about making a good first impression—which Adam clearly doesn't in his *Beam Me Up, Scotty* T-shirt. I mean, as a *Star Trek* fan, I appreciate it, but he has to realise it'll put him immediately in the nerd box in the eyes of everyone he meets today.

"I'm not sure you realise how big Upper Campus is," Adam says as we join the morning traffic on Main Road.

"What? Of course I do. I've seen the maps."

"And I'm not sure you realise how much competition there is for parking, meaning we'll probably be walking from Middle Campus—if we're lucky."

"Yeah, I get that." And I get where he's going with this line of conversation. "And before you continue, yes, I still chose to wear these shoes, and yes, my feet will be fine."

"Okay," he says, his tone implying he knows he'll be proved right before the day is over.

"Besides, you've heard of the Jammie Shuttles, right? The blue busses that are free for students? We can just hop on one of those and get a ride to Upper Campus."

"Okay." That same annoying tone.

"You'll see," I tell him. "Today is going to be awesome."

And it is. I mean, the welcome talk in Jammie Hall isn't all that inspiring, and the campus and library tours aren't exactly thrilling, but simply *being here* is incredible. Walking along Jammie Plaza, seeing the ivy-covered buildings, hearing the laughter and chatter of the students around me … it's everything I've been dreaming of. I have to admit, there aren't many girls dressed as fabulously as I am, but I do see a large number of short dresses and skirts, even if they aren't all as tight as mine and only a few are paired with heels. Okay, so maybe I'll save heels for once a week.

After a traumatising talk about sex education and STDs—don't they know we heard enough of that stuff at school?—we're sent off for a lunch break. I try to attach myself to a group of girls who look like they've always been part of the cool crowd, but before I can greet them and introduce myself, one of them waves to a guy nearby, and they all hurry towards him.

Right. I guess I'll try again after lunch.

I swivel around on the spot, hoping to see a sign pointing me in the direction of food that will satisfy my gurgling, breakfast-deprived stomach. All I see are the many tables, gazebos and umbrellas set up on Jammie Plaza for the clubs and societies promoting themselves this week. I wander towards them, wondering if any of those tables sell food.

There's a club for just about any activity you could ever hope to do. Ballroom dancing, wine tasting, astronomy, film, debating, skydiving, archery—archery! That is epic! I could be the next Green Arrow or Hawkeye. I could be the next Katniss! I wonder where archery ranks in terms of 'cool' clubs, though. Probably not that high.

I continue walking. My eyes glide over hockey, tennis, rowing—

Wait. Is that … Logan?

I take a few steps closer to the busy rowing club table. "Logan?" The laughing guy with the blond hair and the arms and shoulders that are *way* bigger than the last time I saw them looks up. His eyes travel over me, and when they're done, he looks almost as shocked as Adam did this morning.

He stands up and comes towards me. "Livi?"

I cross my arms. "Oh, you remember me?"

"Livi, what do you mean? Of course I—"

"You haven't replied to a single email, text or Facebook message I've sent you over the past year. And you haven't spoken to Adam or Sarah either. What happened? You got here and we were no longer good enough for you?"

"Liv, come on." He reaches out and runs his hand down my arm. He smiles, but I can see the uneasiness—the guilt—in his eyes. "My life is insanely busy here. I'm involved in everything. Res and sports and committees, and then having to study to pass all my courses on top of that. I didn't forget about you guys, I just haven't had time to—"

"Oh, yeah, no time." I nod. "I've seen the pictures on Facebook. I can understand why you'd have no time for us with all those parties you go to."

"Liv, that's not what I meant."

"Look, I get it, okay? Being involved in everything. I mean, I want that too. I want to be the life of the party, not standing on the outside wondering where my invitation is. It just would have been nice if you hadn't ignored your old friends while meeting all your new ones."

Logan looks at his shoes. "I know. I'm sorry." He glances up. "Do you forgive me?"

"Maybe."

"Will it help if I tell you that you're looking amazing?"

"Only if you mean it."

Pretending to look offended, he says, "Of course I mean it."

I relent and give him a small smile. "Thanks."

"Hey, Logan, get over here." Logan looks over his shoulder to where the other guy behind the table is attempting to deal with a large group of people who all seem to want to know about the rowing club.

"I gotta go," Logan says, "but it was awesome to see you, Liv." He gives me a quick hug. "And hey," he adds. "You don't have to worry about being on the outside anymore. I'll make sure you get an invitation to anything you want."

I watch him as he gets back to promoting the rowing club, grinning widely, slapping guys on the shoulder, laughing at jokes I can't hear. My smile slips. Logan may have apologised for ignoring me and promised to get me into any party I want, but I won't delude myself into thinking we're actually friends anymore. Perhaps we could be, if I worked really hard at it, but I can tell it won't come from his side.

I turn away as I remember I'm supposed to be looking for food. I need to rest my feet for a moment, though. I'd never admit it to Adam, but these shoes are *killing* me. I head towards Jammie steps to sit down—I'll have to do some strategic placing of my bag so no one can see up my dress—but before I get there, a group of girls wave to me and call me over. I hesitate, my insecure side telling me they can't possibly be waving to me, but after a quick glance over each shoulder, I walk towards them. They're the same four girls, I realise as I get closer, that I wanted to introduce myself to earlier.

"Hey," one of them says with a wide smile on her pink-glossed lips. She twists a strand of golden blonde hair around her finger. "Do you know Logan Richmond?"

That's what they called me over here for? "Um, yeah. We were at school together."

"Oh my Gucci!" she squeals. "So you, like, *know* him know him."

"Um ..." All I can think of is the Biblical sense of *knowing* someone, and I'm pretty sure—at least, I *hope*—that's not what she means. "Yes, well, we were really good friends, if that's what you mean." I don't add that we are no longer good friends, since being Logan's friend appears to be a good thing. "So, he's quite popular around here, huh?"

"Are you kidding?" another girl says. Her perfect brown curls suggest she woke up even earlier than I did. "He's a legend! I mean, at every res gathering we've been to since we got here, at least one person has said, 'You've heard of Logan, right?' So yeah. He's a Smuts legend."

Smuts. The men's residence on Upper Campus. If I'd got into res as part of Perfect Freshman Year Plan A, I'd know all about Logan the Legend. "So ... you're all in res?" I try to rein in my sad puppy voice, but I may as well paint *Feeling So Left Out Right Now* across my forehead.

"Yes," says Golden Blonde Girl. "Courtney and I are in Graça Machel, and Charlotte and Amber are in Fuller. Oh, and I'm Allegra, by the way." She holds her hand out to me, that beaming smile never leaving her glossy lips.

"Allegra?" My musician brain goes straight to the word *allegro*, and I wonder if the name Allegra means the same thing. The girl attached to it certainly fits the word 'lively.'

"Yes. And you are?"

"Livi," I say, taking her hand.

"You're in our faculty, right?" says Curly Brunette Girl. *Charlotte*, I remind myself. *Charlotte, Charlotte, Charlotte.* The other two names have already flown from my brain, but if I remember nothing else from today, I *will* remember the names Allegra and Charlotte. "I remember seeing you in the library during the campus tour," Charlotte continues. "I was admiring your shoes."

"They're incredible," one of the other two girls says. "I'm so jealous."

"Thanks," I say, remembering a second later to push my shoulders back in a confident pose and flick my hair over one shoulder. "When I saw them, I knew they'd go perfectly with this dress."

"You were so right," Allegra says, nodding. "Anyway, we were just on our way back to Beattie Building for the next orientation thing. You should sit with us."

"Oh, yeah, okay." I try to play it cool as the five of us head back to the Commerce Faculty side of campus, but inside I'm jumping up and down shouting, *Yes!*

"So if you were at school with Logan, then you're also from Durban, right?" Charlotte asks. "Were you in the same year as him?"

"Yes. I took a gap year last year," I explain. "I was an au pair in Germany."

"That is so exotic," Allegra says. "Did you meet any hot foreign guys?"

"Well, there was this one particular guy." The smile I give them is loaded with meaning. "He was kind of … German nobility."

"Oh. My. Gucci." Allegra stops and takes hold of my arm. "You have to tell us *everything*."

From: Alivia Howard <livi-gem@gmail.com>
Sent: Wed 12 Feb, 10:56 pm
To: Carl <cpsb21@yahoo.com>
Subject: Dear Carl

I know you're never going to see this, but I thought I should tell the virtual version of you that you helped me make friends today. Yip. You were an ass and you broke my heart, but it's all good because I wound up at the university I really wanted to go to, and the girls I met today LOVED hearing about our secret romance. So thanks for that. Also, I don't think I told you this in person when I had the chance, but … you should really go jump in a lake. (And seeing as how you *have* a lake, that should be easy.)

MUSIC. A GENTLE, SOOTHING MELODY. IT PULLS ME SLOWLY from the depths of sleep, coaxing my eyes open with its warm, comforting tones. My bedroom is aglow with midmorning light, reminding me that it's Saturday and I can stay in bed all day if I want to. I roll onto my back and close my eyes as the last cobwebs of sleep disappear and my brain finally recognises the music. One of my favourite piano pieces, Beethoven's *Sonata Pathétique*, second movement. Adam—fellow musician geek—must have put it on.

I lie in bed a while longer as the sun's warmth tangles itself around the melody. Swirls of imaginary colour twist lazily around my room. Then, out of the blue, the notes stumble over each other and hesitate. My eyes fly open. *Wait a second* ... This isn't a recording. It's live.

I sit up, grab my glasses from my bedside table, and climb out of bed. The music continues as I open my door and pad down the passage on bare feet. I'm pretty sure this house didn't include a piano last time I checked, but a recording wouldn't have a mistake in the middle of it. I reach the lounge, and there, next to the L-shaped couch Lynda and Mom picked out for us, is an upright piano. And sitting at it, continuing with the second movement of *Sonata Pathétique*, is Adam.

I cross the lounge and stand beside the instrument. "Your piano," I say.

He looks up and smiles, his fingers continuing to play. "My piano," he repeats.

"But … it … how did it get here?"

He stops playing and runs both hands through his messy, not-yet-showered hair. "I thought I could handle no piano. I was just gonna get myself a cheap, second-hand keyboard, remember? But I tried some out at a shop last week, and it's just not the same. So I asked my parents if there was any way they could get my piano here, and my dad made a plan. Some guys with a bakkie who—scarily enough—had never moved a piano before, but somehow managed to get it here in one piece."

"Awesome," I breathe, running my finger gently along the keys. I've always loved Adam's piano. My parents bought me a shiny new piano when I started learning how to play in primary school, back before I chose the violin as my main instrument, but it never had the same character as Adam's piano, with its heavy wood, scuff marks, stained ivory keys, and faded gold lettering indicating who made it. "When did it get here?"

"Yesterday morning, and the piano tuner came yesterday afternoon. You must have missed it when you got home."

"Mmm." I was at Allegra's res until eleven last night. Not doing anything exciting, unfortunately, rather finishing off a group assignment we'd left until the last minute. It was supposed to be handed in yesterday, but the lecturer gave us all an extension.

"It must be in by ten tomorrow morning," she'd said, giving us a stern be-grateful-because-this-won't-happen-often look. "And I shall be outside my office at one minute past ten to remove all assignments from the box."

"Yeah, I was rather late last night," I say with a yawn, then consider the fact that, to most of the student population, eleven probably isn't considered late. Especially not on a Friday.

"So how's everything going?" Adam asks, leaning back with one hand on the piano stool. "I've barely seen you the past two weeks."

"Oh, you know, everything's good. Busy, but good." I flop onto the couch. Hanging out with Allegra means rushing around all the time. Shopping, coffee dates, meeting up with good-looking guys, lectures, more shopping, res parties, more coffee dates. "Lectures aren't that exciting, but my friends are great, and there's this good-looking guy who's in most of my classes, and I'm pretty sure he's been checking me out."

"That's ... cool."

"His name is Jackson," I continue. "If we were back in high school, I'd have no chance with this guy, but now ...

everything's different."

"You're part of the 'in' crowd," Adam says with a sigh, making air quotes with his fingers.

"Well, yes, I think so." I stare at the ceiling and twist a piece of hair around my finger. "There are so many different people here, which means there are so many different kinds of 'in' crowds. But I'm definitely not 'that nerdy girl' anymore. And maybe you think I'm being shallow or whatever, but I like this. I like feeling pretty and confident. I like it that people are friendly purely for the sake of being friendly, and not because they're about to turn around and make fun of me."

"Livi?" Adam waits until I sit up and look at him. "You've always been pretty."

I tilt my head to the side and give him a smile. "Thanks. But you're my best friend, so you kinda have to say nice stuff like that."

"Not really. Friendship is based on honesty, right? So if you were hideous, I'd have to tell you." He turns back to the piano and begins playing a new piece. A slow waltz. "Are you too cool these days to play 'Guess the composer'?"

"Ooh, no. Just give me a minute to get breakfast." I love this game, but my stomach is protesting at not having been fed yet. I dash to the kitchen, get myself a bowl of muesli and yoghurt, and head back to the lounge as Adam continues playing. "Brahms," I say between mouthfuls.

Adam nods before changing to something else. "Okay, how about this one."

It's a lively and instantly recognisable tune, bouncing

happily along as my brain struggles to connect it to the right name. "Oh, I know this one. I know it, I know it." I sit down and continue munching. "It's … that Czech dude with the weird name … Dvořák! And it's one of the *Humoresque* pieces, right?"

"Yes," Adam says, already modulating into the next piece. "And this one?"

A fast waltz this time. Bright and happy. The urge to dance is irresistible. I jump up and start spinning around in circles with my cereal bowl. Adam doubles over with laughter, smothering half the keys as I prance around singing, "*One*, two three, *one* two three, *one*, two three." I bump into the coffee table and say, "Brahms?" Adam recovers enough to shake his head. "No, wait, it's Chopin."

"Yes." He finishes with a flourish.

I drop back onto the couch, and, after another mouthful of cereal, say, "Play that other Chopin one. The *really* fast one."

"Which one? *Minute Waltz* or *Fantaisie-Impromptu*?"

"Oh. I forgot about *Fantaisie*. I was thinking of *Minute Waltz*."

"All right, then." Adam wiggles his fingers as I lean on the arm of the couch so I can see properly. "Bring on the show-off piece."

His hands hover above the keyboard. He breathes in deeply, then takes off. His fingers fly over the keys at incredible speed, stumbling here and there as he tries to play the piece as fast as possible. When the slow part in the middle arrives, I can see he's forcing himself to hold back, playing it as it's written when all he really wants is to speed up. There's the pause, and then … back to the flying fingers, rushing over the keys, his eyes darting back and forth as they try to keep up, notes tumbling over each other like a thousand drops of water, and then … finished!

I jump to my feet, clapping and singing, "Standing ovation! Standing ovation!"

"Um, Livi?" My hands pause mid-clap as I look up. Luke is standing in the doorway holding my phone out to me. "I heard it ringing," he says. "Twice. I thought it might be important, so … here."

"Oh, thank you." I cross the room and take it from him, my face warming up as my fingers brush his. I wonder if perhaps he'll stay with us in the lounge—I've barely spoken to him in the three weeks I've been here—but he disappears before I can say anything else.

"Why does he always go and hide?" I whisper to Adam.

"Maybe he doesn't like your creepy staring."

"I don't *stare*, I just—" I break off as Adam gives me a pointed look. "Oh. I get it. You're reminding me that I used to complain about Luke's creepy staring, and now I'm the one doing the creepy staring. Well, I'm not. I'm just trying to get to know one of my housemates a little bit better."

"Really? You didn't seem interested in getting to know him back when he was Gross Cousin Luke."

"Okay, so maybe I should never have called him that. Maybe I should have …" I trail off as I look at my phone's screen and see two missed calls and three texts from Allegra.

Allegra: Wake up wake up wake up!

Allegra: Are you STILL sleeping?

Allegra: What's your address again, cos I'm gonna be there in an hour. We're going to … THE BEACH!

"Whaaaaat?"

"What?" Adam looks alarmed.

"Oh my foot. Allegra's coming here. HERE!"

"So?"

"So? I have to, you know, make a good impression. I can't lose the group of friends I have now. Everyone's already formed their cliques, so if Allegra and Charlotte reject me, there'll be no one left for me to be friends with."

Adam rolls his eyes. "I highly doubt that's true."

"And I have to paint my toenails and shave my legs and wash my hair and … ugh!" I grab my cereal bowl from the coffee table, knocking my shin into the edge of the couch at the same time. "Flipping ow!" I grasp my chin and hop for several seconds while Adam does a terrible job of holding back his laughter. I glare at him. "Okay, so if you're still here when she's here, just … be cool."

Adam spreads his arms out. "I'm always cool."

"Uh huh."

Back in my bedroom, I assess the scene for signs of nerdiness. My Marauder's Map cushion will need to be hidden. Or will it? Harry Potter is pretty much universally loved, so maybe I can risk Allegra seeing it. She can't hate me for loving Harry Potter, can she? Maybe she's read the books too! My violin and music stand have to go, though. There are too many 'orchestra geek' taunts fresh in my memory to risk that one. I slide them both under my bed, then remove my Star Trek DVDs from the DVD collection on the bookshelf and hide them in my cupboard.

Right. Shower time.

Allegra sends a message when she reaches our gate. I grab my beach bag—towel, sunscreen, sarong, water bottle, *no* book, and the sunglasses I recently borrowed from Charlotte—and rush out of the house. I meet Allegra on the front stairs. "Hey!" I give her a hug. "Cool, let's get going."

"Wait, I want to see your house."

"Oh, don't bother." I conceal my panicked expression with a bored one. "It's nothing exciting."

"Well, yeah, I get that." She lowers her voice and winks. "I want to see the guys you live with." She jumps up the stairs and lets herself in. I follow her, silently praying nothing goes wrong. "Awesome," she says, poking her head into the lounge. "This place is totally vintage cool."

"Thanks," I say with a laugh that hopefully doesn't sound too strangled.

"And where's your room? Down here?" She heads off down the passage before I can answer. Before she gets there, though, Adam appears in his doorway. Fortunately, he's had a shower since our 'Guess the composer' game, so we're spared seeing him in his sleep shorts—although something tells me Allegra wouldn't have minded that. "Oh, hey," Allegra says. She tucks her hair behind one ear, and I'm willing to bet she's giving Adam her shy smile.

"Um, hi." He leans in his doorway, probably trying to look cool as per my instructions. He ends up looking kind of awkward, though. "You're Allegra, right?" he says. "I'm Adam."

"Hi, Adam. It's great to meet you. Livi hasn't told me *nearly* enough about you." She looks over her shoulder and winks at me while I try to figure out who I'm more embarrassed to be in front of right now.

The sound of a door opening makes me turn around. Luke walks out of his bedroom, looking surprised—and a little terrified—to find us all standing in the passage.

"Luke, this is my friend Allegra," I say quickly. "She just stopped by to pick me up. We're on our way to the beach." I grab Allegra's arm and steer her past Luke and back towards the front door.

I've barely closed the door behind us when Allegra squeals. "Livi! You did not tell me he was *that* hot!"

"Shh." I drag her away from the house towards her car.

"And Adam wasn't bad either. I don't know what it is about glasses, but they always make guys look cute."

"Adam already has a girlfriend, and Luke is so shy he basically doesn't talk to girls at all. So good luck with that."

Allegra giggles. "I bet I can help him with his shyness."

I groan, then remind myself that Allegra's reaction is a

good thing. Her liking my hot/cute housemates means she's less likely to drop me as a friend if I happen to do something embarrassingly uncool.

With a heave and a groan, I slide the rusted gate closed across the driveway. The motor stopped working, but the landlord doesn't seem interested in getting it fixed. Dusting my hands off, I ask, "Which beach are we going to?" I follow Allegra to her car. "I haven't been to any beaches here yet."

"You *haven't?*" Allegra gives me the kind of shocked look that suggests I may have committed social suicide by admitting that. Then she smiles. "Wow, Livi, you are going to *love* it. Clifton 4th Beach is gorgeous. And guess who's going to be there." She wiggles her eyebrows at me as she unlocks her car. "Jackson."

CLIFTON IS BUZZING WITH ACTIVITY, MAKING IT ALMOST impossible to find a parking spot. After doing a three hundred-point manoeuvre—Allegra doesn't seem to be able to parallel park, and I'm not about to try it in someone else's car—we manage to get into a gap on the sidewalk. We grab our bags, run across roads, climb down narrow staircases, and eventually the beach comes into sight.

Bronzed bodies in tiny bikinis line the sugar-white sand, guys with rippling abs and gleaming skin toss a volleyball over a net, and several small yachts bob in the gentle waves close to shore.

"Wow." I pause at the foot of the staircase. "So this is where all the beautiful people hang out, huh?"

"Totally," Allegra says, flicking her hair back and sauntering onto the powdery sand.

"I'm not sure I belong here," I say with a giggle, hurrying

after her. "These people are *too* perfect. Like, not a wobbly bit in sight."

"Oh, don't be silly. You're a total stick. I wish I had your figure."

"Um …" I'm not sure what to say to that, because I've tried on some of Allegra's clothes, and after not being able to get the zips up on any of her jeans, it's clear to me she's the only stick around here. Well, aside from all the glamorous sticks already lounging on their towels, their perfect wobble-free skin glistening beneath the sun. "And where are we gonna sit, anyway? This place is packed."

"Yeah, we shoulda been here hours ago, but *someone* decided to sleep in this morning and not answer her phone."

"Well, you know, it is Saturday, so I—"

"But Charlotte and the girls got here a while ago, so they're keeping a spot with a good view for us." She looks over at me. "And you *know* what I mean by a good view."

I'm pretty sure she means the hot guys and not the clear blue sea spread out before us or the mountains rising behind us. "How do you know where they are?" I squint and shield my face from the sun as I search the tanning bodies for three I recognise.

"Oh, we came here a few times during res orientation, so we've kinda decided on a favourite spot. See? Over there." She points to a cluster of rocks, then jogs towards the three girls lying in a row and the two empty towels beside them. "Hey, ladies."

Courtney and Amber raise themselves up on their elbows to greet us. Charlotte simply waves, not moving from her perfect tanning position. "Hello, dears," she says. Her eyes squint at us from behind the brown lenses of her retro sunglasses before closing again.

"Where are the guys?" Allegra asks, glancing at the two empty towels before looking around.

"They dared each other to go for a swim," Courtney says as she lies down and drapes her arm over her eyes.

"Insanity." Allegra shakes her head, but I can see from her small smile she's impressed. "There's no way you'd get me into that water. *Way* too cold."

"Tell me about it," Charlotte murmurs.

Allegra and I lay our towels down on the empty sand beside Charlotte. I kick my shoes off and drop my bag onto the towel just as a male voice shouts, "Hey! Allegra and Livi!" Jackson and his friend Rob jog across the sand towards us, dripping wet from their dip in the waves.

"Hey, you want a hug?" Rob asks, advancing on Allegra. He opens his arms and shakes his head, flinging droplets of water in every direction. I jump out of the way as Allegra squeals and runs past me.

"Stop being an idiot," Charlotte says, sitting up and smacking Rob's legs with a rolled-up magazine.

I look over at Jackson, wondering if he might be about to try the same thing with me. We don't know each other all that well, though, so instead we just stare at each other awkwardly. He seems to remember himself suddenly, and breaks the awkwardness with a smile. He runs a hand over his wet hair.

His muscles flex.

Water glistens on his skin.

I try to remember how to breathe.

Sweet hammer of Thor. He's like a sexy Norse god who just rose up out of the ocean, then slow-motion ran across the sand towards me, because we're clearly soul mates, and his heart cries out for—

Allegra ducks behind me, and Rob, still chasing her, trips over my sandals and rams into me, knocking me face-first onto my towel. Charlotte gasps, and Allegra cries out, "Livi! Are you okay?"

"Yes, fine, totally fine." I sit up hastily, patting my hair and making sure my dress isn't somewhere up around my neck.

"Cool, sorry, Livi." Rob drops onto his towel next to Amber and reaches for a bag of chips from under a bunched up T-shirt.

Allegra seats herself daintily upon her towel beside me. I stretch one leg out, bend the other at the knee, and lean back on my hands, attempting to arrange myself into a sexy goddess pose. When I look up, though, Jackson is heading back to his towel on the other side of Rob.

Great. Sexy goddess pose wasted.

I watch Allegra as she slowly and seductively pulls her dress off over her head. I wonder if it's for Rob's benefit— which would be pointless, since he's currently tipping barbecue flavoured chips down his throat, his eyes closed against the glare of the sun—or simply for all guys in the vicinity. Either way, it makes me want to laugh. And try it out for myself, of course.

I wiggle around until I'm no longer sitting on my dress. I cross my arms, take hold of the bottom of the dress, and pull up. It all goes smoothly until the last step of the manoeuvre, where the dress is over my head and my arms are up in the air. Something catches on something else, the dress stops moving, and suddenly I can't remember if I shaved under my arms or not.

The dress is stuck.

I can't see anything through the fabric.

And I may or may not be flashing hairy armpits to the whole of Clifton 4th Beach.

Panicking, I give the dress a good tug. Something loosens at the back of my neck. The fabric rushes past my face, and the beach comes into view again. I lower my arms and twist to the side—and find myself face-to-face with Allegra's horrified expression. A horrified expression pointed directly at my chest.

I look down—"Whoa!"—and clap both hands over my half-exposed left boob. My traitorous bikini strap dangles over my stomach, which is obviously what led to the triangle of fabric flopping down and causing my indecency.

"Livi! This isn't a nude beach!" Allegra's stage whisper catches the attention of Rob and Jackson, who abandon the barbecue chips and lean across their towels to look past Allegra.

I duck down, using Allegra as a shield as best I can while my hands hastily reposition my bikini. An inferno erupts across my face. Holy smoking embarrassment. I need to leave. IMMEDIATELY. I can NEVER look any of these people in the eye again. Goodbye, Clifton 4th Beach. Goodbye, potential boyfriend Jackson. Goodbye, friends who are cooler than any I've had before. I'll spend the remainder of my varsity career closed in my bedroom, wrapped in many layers of clothing, working hard like a—

"Can you help me with my sunscreen, Livi?" Allegra asks. She hands over a bottle of spray-on sunscreen before twisting around so her back is facing me. "I guess our plan didn't work," she whispers—a proper whisper this time, not one meant for half the beach to hear. "The guys are far more interested in their beach snacks than in rubbing sunscreen over us."

Right. So … the boob-flashing incident is forgotten? Just like that? Maybe I didn't expose as much skin as I thought. I spray sunscreen across Allegra's shoulders, neck and back. I rub it in, then swivel on my towel so she can do the same for me. Our plan was to sit close enough to the guys that they'd end up offering to help us out with our sunscreen, but it's now a bit awkward with Charlotte, Amber and Courtney lying between us and our sexy Norse gods.

"Oh my Gabbana, Livi," Allegra says as she replaces the cap on her sunscreen bottle. "I just thought of something."

"What?" I glance down hurriedly to check I'm not flashing everyone again, but my bikini is in place.

"You would make such a hot blonde."

"What?" I reach up to pat the mess of hair bundled on top of my head. "No way. Really?"

"Yes, totally. Not, like, bleach blonde. But something more natural. Like blonde and gold highlights mixed in with your red. It would be so hot. Please let's do it the next time we go to a salon!"

"Um, okay, I'll think about it." I didn't realise hair colour could make a person so excited, but Allegra seems thrilled by her idea. She rolls onto her stomach and pulls a magazine from her bag.

"Let's look for an example," she says, already flipping through the pages.

"Uh, sure." I lie beside her, wishing I was reading my own magazine, which features an article on the actress playing the lead role in the newest Marvel Comics movie adaptation.

A shadow falls across the page. "Hey, Livi." I look up and see Jackson silhouetted against the bright sun. "I thought maybe you and I could take a walk along the beach. If you want to."

I look at Allegra, who gives me an excited grin, then back up at Jackson.

Be cool, Alivia, I instruct myself. *Just. Be. Cool.*

"Yeah, sure, okay." I sit up, grab my sarong from my bag—*Slowly! Stop looking like you're desperate to be at his side!*— and tie it around my hips before standing.

"Let's walk along the shoreline," he says. "You can feel how cold the water is. Maybe," he adds with a cute half-smile, "you'll be brave enough stick more than just your toes in."

After a glance back over my shoulder to where Allegra is giving me two thumbs up, I follow him.

From: Alivia Howard <livi-gem@gmail.com>
Sent: Sat 1 Mar, 11:48 pm
To: Sarah Henley <s.henley@gmail.com>
Subject: Romantic Beach Scene

Sarah!

Think of every romantic beach scene you've ever written (I don't know if you've actually written any, but just IMAGINE one if you haven't), put them all together, and that's what I had today! Well, aside from the accidental half-flashing of my left boob, which I hope no one EVER mentions again.

Anyway, so you remember Jackson, right? The guy who keeps smiling at me in lectures? The guy who then sat next to me twice last week? And drew cute little doodles along the edge of my notes? (I have NO idea what happened during those two lectures.) Well he was there today. At the beach. And he asked me to go for a walk with him—just the two of us!

We talked about where we grew up, and what our hopes are for the future, and what music we like, and tons of other stuff that's random but seemed really AMAZING to talk about at the time. He splashed me with water (I know, I know, you're cringing right now. Hopefully you never wrote that part in any of your Romantic Beach Scenes, because it's such a cliché, but when it happens to you in real life, you giggle and squeal like a silly girl while your heart explodes with imaginary hearts), and in places where the sand was hot, he even picked me up and carried me so my feet wouldn't burn! (Now that part you CAN write about because it was SERIOUSLY AWESOME!)

We stayed there the whole day, and in the evening we all had sundowners at this place overlooking the beach and the sunset. Jackson even put his arm around me when it started getting cooler. (Swoon!) Sooooo no actual date yet, but there are definitely plenty of magical sparks flying around!

xx Livi

P.S. I apologise for the overuse of exclamation marks.

P.P.S. No I don't!!!!!

____

THREE WEEKS INTO THE SEMESTER, AND I'VE FINALLY RUN out of clean clothes. I managed to sneak some underwear into a load of laundry Adam had already started this morning—and sneak it out as soon as the washing machine started singing its 'I'm finished!' song—but I didn't have time to do anything more than that.

Allegra picked me up and we spent the morning dashing around Canal Walk, getting our nails done and each looking for a new dress to wear tonight. In their first week here, Allegra and Co. discovered a nightclub called The Banana Pearl, and they've been wanting to take me there ever since I became part of their group. Instead of admitting that nightclubs have never held much fascination for me, and that I've never actually been to one—NOTHING on this earth could force me to confess that little detail—I simply act excited every time they speak about it.

But now, after three weeks, they've made a plan to return to The Banana Pearl with a bunch of other people we sometimes hang out with. And that bunch of other people includes Jackson—a fact that makes The Banana Pearl suddenly become a whole lot more interesting. Jackson and I have sat together in lectures, we've doodled on each other's notes, and I even visited his room in Smuts once with Charlotte and Amber while Allegra was busy.

But he hasn't asked me out yet.

So TONIGHT could be the night where I show him just how amazing and desirable I am.

My hair is straight and sleek, my dress is short and tight, my heels are dangerously high, my make-up is dark and sparkly, and all exposed skin is covered in shimmery powder.

I'm ready to go.

I'm also horrendously hungry.

I barely ate anything all day in order to avoid the bloated stomach look tonight. I'm looking fabulous in this dress—if I do say so myself—so missing lunch was worth it, but I'm starting to think I need to eat *something* before I go out. I *clip-clop* my way to the kitchen and grab a jar of peanut butter and a spoon. I lean against the counter, remove the lid on the jar, and scoop out a spoonful of peanut butter.

"Hey, Liv, do you want—Oh, wow. I guess you're going out, huh?"

"Mmm." I remove the spoon from my mouth as Adam enters the kitchen. "Yes. What were you going to ask me?"

"Oh, uh, I've got some friends coming around to play

Xbox, and I wondered if you might want to join us. You haven't played in a while, and I don't think you've met any of my new friends yet."

"Oh, that would have been great. I'm sorry I can't join you." I stick a second spoonful of peanut butter into my mouth.

Adam nods. "Yeah. You've, uh, got a busy diary these days. I should have known you'd already have plans." There's something a little bit … off in his voice. He crosses his arms and leans against the fridge. "Where are you going tonight?"

"The Banana Pearl," I say as I screw the lid back onto the peanut butter jar. "In Long Street. You heard of it?"

He nods again. "Yes, I've heard of it. I've heard about … things that happen there."

Ah. So that's what was off in his voice. That's what the look is about.

Disapproval.

I place the jar on the counter and cross my arms. "Don't give me that look."

"What look?"

"That look that says good girls like me shouldn't be going out to clubs like The Banana Pearl. Or shouldn't be going to clubs at all. Or wearing clothes like this. Or make-up like this."

"I don't have a look like that."

"You're giving me that look right now!"

"Maybe you're giving yourself that look."

"What? That makes no sense."

He shrugs. "Whatever. If I *was* giving you a look, it would more likely have been a look that said, 'Thanks for spending absolutely *no* time at all with your old friends.'" He pushes away from the fridge with a sigh. "It's clear your new friends are more important."

Guilt needles my insides. Adam's words sound awfully similar to the ones I said to Logan when I confronted him during orientation. "Hey, come on, that's not fair. I'm trying to—"

"Don't worry about it, Liv," he says. "It's a little sad to think that soon we won't have anything in common anymore, but that's the way life is, right? People change." He turns and disappears through the kitchen door.

"Adam!" I shout after him. "Hey, don't walk away like that." I follow him, wobbling slightly on my heels. "This isn't all my fault. It's not like you're always around. You disappear to that—that—hippy cafe place down the road—"

"Which I've invited you to several times," he says before turning into his room.

"You can't expect me to be available for everything at the last minute, Adam. I have *plans*. I'm a plan-making person."

"My point, Alivia," he says, sticking his head out of the doorway, "is that you only ever have time to make plans with one person. That one person who is your gateway to all things Cool. Your pathway to—"

Right on cue, Allegra's headlights slide across the glass pane of the front door, and my cell phone starts ringing. I stomp—if it can be called stomping in impossibly high heels—into my room and grab my purse.

"Enjoy The Purple Banana," Adam shouts before slamming his door shut.

"It's The Banana Pearl!" I yell back.

The Banana Pearl turns out to be a less glamorous version of what I've seen in movies. Movies give you flashing coloured lights, sexy bodies, smoke machines, and the best dance music. The Banana Pearl got the flashing lights right, but the bodies are sweaty, the only smoke in here comes from cigarettes, and the music is so loud it's more distortion than actual music. Or perhaps that's the sound of my eardrums caving in.

Movies. Full of lies, they are. Planes are quiet, people have actual conversations in nightclubs, everyone is beautiful, and sex is perfect. And not that I've had first-hand experience in the sex department, but I've heard enough to know that The Perfect Sex Scene doesn't exist in real life.

I hold onto Allegra's hand as she pulls me past dancing bodies, people on high stools grouped around small round tables, and a lounge area. We reach the bar, where the music doesn't seem to be quite as loud, but I still can't hear anyone speak. I have no idea how one orders a drink here.

We find our group of friends at one end of the bar. Charlotte, Amber and Courtney. Rob and a bunch of other people I vaguely know.

But no Jackson.

Why is there no Jackson?

I cup my hands around Allegra's ear and shout the question to her. She frowns at me and shakes her head. "What?" she yells.

I try again, but I get the same confused look from her. So I simply yell, "JACKSON!" until I see recognition on her face.

She looks around, speaks to a few people—how? How does she speak to them? Am I the only one who's nearly deaf?—then yells something into my ear. "Jackson ... work ... couldn't come."

I miss at least half of what she says, but the message gets through: he couldn't come. I try not to feel as though my whole evening has just fallen apart. I can still have fun, right? I can dance. I like dancing. It's happened mostly in the privacy of my own bedroom in the past, but I don't think I'm that bad at it.

If only Jackson were here to see my sexy dancing ...

I grab Allegra's arm and motion to the dance floor with my head. If Jackson's not here, and it's too loud to chat to anyone, then the only thing left is dancing.

The lights are out inside the house when I get back just before 1 am. I stand in the doorway and yawn, my eyes squeezing shut and my jaw just about unhinging itself. I keep telling myself that it isn't all that late, but my body doesn't seem to agree. Allegra and I would have stayed out longer, but I was getting bored with no Jackson there, and Allegra quickly lost interest after Rob started salivating all over a girl he'd only just met. We yelled our goodbyes to everyone, saying we had somewhere else to be.

Yeah. Somewhere like bed.

After locking the door, I remove my heels and tiptoe down the passage to my bedroom. A strip of light shines beneath Adam's closed door, and I can hear the sound of muffled voices and studio laughter. He's watching series again.

I flick my light on and toss my shoes onto the armchair in the corner. I place my purse on my desk and notice something odd: a pair of polka dot underwear sitting on top of my laptop. Beside it is a note in Adam's handwriting. *Thanks, but I don't think these will fit me.*

Oops. I guess I missed this pair when I was fishing my undies out of the washing machine earlier. Smiling, I head to the bathroom and turn the shower on. I wash the glitter from my skin and the smoke from my hair. Once I've got my PJs and glasses on, I tap lightly on Adam's door.

The TV series laughter pauses, and Adam says, "Come in?"

I open the door, but don't step into the room. After our conversation earlier, I don't know if I'm welcome in here anymore. "Hey," is all I manage to say.

"Hey," he answers. He's turned the computer screen on

his desk so it's facing his bed. I recognise the paused characters on screen, but I ask anyway.

"What are you watching?"

"*The Big Bang Theory*. Season three."

I nod. It's one of my favourite series too. "I'm sorry about earlier." My voice is so quiet it's barely a whisper.

He sits up on the bed and crosses his legs. "Me too. That probably wasn't the best way to say what I was thinking."

I close the door behind me, cross the room, and climb over him to sit on the other side of the bed. I reach for the spare blanket at my feet and pull it over my legs.

Adam hits the Play button on his remote, but turns the volume down so we can only just hear the characters. "How was The Purple Banana?"

I roll my eyes but don't correct him. I know he's doing it on purpose now. "It was fine. No one offered me drugs or tried to do anything inappropriate. The music was cool—when it wasn't too loud—and the dancing was fun."

"But?"

"Well, Jackson was supposed to be there, but he wasn't."

"Okay." Adam nudges his glasses up.

"How was your evening? Did you kick everyone's butt at whatever game you were playing?"

"Of course." He nudges my shoulder. "If you'd been there I would've kicked your butt too."

He probably would have, considering how long it's been since I played. I pull my knees up and pick at a stray thread coming loose from the blanket. "I miss playing Xbox. I miss playing my violin. I miss reading and searching for new music to listen to. There just … isn't time for everything."

"I know," Adam says with a sigh. "That's why you've got to prioritise. Choose the things that are most important to you. And … I guess the things that are important to you might not be the things that are important to me, and … that's okay."

I nod. It is okay, but for some reason it doesn't feel that way. It feels like I'm losing something. I lean my head against his shoulder. "You're still important to me," I murmur.

After several moments of watching Sheldon try to explain some equations on a whiteboard to Penny, Adam whispers, "Your hair is making my shoulder wet."

"Well, you're hogging all the pillows," I whisper back.

"They are my pillows."

I crawl to the foot of the bed and grab the cushion from his wheeled desk chair. The chair slides to the side, knocking a notebook that was jutting over the edge of the desk onto the floor.

"Oops."

"Princess Clumsy."

I settle back on the bed with the cushion behind me. "Clumsiness is my superpower. We've already established this."

We watch as Sheldon attempts to begin his explanation from the beginning again while Penny grows more and more frustrated. My eyes start to slide closed.

"Don't you have a test on Monday?" Adam says.

"Mmm." *Don't think about that.*

"So … you should probably go to bed soon so you can study tomorrow."

"Mmm." *You're not nearly that sensible, are you, Livi?* With considerable effort, I open my mouth and say, "My other superpower is scoring spectacularly high marks in a test I am superbly unprepared for."

Adam snorts. "If only that superpower existed."

From: Alivia Howard <livi-gem@gmail.com>
Sent: Sun 9 Feb, 2:38 am
To: Carl <cpsb21@yahoo.com>
Subject: Dear Carl

Why can't they make clubs that are awesome like in movies? Like, classy. With clean floors. And music that is always at the perfect volume. And—cherry on the top—that guy you're crushing on must always show up right when you want him to.

Note to self: make a club like this one day.

Also … figure out how to be obsessed with *The Big Bang Theory* while retaining cool clubbing image.

Damn …
So …
Tired …

I mean so damn tired.

9

WHEN MORNING ARRIVES, I REGRET NOT LISTENING TO Adam. My head aches, probably from a combination of deafening music and a lack of sleep, brought on by too many episodes of *The Big Bang Theory*.

After hitting my snooze button seven times, I manage to sit up. I stare at the gap between my curtains for a while. Dark clouds. Some drizzle. A bad day for the beach and a perfect day to stay inside studying.

Ugh.

I shove my glasses on, shuffle over to my cupboard, and remember that the only clean clothes I have are a few pairs of underwear. I can't sit in my underwear all day. Or can I? Some of my underwear looks just like—

No, don't be ridiculous, Alivia. Pyjamas. You can stay in your pyjamas.

I push my glasses up and rub my eyes. Sheesh. Studying

is *not* going to go well if my brain is in the kind of state where it thinks wearing underwear and nothing else is acceptable. Especially with the cold breeze blowing in through the window this morning. I should probably wait a while before attempting to work. I should … do my laundry.

I pick up one of the two close-to-overflowing laundry baskets from the corner and shuffle out of my room with it. I pass Adam's open door. He isn't home. He knocked on my door about an hour ago to say he was going with Luke to … somewhere. I think I fell asleep halfway through his sentence.

The tiny room off the kitchen serves as our laundry/pantry. I open the lid of the washing machine and empty my laundry basket into it. It appears I have far too many dirty clothes, though, because at least half of them land on the floor on either side of the machine. With a groan, I return them to the basket. I locate the little tray thingy for the washing powder, then spend several minutes examining the dials and buttons on the outside of the machine. After all, it's not like I've done much laundry in my life. We've always had at least two domestic workers at home to take care of things like that, and last year in Germany … well, I lived in a castle, so it goes without saying that there were staff employed to do the laundry.

I'm so glad Adam isn't here right now to see this. I press the start button and step back. A humming noise begins, which I think is supposed to happen. I leave quickly, hoping the machine doesn't explode or leak or eat all my clothes.

I make myself a cup of pomegranate flavoured rooibos tea before heading back to my room to begin the arduous task of pretending to study.

Afternoon status: I've almost fallen asleep twice, sent three different cat videos to Adam, and been on Facebook at least once every twenty minutes. I found Jackson on Facebook and contemplated adding him as a friend, but I didn't want to seem desperate. Allegra says I should be doing the hard-to-get thing.

I also did some studying. The content itself isn't all that difficult to understand or remember. It's just tremendously boring.

I hear laughter coming from Adam's bedroom. He could be laughing at the cat videos, *The Big Bang Theory*, or something entirely different. Whatever the cause, I'd far rather be in the fun room than in the forcing-myself-to-study room.

Time for a break.

I jump up and cross the passage to his room. I tap on the door, then open it. "Have you watched the third one yet?" I ask. "Because that one is the—Oh, sorry." Adam's sitting at his desk in front of his computer, but it isn't a cat video or a TV series on the screen. It's his girlfriend.

"Is that Livi?" she asks.

"Yes." Adam tilts the screen slightly so the webcam can see me.

"Hey, Jenna." I take a few steps forward and wave, kicking a pile of Xbox controllers at the same time. "Oh, crap, sorry," I say to Adam, who's giving me an odd look. I crouch down and slide the controllers to the side of the room. "Hey again!" I say with a cheery smile and another wave as I jump up. "How's matric going?"

"Oh, you know, it's not too bad so far," Jenna says. "I just can't wait for this year to be over so I'll finally be done with high school, you know?"

"Yes, I know exactly what you mean."

She smiles—the kind of awkward smile that tells me she's not sure what else to say.

"You're so lucky to have Adam as your boyfriend," I tell her as I lean against his chair. "I think I can safely say he's the *only* reason Sarah and I passed physics."

Jenna nods. "Yeah, I know, I'm very lucky to have him."

Adam's ears turn pink.

Jenna's gaze moves back and forth between the two of us.

Right. My cue to leave.

"Anyway, you guys enjoy your chat. Nice to see you, Jenna." I hurry out of the room, being careful not to walk into anything else.

I plop myself back down at my desk and stare at my textbook.

Focus.

Read.

Understand and remember.

Somehow, I find myself getting into it for the first time all day. It's not as though it's become any more interesting, but I'm less distracted. It grows darker outside, rain patters down, and I keep reading, highlighting, and making notes from my textbook.

"Hey."

I look up and see Adam in my doorway. "Oh, hey." I replace the cap on my yellow highlighter.

"You're wearing my jersey," he says.

"What?" I look down at myself. "Oh, yeah. Mine are all dirty. I mean, I know it's summer, but the aircon is always on in those lecture theatres, and it ends up freezing. So, yeah. All dirty." I start to feel uncomfortable beneath his unblinking gaze.

"You know that your clothes will continue to be dirty unless you wash them, right?"

"Yes, I know. I actually did some laundry this—Oh, crud, I forgot. My clothes are still in the machine." I push my chair away from the desk and stand up. "So much laundry, so little time," I say with a laugh, trying to lighten the atmosphere that suddenly feels way more tense than it should.

"Maybe if you spent some of your early mornings doing laundry instead of doing your hair, you wouldn't have this problem."

"Well, yes, but then I'd have hair problems." Another smile. Another attempt to make him laugh.

Another fail.

"And did you know it was your turn to do the grocery shopping this weekend? Luke ended up doing it yesterday because there was hardly anything left in the fridge."

"Oh, shoot, really? I totally forgot." I think of the shopping schedule stuck to the fridge. The shopping schedule I haven't looked at since we sat with our mothers and drew it up.

Adam crosses his arms, still no trace of a smile on his face. "Real life getting too much for you, princess?"

"*Excuse me?*"

"You heard me," he says, his voice raised. "I know you've spent your entire life inside Chateau Zimbali, but it's time to join the real world. This only works if we all take responsibility, okay? We all do the cleaning, we all do the laundry, we all do the shopping. We all *contribute*."

"I KNOW. I said I was sorry, okay? I forgot about the shopping. I'll pay Luke back for whatever he bought yesterday. Jeez, what is wrong with you?" I pull off the jersey and throw it at him. "I wear one piece of your clothing and suddenly you're yelling at me about everything I'm doing wrong. You could just *talk* to me instead, you know."

His fingers clench around the jersey. "What is wrong with me?" he repeats. "What is wrong with me? You walk into *my room* wearing *my clothes* while I'm having a video chat with *my girlfriend*, and then I have to spend the remainder of our conversation trying to convince her that there's nothing going on between you and me. That is what's wrong with me right now."

I stare at him, letting the ridiculous words sink in. "What? Seriously?"

"Yes."

"She honestly thought there might be something going on between us?"

"Yes."

I let out a faint laugh. "That's insane. Obviously you told her she's got nothing to worry about, right?"

"Obviously. But she's there, and you're here, and she isn't exactly happy about that."

"Yes, but …" I don't see what the problem is. "Doesn't she know you're, like, a thousand percent committed to her?"

Adam shuts his eyes and sighs. "Just don't wear my clothes again." He turns and walks back to his room, the jersey bunched in his hand. He closes his door.

I blink back tears as I head to the laundry/pantry. I open the washing machine lid and take hold of a fistful of wet washing. I pull it out and stare at it, my lower lip starting to shake.

My white clothes are now blue.

From: Alivia Howard <livi-gem@gmail.com>
Sent: Sun 9 Feb, 8:14 pm
To: Carl <cpsb21@yahoo.com>
Subject: Dear Carl

It shouldn't be this hard to do laundry. Maybe I should just shower with my clothes on. That way they'll end up clean. Good idea? No? No. I didn't think so either.

Real life sucks.

MONDAY, FIRST PERIOD. I DIDN'T HAVE TIME TO straighten my hair, the clothes I'm wearing were hastily half-ironed this morning, and I've got glasses on instead of contact lenses. My eyes need a break after staying open until 3 am trying to cover all the work in today's test. Seriously. How did we manage to get through so much material in only three weeks?

I scurry into the lecture theatre two minutes before our test is meant to begin. I half expect my four friends to point at my glasses and shout, "Nerd! Be gone!" Honestly, though, they don't look in spectacular shape either. Well, except for Charlotte, who has the ability to whisper, text, pass notes, and still know exactly what's happening in every class. She was most likely getting her beauty sleep at 3 am while the rest of us were studying.

I slide into a seat at the end of the row beside Allegra. "You guys ready for this thing?" I ask.

Allegra rubs her eyes. She isn't wearing any make-up. I've *never* seen her without make-up. "I hope so. I made the mistake of mentioning this test to my parents. They want me to send a photo of the result when I get it back."

"A photo?" Charlotte says. "Wow. That's extreme."

"I, uh, may have had a habit of lying to my parents about test results at school. They like to see proof now. They— Hey, since when do you wear glasses?" she says to me.

"Uh, since always," I admit. "I usually wear contacts."

"Oh." Allegra tilts her head as she examines my face. "They're cute. You should wear them more often."

"I should? You don't think glasses are too … nerdy?"

"Well, spectacles do sort of have that nerd vibe," Charlotte says, "but as long as they're a trendy design and the shape suits your face, they can make you look both intelligent and attractive at the same time."

Allegra nods. "Yeah. That. I'm just a bit too tired right now to make my thoughts come out clearly."

At the front of the lecture theatre, Professor Batch organises a pile of papers. "No more talking, please," he booms. "I'm about to hand out the question papers."

I try to quiet my brain and recall the main points from all the summaries I made in the past twenty-four hours, but I'm distracted by the guy three rows down who just turned around. The guy smiling at me and mouthing, *Good luck*.

Jackson.

Focus, Livi, focus.

I smile back, then turn my attention to the paper that just landed on the desk in front of me.

"That wasn't so bad, huh?" Jackson leans in the doorway of the lecture theatre, waiting for me. He's never waited for me before. Something must be different.

"Yes, I'm quite surprised," I say. "I was expecting it to be a lot worse." I reach up to tuck my hair behind my ear, mainly because I don't know what else to do with my hands.

Allegra and Co. walk past us. Allegra winks while Charlotte and Amber argue about question twelve.

Jackson tilts his head to the side. "I like your hair like that. It's … natural."

Holy pink Power Ranger. Here I am on my worst day ever and I've already received two compliments? I've obviously missed something about the way the world works.

"Come on, let's get to Stats," Jackson says.

I manage to refrain from squealing as we head to our next lecture venue together. I let my hand dangle casually between us, just in case he wants to hold it. Oh my hat, I am *pathetic*. Here I am getting all giggly-excited about HAND HOLDING. I can't help it, though. I've only ever had one boyfriend, and he didn't wait after class for me. He didn't hold my hand in public, either. We exchanged smiles across the corridors and notes during English and History, but we kept our hanging out for after school. As if it would have been weird to be seen together in front of everyone else. Or something. I can't remember. We were both orchestra geeks, so perhaps that explains it.

Of course, my German prince Carl held my hand, but it never happened in public. None of our exchanges ever took place in public.

"So, uh, we missed you on Saturday at The Banana Pearl," I say with a sideways glance at Jackson. I add in a half-smile that's supposed to look cute and upset at the same time.

"Ya, I wish I coulda have been there. I had to take on a late shift at work. Only got home around midnight, and then ..." He gives me an apologetic look. "Well, I was kinda beat."

"Oh, yeah, okay, that's cool. Where do you work?"

He scratches his head. "Uh, at the cinema. Kinda lame, I know."

"What? No. That's really cool. Do you get to watch all the movies?"

He laughs. "Not exactly. I do more of the glamorous work like collecting tickets and sweeping popcorn off the floor."

My laughter joins his. My mother would be horrified to learn that I'm interested in a popcorn sweeper, but Jackson's job—and the fact that he can joke about it—makes him even more adorable to me.

If only he would attempt to hold my hand now.

No such luck. We make it to our Statistics lecture without our hands even brushing, but it's hard to feel disappointed when I've got a whole period of sitting next to him to look forward to. I scan the lecture theatre and find my four friends and two of his in our usual spot: roughly the middle row. But instead of joining them, Jackson leads me to the back row. The row where the loner Indian girl and the two guys with the dreadlocks always sit. And that other guy who only comes to lectures to sleep.

Jackson walks along the row, picks a seat in the middle, and gestures to the seat next to him. Right. As if I had any intention of sitting anywhere else. I flash what I hope is an alluring smile as I slide into my seat and place my bag on the floor between us. I lean down—this isn't a cleavage-exposing shirt, so it needs a bit of help—and slowly remove my notebook and a pen from my bag. I open the notebook to the last page I wrote on, then cross one leg over the other. Slow and sexy. I stare ahead and focus on breathing normally. *I'm cool. I'm so cool. Sitting in the back row with the guy I have a mega crush on is not affecting me in the least. I'm going to pay attention to the lecture now. And look! I have glasses on, which make me appear both intelligent and—*

"Recovered from the test yet?" our lecturer asks. She's young, but her horrendous taste in clothes combined with her long, non-styled hair that just *hangs* there makes her look at least a decade older than she is. Charlotte keeps talking about abducting her and performing a makeover. "Yes, I know all about the test most of you had in first period," she says, nodding to us. "Don't look so surprised, Mr Fischer. But I need you to forget about it now and concentrate, because today we'll be doing—"

I have no idea what we'll be doing today, because Jackson just reached over and started drawing on my open notebook, completely shattering my focus. All I see is his hand and the neat lines coming together to form a picture. It's a little cartoon guy. He's waving at me. No, wait, he's holding a bunch of flowers out to me.

Oh, that is so cute!

I pick up my pen and write, *If I could draw a little girl accepting the flowers, I would.*

Underneath my words, he writes *HA HA HA!* in large capitals, then proceeds to draw little stick figures climbing all over the letters.

I write, *Cute!*

He then spends a while bent over the corner of my notebook, eventually revealing a cartoon version of our lecturer pointing at a projector screen with nonsense written on it. I laugh quietly, then nudge his knee with mine. "You're really good at this," I whisper.

He gives me a heart-melting grin. Then he picks up one of my hands from my lap. He holds it in his left hand and starts drawing on my palm with his right.

He's drawing on my hand.

HE'S TOUCHING MY HAND.

Don't pass out. Don't pass out. That would be seriously uncool.

He holds my hand up so I can see his artwork. Not a picture this time, but words. *Saturday night. 7 pm. You and me. What do you say?*

What do I say? "Are you … is that …"

He nods and whispers, "I'm asking you out."

I try to conceal my absurd happiness with a teasing smile. "You could have just *asked* me, you know."

"But then I wouldn't have had an excuse to hold your hand."

My insides melt.

"You two at the back there," our lecturer calls out. "I hope you're paying attention because the next question is for you."

ALLEGRA IS *ALLEGRISSIMO* TODAY, DASHING AROUND THE mall, scouring every shop for the perfect dress for my date tonight, sampling nail polish, and snapping up deals before other shoppers can get to them.

"Okay stop," I say eventually. "I need a break. My hair appointment is in twenty minutes. Can we sit down until then?"

"You know you'll be sitting the whole time you're having your hair done, right?"

"Well, yes, but that doesn't change the fact that my feet are sore now."

Allegra sighs and mutters, "Amateur." She links her arm through mine. "Fine, we can sit at the salon and look at magazines."

"Great."

I kept telling Allegra it was too expensive to colour my

hair, but then she found a Groupon for a salon here at Cavendish, and we both decided my first date with Jackson would be an excellent occasion on which to make my debut as a blonde. The kind of blonde who has a head full of 'natural' highlights from caramel to gold to platinum. Or something like that. Sometimes I zone out when Allegra talks too much.

I plop onto a couch, squeeze the magazine in my hands, and say, "I'm so excited!"

"I know, right? Your hair is gonna look amazing."

"Not about my hair, silly. About my date. Do you think he'll try to kiss me?"

Allegra lets out a hoot of laughter. "He's not a fumbling thirteen-year-old. Of course he's going to kiss you. Why else do people go to movies?"

Well, I thought they went to movies to actually watch movies, but I guess that's what they do with their friends, not the hot guy they've been crushing on for weeks.

"What about you?" I ask. "Is there anyone who's caught your eye since Rob decided to be a jerk last weekend?"

"Well, since you brought it up," Allegra says, flipping her magazine shut and grinning at me. "There is actually someone. Remember when you got Logan to invite us to Smuts on Monday evening and we were hanging out in his room? And that guy who stays in the room across the landing came in to talk to him?"

"Yes?"

"That guy. Damien." She sighs. "Isn't that the sexiest name?"

"Um, sure. Very sexy." Damien seemed more like the quiet, studious type, not like the loud, confident guys Allegra usually goes for. But what do I know?

A woman with short black hair, black clothes, and black shoes ushers me towards one of the chairs in front of the mirror. I sit, fold my hands in my lap, and take a look at my reflection. I breathe in deeply and say to Allegra, "Are you sure about this?"

"Am *I* sure about this? Am I sure I want to see my friend as a hot blonde? Oh yes. The question, Livi, is whether *you* are sure you want to see yourself as a hot blonde."

I tilt my head to the side and practise my flirty smile. "I am. Let's do this."

So here I am in my tight new dress—note to self: STOP BUYING NEW CLOTHES. YOU'LL RUN OUT OF MONEY SOON—crawling around on my bedroom floor, holding my perfectly styled hair back with one hand, and patting the floor with the other in the hopes of coming across the earrings I just dropped. One, they go perfectly with this dress, and two, they don't belong to me. I have to find them.

Eventually I feel something small and sharp beneath my hand, and when I look closer, I see a small aqua coloured stud glinting at me. Now to find the other one.

When I'm finally back on my feet with both earrings in

and my knees dusted off, it's almost time to go.

Shoes, handbag, one last mirror check, and I'm ready.

"Hey, Luke, I'm back." The sound of the front door closing accompanies Adam's voice. "I'll be ready in ten minutes."

Great.

Adam and I haven't spoken since the clothing argument almost a week ago. Considering we live in the same house, I thought it would be more difficult to avoid him, but these days it seems like he's always gone when I wake up and out when I get home late, and the rest of the time I'm on campus or with Allegra. It's been remarkably easy for us to ignore each other.

What will he say about my hair?

My hair turned out to be gorgeous, of course—every shade of blonde mixed in with a hint of my original red— but Adam will no doubt find a way to link it to the fact that my new friends have more influence over me than my old friends. Maybe I can get out of the house without him seeing me.

I lift my keys quietly from my desk, then listen at my door. No sound. No one speaking. No footsteps walking down the passage towards Adam's bedroom. Where did he go?

I check the time on my phone. Crumbs, I really need to get going. Jackson's shift at the cinema finished five minutes ago, which means he'll be waiting for me. He offered to be a gentleman and rush over here to pick me up, but we'd miss the beginning of our movie if he did that, so I told him not to be silly. And then I kissed goodbye to my brilliant hard-to-get skills and I added that he'd have plenty of opportunities to pick me up in the future.

Cringe.

I step out of my bedroom and head for the front door as quietly as I can in heels. *Clip-clop.* No Adam. *Clip-clop.* Still no Adam. I'm almost there when the front door swings open, revealing the last person I want to see: Adam.

Crapazoid. He must have gone back to his car for something.

He freezes in the doorway, his eyes a little wider than normal as he takes in my hair. He stares. Blinks. Stares some more. Then he shakes his head and walks past me, leaving the front door open.

"What?" I shout after him. "WHAT? You want to say something?"

"I don't know who you are," he shouts back.

"Loser," I mutter, slamming the door behind me as I leave.

I put Adam out of my mind, drive as quickly as I can, and arrive at the cinema seven minutes after the time Jackson and I agreed to meet. Seven minutes is good, right? Not too eager, but not annoyingly late.

I reach the top of the elevator and look around. People waiting in line to buy popcorn, drinks and snacks. People fighting over salt canisters. People coming in and out of the toilets. People crowding around the poor guy checking tickets. People, people, people. How am I ever supposed to find—

"Hey there, sexy."

Butterflies flit around my insides—HE THINKS I'M SEXY!—but I manage to pull off the look I practised in my mirror this afternoon. The glance down, smile shyly, then peek up through long lashes look.

Jackson swallows.

Yes! Score! I rock at this flirting business. Jackson's also pretty good, though, so he recovers quickly from him nervous swallowing moment. He steps forward and gives me a hug. It's a smooth, quick movement, over in two seconds, but I'm pretty sure his lips brushed my cheek. "Your hair looks great," he says.

"Thanks." I clear my throat. "So which movie are we watching?"

"I thought you might enjoy that chick flick," he says, pointing to a poster showing a startled guy with a woman on each arm, "rather than the new superhero release everyone's here to see. And we'll have more privacy this way." He winks.

Privacy. I like the sound of that.

I also *really* like the sound of the new superhero movie. I've been looking forward to it ever since I saw the first trailer months ago. But I don't want to miss a second of it, so it's probably a good thing Jackson and I won't be watching it tonight.

Eventually we get through the crowds of superhero fans, past the ticket-checking guy, and into our movie. We sit down as the lights go out and the first advert comes up. I put my handbag on my lap, then settle back with my arms on the armrests. Obviously. Because that's universal sign language for 'Hold my hand,' right?

Jackson leans across the armrest and whispers, "I told you we'd have more privacy in here." He nods to the other side of me, where there are four empty seats and then three girls. On Jackson's side of the row, there's no one.

"Well done," I whisper.

He grins. When he sits back, I realise his hand is holding mine.

Wow. He's good. Guys should take lessons from him.

The butterflies in my stomach continue their flapping as the movie begins. It's a movie stuffed full of chick flick clichés, so I can't help making fun of it. Fortunately, instead of finding this annoying, Jackson seems to enjoy this game. It becomes a race to see who can point out each dumb movie cliché first.

We're about half an hour in when we both turn to each other at the same time, ready to make fun of the same idiotic movie moment. We both start laughing, quietly shaking as neither of us looks away. Our laughter subsides to smiles. And we're still not looking away. Jackson's gaze moves to my lips, then back up again. He leans towards me.

Breathe, Livi. Don't pass out. Breathe!

I breathe in as I lean closer to him. My heart hammers. The butterflies' wings catch fire. His lips touch mine. Slow and soft and sweet. His hand slides through my hair and pulls me closer—and I melt against him.

I'M STILL SMILING WHEN I GET HOME. EVEN THE FACT THAT I have to park in the road because the driveway is blocked by Adam's friends' cars can't turn my lips down. I sit in my car, humming a song and replaying the night's events, that same silly smile on my face and my insides almost as jellylike as when Jackson first leaned over to kiss me. I don't remember much of the movie after that first half hour, but I've become intimately acquainted with Jackson's lips.

Our plan was to have a romantic dinner somewhere after the movie, but at 8:30 pm on a Saturday evening, everywhere decent was already full. We ended up in the mall's food court at the Burger King, which I hadn't exactly pictured as part of our Perfect First Date—I was certainly hoping my new dress would get to see finer cutlery than the plastic stuff they throw into the takeout bag—but I was with Jackson, so it didn't matter where or what we ate.

A sigh escapes my lips as I think of our chocolate milkshake-flavoured kiss as we leant against my car in the parking lot. Jackson wanted to drive me home in my car so he could kiss me goodnight outside my own house, but I told him—with a flirtatious smile—that he could save that for next time.

I wake up from my reverie and remind myself that I'm just about asking to be hijacked, sitting here in the dark with my keys in the ignition. I hurry up the driveway, across the garden that is once again approaching jungle status, and into the house.

Laughter, shouting and music greet me. I remove my heels and hold them in one hand as I walk to the lounge doorway. Five guys—probably all computer science nerds like Adam—are squashed onto our L-shaped couch. Adam and another guy are holding Xbox controllers and sitting forward, staring intently at the TV. Even though I can't see the screen from here, I know they're playing *SoulCalibur*. I recognise the music. Adam shouts "Yesssss!" just as his friend shouts "Awwwww!" and flops back onto the couch. Then someone else notices me standing in the doorway, smacks his friend on the arm, and seconds later they're all staring my way.

"Uh, hey, everyone. I'm Livi." I wave. A chorus of enthusiastic greetings follow. After exchanging an awkward glance with Adam, I say, "Well, I should—"

"Hey, do you want to play?" one of them asks, holding a controller out towards me. "Adam told us you're pretty good."

Really? He didn't tell you I'm a shallow-hearted, friend-abandoning snob?

"Um, thanks, but I'm really tired. I'd be more than happy to kick your butt next time, though."

"Oooooh." Someone else punches the guy still holding the controller out to me.

His arm droops as everyone starts laughing, but he shouts, "Deal!" above the noise.

With a laugh and a shake of my head, I walk to the kitchen. I switch the kettle on, then lean against the counter and begin typing my email version of Dear Diary.

From: Alivia Howard <livi-gem@gmail.com>
Sent: Sat 15 Mar, 11:01 pm
To: Carl <cpsb21@yahoo.com>
Subject: Dear Carl

Okay, so Burger King was not on my list of Top Ten Perfect Dates (it certainly couldn't compare to all our secret rendezvous beside the lake), but SO WHAT. His kisses more than made up for that, and the WAY he asked me out—writing on my hand so he'd have an excuse to hold it—was really cute. Points for that.

And points to me for perfecting the art of looking sexy while eating fries.

So. Grand total of guys Livi has kissed: two.

No, wait, three. I always forget about that slobbery spin-the-bottle experience. ANYWAY. Kissing Jackson was far better than that. It was better than kissing you too, so take that!

(Livi, you're talking to someone who isn't there. You might be crazy.
Really? I don't think so. That's what writing in a diary is all about. No one expects the diary to respond. Duh! Talking to MYSELF on the other hand ... that is crazy.)

Crazy Livi signing out.

"So ... you and Adam are fighting, huh?"

I look up from the rubbish I've just sent out into cyberspace where no one will ever read it and find Luke standing on the other side of the kitchen table. "He speaks," I say before I can stop myself.

"Uh, yes." He scratches his head. "I speak."

I put my phone down. "It's just that most of the time ... you don't."

He shrugs and opens the fridge. "Strong, silent type, I guess."

Well that's the biggest understatement ever. I turn around and pour boiling water over the teabag in my mug. I add a squirt of honey, then move the mug to the table and sit down. Luke is still in the kitchen, making himself a toasted sandwich. And not speaking. "Okay, I'm just gonna be blunt here," I say. "You're really good-looking."

"Uh ..." Luke's eyes dart around, probably looking for

the nearest escape route.

"But you're also really shy. Is that why you don't have a girlfriend? Because I expected there to be, like, hundreds of girls beating down the front door trying to get to you."

He blinks. "That would be … mildly terrifying."

"Have you ever had a girlfriend?"

Luke sits down at the table with his plate and sandwich. Holy hippogriff. I feel an actual conversation coming on. "I had a girlfriend in high school," he says. "She was the one who introduced me to gym, which, um, is where I spend a lot of time now. She did the whole makeover thing on me. Then she dumped me."

"Ouch. That sucks."

He nods. "The girlfriend I have now is a lot nicer. She lives in East London, so that's why you haven't seen her around."

"Oh. So you *do* have a girlfriend." Well, thank goodness I didn't throw myself at Luke on my first day here when I was dazzled by his unexpected hotness.

"Yes."

"Why didn't you say anything?"

He gives me a confused look. "You didn't ask." He takes a bite of his sandwich. A string of melted cheese stretches between his mouth and the bread. I blow on my tea, then sip it. We sit in silence. I wonder if he's planning to eat his sandwich and leave without saying anything else. If I have any more questions for him, I'd better get them in now. Who knows when another opportunity might arise.

"Why do you always avoid talking to me?"

"I …" He looks cornered again. Jeez, am I really that scary? "I used to make you uncomfortable," he says, staring at his plate. "You and Sarah. When we were all younger and I was … even shyer than I am now. I guess I'm still embarrassed about that."

"*You're* embarrassed? Luke, I'm the one who should be embarrassed. Sarah and I used to tease you about staring at us. We … well, we called you names, and we shouldn't have. I'm—" I pause, staring at the blank space of wall above the fridge. I frown. "I'm having a light bulb moment," I murmur. I put my mug down and look intently at Luke. "Do you think everyone gets bullied at some stage in life? I only ever thought about the kids who were mean to *me*. I only ever thought of myself as a *victim*. But I was mean to you. I recognise that now. And maybe the kids who were mean to me were all bullied by someone else at some stage. Like a meanness cycle."

Luke finishes chewing. "Everyone's been hurt by someone else at some point, right? Even if it wasn't intentional."

I nod slowly. "I'm really sorry, Luke. I didn't realise back then that I was being mean."

He stands and carries his empty plate to the sink. When he turns around, he gives me a small smile. "Don't worry about it. It's all in the past."

After he leaves, I pick up my tea, handbag and shoes, and head to my bedroom. After my shower routine, I climb into bed with my laptop and the first season of *Battlestar Galactica*. It's about time for me to watch the series again.

And it'll distract me from the almost overwhelming urge to text Jackson—something I'm pretty sure it's too soon to do.

I settle back and get ready to lose myself in the war of the humans against the Cylons. It's just as captivating as the first time I watched it. I've just started episode three—after convincing myself that I'll watch *just one more*—when my phone's screen lights up. I press pause on my laptop and pick up my phone. Dad. Why is he calling so late?

I sit up and answer the call as mild panic grips my insides. "Dad. Is everything okay?"

"Livi, hi."

"What's going on? Is Mom okay?"

"Yes, yes. She's—she's fine."

"Oh, okay." I lean back and push my laptop out of the way so I can stretch my legs out. "It's just that you don't usually call so late." Or at all. I've spoken to Dad twice in the past five weeks, and both of those calls were on speaker phone with Mom.

"Yes, I ..." I hear him taking a deep breath. "How are you doing?"

"Fiiiiine. I'm just watching DVDs in my room."

"Okay, great."

Pause.

"And how are you?" I ask.

"Good, good." Another pause. "Actually, not so good."

"Why?" The panic starts crawling back. "What's wrong?"

"I ..." He groans, then mutters, "I can't believe I have to do this."

"Dad, what's going on?" I sit up and grip the duvet with my free hand.

"I have to tell you about something. Something that's … complicated and … very difficult to talk about. Something that happened a long time ago, but it's now come to light, so I … need to tell you about it."

I wait, my heart hammering as hard as it did in the cinema earlier, but for an entirely different reason.

"A number of years ago, when you were less than a year old, and I was working a lot between here and Joburg, I …" He sighs. "I had an affair."

Pause.

"You WHAT?"

I sit on Adam's bed with my knees drawn up and my arms wrapped around them. My shocked brain is playing through the same words over and over. *It can't be true. Dad would never do something like that.* But he did. And beneath the shock, something else is beginning to burn.

Anger.

I stare unblinking at Adam's cupboard doors as tears slowly distort my vision. I hear Adam saying goodnight to his friends. They all traipse outside. The front door closes and Adam's footsteps move towards his bedroom.

He stops in the doorway. Sighs. "Livi, do we have to do this—" His words falter. "What's wrong?"

"My dad," I say, my voice coming out strangely hoarse. I'm still staring at the cupboard doors, but they're swimming now. Swimming through furious, unshed tears.

Adam is across the room in a second, sitting on the bed and leaning towards me. "What happened? Is he okay?"

My head moves slowly from side to side. "No. He's a lying, cheating bastard."

"What? Why?"

I blink. A tear drops onto my cheek. I swipe at it before turning to look at Adam. Four words boom inside my head. Four words demanding to be said out loud. Four words I'm terrified of saying, because uttering them will make them real. Four words I have no hope of holding in.

"I have a sister."

Adam's eyes grow wider.

The words sound foreign. Ridiculous. So I say them again. "I have a sister."

"You … have a sister?"

The rage boils over. "I HAVE A SISTER. A seventeen-year-old half-sister. Because my father couldn't keep his hands off some other woman. Because my mom and I weren't good enough for him. Because he clearly didn't give a damn about the fact that *he was married*!" I grasp the sleeve of Adam's T-shirt in my fist. "How could he do this to us? To my mom? How could he *lie* to us all this time? And this other woman. How could she go after a man who *already belonged to someone else*?"

Adam carefully removes my fist and holds my hand in both of his. "How did you find out?"

"He phoned to tell me. He—he said it 'came to light,' so now he had to tell me about it, and I don't know what that means because I put the phone down after he reached the part about having another daughter. Another daughter! *I'm* supposed to be his only daughter!"

Adam rubs my hand. "Have you spoken to your mom?"

I close my eyes and shake my head. "I want to. And then I don't. I don't know what to say. If I'm feeling hurt, can you imagine how she must be feeling? And it's really late. She's probably … I don't know. I just don't know." I grab a cushion and climb off the bed with it. I hug it to my chest as I pace. "I can't figure out what to feel. One moment I'm furious, and then … I think about how … he didn't want us." I stop pacing. "He wanted someone else. And then I just want to cry. And crying's so stupid. He's not worth it." I continue my angry stomping. "Horrible, lying, cheating—STUPID SHOES!" I yell as I trip over a pair of running shoes on the floor. "Why do things *always* jump in front of me when I'm trying to walk?"

"Well, uh—"

"Don't answer that." I sit on the edge of the bed with my arms wrapped around the cushion. "I'm sorry. We haven't spoken all week, and now I'm dumping my problems on top of you."

"Livi, we've been dumping our problems on top of each other for six years. That's what friends do, remember?"

I shrug. Does that mean I should be telling my new friends about this? Somehow, I can't imagine sitting down with Allegra, Charlotte, Courtney and Amber and talking about my father's secret relationship with another woman and how I suddenly have a sister. I imagine it would be more like discussing the latest scandal in their favourite TV show than them providing support for me through a difficult time.

Fortunately, I have Adam. And Sarah. Who will be receiving a call from me first thing in the morning.

"I think I should go to bed," I say.

"Will you be able to sleep?"

I rub my eyes. "I don't know." Both my mind and body feel unbearably weary all of a sudden, so I sure hope so. "I'll just … try to think of nothing."

From: Alivia Howard <livi-gem@gmail.com>
Sent: Sun 16 Mar, 1:34 am
To: Carl <cpsb21@yahoo.com>
Subject: Dear Carl

Dad is a gigantic ass.
And … I have a sister.
In. Sane.
(And I want to punch Dad.)

"Can I get you anything else?" Adam asks, eyeing my mug of tea and the open jar of peanut butter on the table in front of me.

I pull the spoon out of my mouth and shake my head. I don't feel like eating anything in particular, but I'm hungry, and I like peanut butter. So here I am eating it for breakfast.

Adam turns back to the frying pan on the stove and cracks several eggs into it.

"My mom phoned this morning," I say, slowly stirring my tea.

Adam swings around. "Oh. How is she? What did she say?"

"She's ... I don't know. Angry, confused, hurt. She's staying with my grandparents in Hillcrest. She found out about the affair on Friday night and left home yesterday morning."

"Did she say how she found out?"

"Yes. So, um, apparently my parents never use each other's laptops, but my dad was supposed to forward something to my mom—some document they both needed to sign or something—but the email didn't go through. Dad said he sent it, but Mom said she never got it. Dad was in the shower, and Mom was frustrated that she hadn't got this thing yet, so she opened up his laptop and looked at his emails. She couldn't find it, so she thought maybe he'd deleted it by accident. She went to the Trash folder, and amongst all the other stuff there, she saw something that said, 'Please can I meet you.'" I stare at my tea for a while, then sip it. "Imagine if she'd just thought it was spam and hadn't opened it. Everything would still be fine."

Adam scoops his fried egg onto a piece of toast, turns the stove off, and sits down. "I'm guessing the email was from your ... half-sister."

My eyes flick up to his. "It's weird saying it, right?"

"Very."

I take a deep breath. "Yes, it was from her. She explained who she was and how her mother had always refused to tell her anything about her father, but that she'd finally found out who he was. Dad hadn't replied to the email. I guess he just deleted it. Mom almost thought it was one of those hoax emails, but the girl wasn't asking for money. She was asking to meet. So Mom confronted Dad about it, and that's how it all came out."

"Your poor mom," Adam says quietly. "It must have been such a shock."

I scoop more peanut butter from the jar and nibble on it. "She said she never suspected a thing. Never doubted his loyalty. Never believed he could lie to her so convincingly." I lick the spoon clean. "Part of me is really mad at this girl for sending the email. If she had no interest in meeting Dad, the affair would probably have stayed a secret forever and we'd all be happy."

"And the other part of you?" Adam asks.

"The other part of me is … curious," I admit. "About her. What she's like. Anyway, it doesn't matter. I don't want to think about it now. Um, so where have you been going every morning this past week?" I tap my spoon against the side of my mug. "Every day I woke up and you were already gone. Which was great, since things were awkward between us and I was avoiding you, but where were you?"

"Gym," Adam says, swallowing his final mouthful. "With Luke."

"Gym? Since when do you go to gym?"

"Hey, this magnificent body does not maintain itself, you know."

I start laughing. I didn't think I'd be able to laugh today, but here I am laughing at Adam's apparently magnificent body. "You're right. Your body has been mind-bogglingly magnificent ever since you got back from America. What exactly were you doing at summer camp? Weightlifting the campers?"

"Yes. I jogged around every morning with a camper over each shoulder." His smile slips as his phone dings and he picks it up to check the message. With a frown, he places the phone screen-down on the table.

"Everything okay?" I ask.

"Yes." He smiles. "What are you doing today?"

"I'm going to a vintage market with Allegra and Courtney. I thought about cancelling, but, you know, then I'd just sit around here thinking about how my father has ruined my family. So … yeah. Want to come with?"

"I'd rather be draped naked over a beehive."

"Still not a fan of markets, huh?"

"Nope. But … maybe we can do something later? This evening? Unless you have, I don't know, a date or something."

"Nah, that was last night."

Surprise colours Adam's expression. "Really?"

"Yes."

"Oh, that guy you said was checking you out in class?"

I nod, pleased Adam remembers me telling him about Jackson. I thought he tuned out whenever Sarah and I started talking about guys. "Yes, that's the one. Movie, dinner, and lots of making out."

"Uh …"

"Sorry. Too much info?"

Adam clears his throat. "Right, so that explains the dress and the hair and everything last night."

I twist a golden strand of hair around my finger. "You hate it, don't you."

"What? No, I don't hate it. I just … liked you as a redhead."

I roll my eyes at him. "Gingers aren't cool. People make

jokes about them."

"Firstly, so what? Secondly, you're definitely more of a redhead than a ginger. And thirdly, if red hair wasn't cool, there wouldn't be so many celebrities dying their hair that colour. And don't forget about all the kick-ass fictional redheads. Like Jean Grey and Ariel and Princess Fiona from *Shrek*."

"And Dumbledore."

"Exactly. Let's not forget Dumbledore."

"Well, anyway, Jackson called me sexy, so the blonde hair was worth it."

Adam sighs and says nothing.

"You're trying really hard not to roll your eyes or mime puking, aren't you?"

"Pretty much."

I stick my tongue out, then push my chair back and stand up. "Time to shower. Unless you want to go first?"

"No, go ahead." Adam places my mug and his plate in the sink.

"Thanks. And, um, I'll do the dishes before I go out. You can leave them." *See? I can take responsibility.*

He smiles. "Thanks, Liv."

"And Adam? Can I say something else?"

"Yes?"

"You were right. Which I guess isn't surprising, since you turn out to be right about ninety-nine percent of the time. And in this case you were right about me, um, struggling a bit with—as you put it—'real life.'" I add the air quotes with my fingers. "But I'm trying. I paid Luke back for the grocery shopping he did last weekend, and I saw the milk was finished on Thursday, so I bought more on my way home. And I managed to get most of my laundry done this week, so I won't be borrowing any more of your clothes."

I half expect Adam to give me a slow clap and a sarcastic 'Well done'—after all, as far as accomplishments go, buying milk and doing laundry aren't exactly high up—but instead he looks at his feet, shrugs, and says, "It wasn't … such a huge deal. I didn't—I mean—yeah, anyway. Thanks."

I watch him as he leaves the kitchen. "Weird," I murmur to myself.

ALLEGRA AND COURTNEY WANT TO KNOW EVERY DETAIL of my date with Jackson last night, but after all the family drama that's occupied my mind since then, the date seems light years ago. And a whole lot less important. Nevertheless, I open up my Bag of Appropriate Responses and pull out my squeals, sighs, and giggles.

We're halfway to the vintage market when Courtney receives a text from Logan the Legend saying he's free now if she still needs help with the section she's been struggling with in Stats. Apparently he aced the course last year, which added to his legend status, because after that, everyone knew he could party hard *and* work hard. Allegra tells Courtney to ask Logan if Damien is around. When the answer comes back—yes—we're all thrown against our seat belts as Allegra hits the brakes, performs an illegal U-turn, and accelerates back towards campus.

I close my eyes and try not to groan out loud. I wanted a *proper* distraction today, and sitting in a guys' res watching two of my friends flirt-study doesn't count. I pull out my phone and text Jackson. I know I'm supposed to wait for him to contact me first so I don't come across as desperate, but maybe if I make the message casually flirty, it'll camouflage the desperation.

Livi: Hey ;-) In case you couldn't tell, I had fun last night ;-) Anyhoo, Allegra, Courtney and I are gonna be at Smuts in about 20 min. Just letting you know in case you're free to come hang out with us. xx L

I then spend the next ten minutes examining every word I wrote and cringing over all the things that shouldn't be there, like the two winking smileys (too much? Should one have been a normal smiley?) and the word 'Anyhoo' (do people actually say that?) and—oh, terrific—the fact that I signed off as 'xx L.' Which is basically the same as XXL. *Hello, my name is Extra Extra Large, and I am an IDIOT.*

Jackson: Hey, sexy bunny. Sorry, I've got a family thing on. Forgot to tell you about it last night. Must be because I was having fun too ;) I'll see you Monday. J

J. Now that's a heck of a lot cooler than XXL. Disappointed, I return my phone to my handbag and watch the scenery flashing by outside. Jackson lives at home because his parents' house is only twenty minutes from

UCT, which means he gets roped into the kind of family stuff that those of us living far from home don't have to get involved in. He complains about it, but I know he enjoys not having to worry about buying food or doing laundry.

I close my eyes and try to remember the feel of his hands around my waist and his lips on mine, but the memory of Dad's phone call—and the two calls I've ignored since then—keeps getting in the way. I can't stop thinking about him (I hope he's wracked with guilt) and Mom (is she falling apart? Is she dealing with this devastating news by working even harder than normal?) and the other woman (is she prettier than Mom? More intelligent? A husband-seducing minx?) and my half-sister (what does she look like? Does she know about my mother? Does she know about *me*?) and the dreaded D-word that no one has said but everyone must be thinking.

Allegra pulls up outside Graça Machel Hall, and Courtney runs inside to fetch their notes. "You can share with us, Livi," Allegra says, checking her reflection in the rearview mirror.

"Yeah, okay." I actually have a semi-decent understanding of what's going on in Stats—as does Allegra—but when I offered to help Courtney, she said she could figure it out on her own. I should have known that 'needing help' was just another flirting tactic.

I look out the window and try to calculate how long it will take me to walk home from here. Fifteen minutes maybe? Twenty? I'm not too sure, but I'd be happy to walk an hour or more if it means I don't have to watch Allegra and Courtney bat their eyelashes and try to make the words 'probability distribution' and 'linear regression' sound sexy. In fact, what I'd like more than anything else right now is to walk. Slowly. Unintentionally. Letting my mind wander. Breathing in fresh air and breathing out all the complications brought on by my father's—

"Okay, I've got everything! Let's go!" Courtney jumps back into the car, and then we're zipping up the hill to Upper Campus. We park on Rugby Road and walk up the steps to Smuts Hall. We're busy signing in at reception when I decide there's no way I'm spending my afternoon here.

"I'm not feeling so great," I say to Allegra. "I think I'm gonna walk home."

"*Walk* home? From here?"

"Yes. It's not that far."

"Don't be ridiculous, Livi. You can't walk from here. This is South Africa. You'll get mugged."

Allegra sounds so much like my mother at this point that I can't help laughing. "It's the middle of the day, Allegra. And thousands of students walk on the roads around here all the time. I'll be fine."

"But you said you're not feeling well. Maybe I ..." She looks over her shoulder to where Courtney is telling the receptionist which room to buzz to get Logan to come down and fetch us. "Maybe I should quickly take you home."

"No. Seriously. I'll be fine." I give her a quick goodbye hug and add, "You don't want to miss out on any time with Damien, do you?"

She smiles. "I guess not. Okay. Be safe."

I head outside, and once I'm down the stairs and out of view of the front door of Smuts Hall, I pull my phone out and open the maps app. I may be happy to wander the streets of Rondebosch as I slowly make my way home, but my direction sense is terrible and I'd like to know that I'm at least heading *towards* Toll Road and not away from it.

It takes me almost two hours to get home because, after reaching Main Road, I decide to make dinner for Adam tonight as a way of making up for neglecting our friendship. Which means that I then spend an unnecessarily large amount of time wandering the aisles of the closest shop searching for recipes on my phone and ingredients on the shelves. And then I have to lug heavy shopping bags all the way home, which I didn't think about when I first came up with my brilliant dinner plan.

I change my sweaty clothes as soon as I get home, then lie on my bed looking through recipes on my laptop and ignoring another call from Dad. Adam and Luke are both out, so I turn my music up loud and sing along while creating a Pinterest board of the best recipes I come across. I'll have to make more time to stay at home so I can try these out.

As evening draws closer, I turn my music off and head to the kitchen to start my cooking extravaganza. At least, that's what I plan for it to be. And if so many people cook, it can't be that hard, right? You just follow the recipe.

I gather my ingredients on the table, then search the kitchen for a chopping board. "Where are you?" I murmur as I search the cupboards. Finally, in a cupboard above the counter, on the highest shelf, I see a collection of chopping boards. *Why? Who puts chopping boards so high up that regular people can't reach them?*

Absently humming the song that's currently stuck in my head, I drag a chair to the counter and stand on it. It's the wobbly type, which isn't great, but I'm sure I can manage to balance for less than a minute. I remove the pile of chopping boards—who knows, I might need them all—and close the cupboard.

"What are you doing?"

Startled, I almost fall off the chair. The chopping boards slide off my hand and clatter onto the floor. I cringe at the noise. When they come to rest, I turn slowly and find Adam beside the fridge. "Nothing. I'm doing nothing."

His lips twitch as he suppresses a smile. "Your clothing suggests otherwise."

"Huh?" I look down at my *I solemnly swear that I am up to no good* Harry Potter tank top. I look up again. "Okay. That is an unfortunate coincidence."

"So you're not up to no good?"

"I'm—no, I'm—Okay, fine." I climb off the chair and cross my arms. "I was going to surprise you with dinner."

His eyebrows climb up his forehead. "You can cook?"

"Of course I can cook."

I have no idea if I can cook. I haven't cooked dinner here once. The last time I even ate dinner here was the night we sat on the floor eating sandwiches with our moms. Ever since then I've either skipped dinner or been with Allegra. We often get food together somewhere nearby, or end up in her room at res eating takeout.

"I think I have a better idea," Adam says. "How about we go to Jazzy Beanbag down the road and get dinner there?"

I place my hands on my hips. "You're avoiding my cooking."

"I'm … looking out for my general wellbeing. And yours," he adds hastily as I throw an onion at him.

"But I've been looking at recipes all afternoon. I want to show you that I'm not Princess Useless who can't do anything for herself."

He gives me a smile that makes me think Allegra might have been right when she called him cute. "I never called you Princess Useless."

I point a spatula at him. "But you were thinking it."

"No. I might have been thinking Princess Chopping Board Challenged, or Princess Kitchen Hazard, but never— Ow!" The second onion catches him on the ear before landing on the floor and rolling into the passage.

"You're supposed to *catch* the onion, moron," I tell him. "Now I'm an onion short."

"Oh, come on, the onion is fine. Especially now that it's made its escape," he adds with a cheeky grin before dashing into the passage so I can't throw anything else at him. I press my lips together, shake my head, and work really hard at not laughing. "Truce?" Adam says. His arm appears around the edge of the doorway and waves the onion at me.

"You're supposed to have a white flag."

"The onion is white inside."

I allow myself a smile. "Fine. You can come back and I'll consider not throwing anything else at you."

He walks back in and sets the poor battered onion on the table. "Plan B," he says. "I help you cook dinner so that you don't set the house on fire or create something inedible, and afterwards we go to Jazzy Beanbag for wine or cocktails or beer or something."

"They serve all that stuff?"

"Of course."

"Hmm. This cafe might be better than I thought."

Jazzy Beanbag is down the road and takes us about five minutes to walk to. The outer walls are covered in peeling paint, and the windows are tinted just enough to be difficult to see through, which is why I always thought it rather a dodgy place. Inside, though, it's entirely different. It's larger than it appears from the outside, oddly shaped with nooks here and there. Warm lighting illuminates a mishmash of couches, chairs, tables, and beanbags. Several walls feature canvases of abstract art, while others are covered with sheet music or the pages of books. A bar runs across the length of one wall, and a stage across another.

"They have live music here," I blurt out the moment I see the band.

"They do."

"That is seriously cool."

"Of course it is," Adam says. "Do you really think I'd keep inviting you here if it wasn't awesome?"

"I guess not." I tap my foot to the beat, taking in the vibe as I look around at the groups of people enjoying everything from drinks to snacks to full-on meals. "It's just that none of my friends have mentioned this place, so I thought it was kind of lame."

Adam shrugs. "Maybe you're hanging out with the wrong crowd."

I try to elbow him in the ribs, but he grasps my arm and pulls me towards a table against the wall next to a red leg-shaped lamp with a feathery lampshade.

"Seriously, though," I say as we sit down. "How come more people don't know about this place?"

"They tend to feature new bands that hardly anyone's heard of, so I guess they don't have famous names bringing in more customers." He leans over and grabs two menus from the empty table next to ours. "They're non-existent on social media, and they've done almost no marketing since they opened two years ago, so if you think about it, it's actually a miracle they have as many customers as they do."

"Word of mouth, I guess."

Adam nods. "I asked the owner why he isn't doing more to market this place, and he said he likes it the way it is. He doesn't want it to become the kind of place where people have to book a table days in advance or queue out the door and around the corner."

"You spoke to the owner?"

"Yes, he's the guy behind the bar."

A waiter, tall and skinny with an electric shock of white hair, walks up to our table and grins at Adam. "Hey, man, what are you doing back here so soon?"

"Just thought I'd introduce Livi to the cool beats of *The Flying Monkey Train*."

"Oh, hey, you're Livi. I'm Hugo." The waiter reaches out and shakes my hand, his expression suggesting he's heard of me before. Which is a little weird.

"Um, hi."

"Anyway, can I get you guys anything?"

Adam asks for a beer, and, after a quick look at the drinks section of the menu, I order a glass of red wine.

"Ooh, sophisticated palate," Hugo says. He nods appreciatively, then heads back to the bar.

I turn to Adam with narrowed eyes. "What aren't you telling me?"

"Uh … I may have neglected to mention that I now work here. I guess I told Hugo about you and Luke when we were chatting." Adam leans over and whispers, "Hugo's in third year and still lives with his parents, but he'd appreciate you not mentioning that to anyone, especially the drummer of the *The Flying Monkey Train*, whom he happens to have a crush on."

I look over at the tiny brunette girl behind the drum set,

then back at Adam. "Wait. Back up. Since when do you work here?"

Adam settles back in his chair. "Not long. For about a week now."

"Oh. I didn't realise you were planning to work this year."

"Well, uh …" Adam runs his finger along the edge of a menu. "I wasn't. But living away from home is turning out to be more expensive than I anticipated, and my parents … Well, my dad isn't getting as many clients as he used to, so things are tight for him and Mom. So I don't want to bug them for money."

I nod, but I'm not sure what to say. Money has always been an awkward topic of conversation for us, mainly because my family has far too much of it and Adam's family has never quite had enough. Fortunately, his parents managed to produce two brilliant children, so their education has always been taken care of by scholarships. But they always had second-hand, falling-apart versions of all the things I took for granted.

The Flying Monkey Train finishes their current song with a cymbal crash so loud, even the tiny drummer who created it looks startled. After a smattering of applause, the lead guitarist launches into a slow solo. His deep, husky voice captures the attention of the room, bringing in some enthusiastic applause after the first few lines of song, and even a 'Woohoo!' from several of the tables.

"Could be you up there soon, hey?" Hugo says to Adam as he sets our drinks down in front of us. "Charming the ladies with your guitar skills."

I pick up my wine glass and open my mouth to tell Hugo that Adam doesn't play guitar, but Adam's already saying, "We should get Livi up there on open mic night."

"Whoa, what? I don't think so." I swirl my wine and bring it to my nose to sniff it. English toffee and … something berry-ish. My parents are wine snobs, and this is one of their recent favourites, which is how I know I like it.

I wonder if they'll ever drink wine together again.

"Come on, Livi," Adam says. "You're always singing at home. You should share your talent with others."

"My talent?" I start laughing. "What talent?"

"You were in the choir," Adam reminds me.

"Right. *Group* singing."

"You did a solo once at a school function."

"Which was a terrible mistake." I turn to Hugo, who's leaning against the empty chair on the other side of the table. "I was so nervous I could hardly breathe. And, as I'm sure you know, breath is required for singing."

He smiles. "Sounds embarrassing."

"It was a nightmare. So—" I lean back and raise my wine glass towards the band on stage "—how about we enjoy our drinks and listen to the people who *can* sing."

Adam picks up his beer bottle and taps it against my glass with a *ping*. "Excellent idea."

From: Alivia Howard <livi-gem@gmail.com>
Sent: Sun 16 Mar, 11:02 pm
To: Carl <cpsb21@yahoo.com>
Subject: Dear Carl

You know what? You might have had a grand castle with beautiful grounds and tennis courts and a lake and a helicopter to fly you to every European royal's birthday party, but sometimes the only thing a person needs is a comfy seat, great music, an excellent glass of wine, and good company.

(And a red leg-shaped lamp covered in feathers. Just because.)

AFTER A WEEKEND OF NO STUDYING AT ALL, I HAVE TO bury myself in my notes and textbooks in order to survive the Stats test on Tuesday and the Ecos test on Thursday. With only three weeks left until the end of the quarter, we can't go anywhere without having tests and assignments thrown at us.

By the time Thursday evening rolls around, I'm desperate to spend time with Jackson—although I don't tell *him* that, of course. The last person I want to speak to is Dad, but it's his face I see on my ringing phone seconds after I arrive home and dump my varsity bag on my bed. I've ignored every call since the first one last Saturday evening, which probably makes me childish and immature, but I didn't want to have to listen to a stream of excuses and apologies. The past few days have given me time to come up with some questions, though. And Dad is the only one who can give me the answers.

I accept the call and bring the phone to my ear.

"Livi? Hello?"

"Hi." I sit on the edge of my bed.

"Oh, Livi, I'm so glad you answered. I just … I just want to talk."

"I gathered."

The silence on the other end of the line tells me he isn't quite sure where to go from here. "Our, uh, last conversation ended rather abruptly," he says. "You didn't really get a chance to tell me what you were thinking and … and feeling."

"Really, Dad? You can't figure that out for yourself? You want me to *tell* you that I feel hurt and betrayed and not good enough?"

"Not good enough? Livi, you have always been the most—"

"Stop." Dad sounds close to tears, and I don't want to feel sorry for him. "If it wasn't because Mom and I weren't enough for you, then what was the reason?"

"It …" He sighs. "I know this isn't what you want to hear, but it was complicated."

"Great. Question number two, then. How long did it go on for?"

"Only a few months—"

"Months!"

"—and then I ended it. Things were already over when I found out Helen was pregnant."

Helen. I've never hated a name so much. "So then what?

You abandoned your lover and your illegitimate daughter?"

"Livi …"

"Oh, I'm sorry. Are we supposed to be sugar-coating this? Would you like me to say *Helen* instead of *lover*?"

Another sigh from Dad. "I did not *abandon* them. Helen and I agreed to go our separate ways. I already had my family, and she didn't seem to mind the prospect of being a single mother. I send money every month, but that's the only role I play in their lives. *You* are my daughter, Livi. You and your mother are my family. I don't want to lose that."

"Well, you really messed up then, didn't you."

"I did. I know I did. But I want to fix this. I want to be a family again. I've … I've been to a counsellor, and she suggested it might be a good idea for you and Mom and me to have some sessions together as a family. I was thinking that when you come home in April, we could—"

"Have you run this idea by Mom yet?"

Dad hesitates. "I … I still need to sort that out."

"She isn't speaking to you, is she?"

"Livi, that's between your mother and me. Most of this, actually, is between her and me. You can ask your questions, and I will be as transparent as possible wherever appropriate, but there are some things you don't need to—"

"What's her name?"

Dad doesn't need to ask who I'm talking about. There's only one other person in this mess who hasn't been named yet. "Andrea." Dad clears her throat. "Her name is Andrea."

Andrea. I try to hate the thought of her, but I can't.

"Livi, please will you consider the counselling option."

"I don't know if—" I break off as I hear a shout from Adam's room. "Hold on." I stick my head into the passage. I can hear Adam's raised voice on the other side of his door, but I can't quite make out what he's saying. I bring the phone to my ear again. "I need to go, Dad."

"Okay. If you want to talk about anything, please phone me. No matter what time of day or night. I will answer." Coming from the guy who's spent most of my life in meetings, I'm not sure I believe that one.

I end the call and throw my phone onto my bed. I cross the passage and stand in front of Adam's door. I listen carefully, but there's no sound. No shouting, no talking, no music, nothing.

I knock.

No answer.

I knock again.

"Not now!"

I frown at the door. Something's definitely happened. Should I go in? See if I can do anything to help? I raise my hand to knock a third time, but something holds me back. The anger in his voice. The anger that might explode all over me if I go in there.

I lower my hand, walk to Luke's room, and knock on his door instead. An uncertain "Come in" follows, and I open the door and look inside. I've never been in here before, and I'm surprised at how messy it is. Unmade bed, clothes on the floor, a bowl and several mugs on the desk.

"Oh, hi, Livi," Luke says from his seat at the desk.

"Do you know why Adam's upset?" I ask.

Luke frowns. "Adam's upset?"

I sigh. "Okay, never mind."

I head back to my room, flop onto my bed, and type a message to Jackson to ask if he's finished playing squash with Rob yet. My thumb is hovering over the send button when the phone starts ringing and Jackson's name shows up on the screen. A thrill shoots through me as I force myself to let it ring a few times before answering. "Hey, Jackson."

"Hey, sexy bunny. Have you been missing me?"

I bite my lip, but that doesn't stop the smile spreading across my face. "Perhaps. Just a little bit."

"Do you want to go watch another movie tonight?"

I roll onto my tummy. "You mean do I want to make out with you in the dark again?"

He chuckles. "Well, you know, I was trying to keep it classy by *not* saying that, but ya. That's pretty much what I was getting at."

I giggle. "In that case, I would love to watch another movie with you tonight."

After giving him my address so he can pick me up this time, I examine my wardrobe for an appropriate outfit. Jeans? No, I enjoyed the feel of Jackson's hand on my bare knee last time. Maybe the skirt I bought when—

Adam's door opens. I hurry across my room and look out the doorway, but Adam's already at the other end of the passage. "Adam?" I call after him. He doesn't answer, disappearing into the lounge instead. "Adam, is everything okay?" I take a few steps out of my room as he exits the lounge while pulling a jacket on. "Did I do something wrong?" I ask. *Certainly wouldn't be the first time.* "Are you mad at me?" He stops at the front door, his hand on the doorknob. "Please talk to me, Adam. I just—"

"Not everything is about you, Alivia!" he yells, swinging around to look at me. In that moment before he yanks the door open, I see red-rimmed eyes. He walks out and slams the door shut.

Crying. He's been crying. I've *never* seen Adam cry.

I run into the lounge and look out the window. Adam slides the gate open just wide enough to squeeze through, then lets out a yell and kicks it when it gets stuck and won't close properly. He heads down the street and out of sight.

My second date with Jackson is similar to the first, although it takes us less time to get to the making out, and we skip the Burger King dinner afterwards because I ate something at home earlier and Jackson got takeout with Rob after their squash game. After driving me home, Jackson suggests we continue our make-out session in his back seat—cliché style—but I remind him that we both have early lectures tomorrow, and with more tests next week, we should be responsible and get to bed at a decent hour. I don't add that I'm worried about Adam and want to get inside to check if he's home. Jackson probably wouldn't appreciate the fact that my thoughts are occupied by another guy.

I hurry to Adam's room the moment I get inside, but his

door is open and he isn't there. I check the rest of the house, but I already know I won't find him. I pull out my phone and call him, but he doesn't answer. I check the time. 10:51 pm. Where would he have gone on foot? Jazzy Beanbag? Well, it seems a good place for me to start looking. Maybe I shouldn't go searching for him, though. I mean, he's probably fine, and when I do find him, he'll get mad that I'm interfering. Trying to get involved.

Not everything is about you, Alivia!

The echo of his words hurts almost as much as the words themselves did when they were flung at me.

I press my fingers to my temples. *What do I do, what do I do?*

I hurry to my room, remove my skirt, and pull on a pair of jeans. I push my feet into a pair of Tomy Takkies, then rummage in the drawer of my bedside table for my car keys. I clutch them in my hand, sit on the edge of the bed, and stare at my phone. I'll give him until 11 pm. If I haven't heard from him by then, I'm—

My phone's screen lights up.

The *Pirates of the Caribbean* main theme blasts forth.

I grab it and answer. "Adam? Are you okay?"

"Hi, Livi," says a voice that isn't Adam's. "This is Hugo. From Jazzy Beanbag. Um …"

Oh crap oh crap oh crap. "What's wrong? What happened?"

"No, nothing serious. It's just … Adam's had a bit too much to drink."

I let out a groan of relief. "Okay, next time you need to start with, 'Hello, this isn't Adam, but Adam is fine.'"

"Right, sorry. Anyway, he's not, like, hectic drunk. He can still walk—sort of. But I'm worried if he walks home alone, he might pass out on the way or something. Are you nearby? I mean, are you able to come get him? If you're not, that's cool. I can probably take him in about twenty minutes. It's just quite busy here right now and—"

"I'm coming now," I say.

"Great. Thanks."

I feel ridiculous driving to a place that's so close, but it'll be easier to get Adam home in a car than to drag him by foot. I park and run inside. Hugo, having just collected a tray of empty glasses from a busy table, looks up and walks over to me. "Hey, thanks for coming. I moved him to a table around the corner where fewer people are disturbed by his random shouting."

"His random shouting?" I repeat as Hugo leads me to Adam's table.

"Yes. Things like 'All girls are just out to break your heart' and 'My ex-girlfriend is the devil.'"

"Oh, crapazoid," I mutter. "Jenna broke up with him."

"Yes. He didn't actually say that, but I'm ninety-nine percent sure that's what happened."

We find Adam with his arms on the table, his chin resting on his hands, and his eyes staring half-open at the band on stage. He raises his head. He looks at me, then at Hugo. "Thanks a lot, dude," he slurs. "A babysitter is exactly what I need right now."

"Well, at least he recognises me," I say to Hugo.

"I can hear you, you know," Adam says loudly.

"Great. Hopefully you can stand too."

Adam can stand, but walking straight turns out to be a challenge. He bumps into three tables trying to get out of Jazzy Beanbag, and, once we're outside, he walks into a rubbish bin while trying to avoid the street light pole beside my car. I open the passenger door for him and push him inside.

"Stupid cow," he mutters.

"Excuse me?" I might have to dump him on the sidewalk after that one.

"Not you," he says, leaning forward and grasping his head. "My demon ex-girlfriend."

I climb into the driver's seat and start the car. "I'm really sorry, Adam." I touch his shoulder, then pull out of the parking spot and use a side road to turn around in.

"She cheated on me," Adam says to the floor between his legs. "Did I tell you that? And it wasn't just a kiss. Oh no. No no no stupid cow. She slept with some other dude. Slept. Sex. The thing we were waiting for. We were waiting for each other. And I'm ..." He sits up and leans his head against the window. "I'm ... such a loser. A virgin loser."

"Adam, you're not—"

"Loser loser loser," he mutters.

I stop in our driveway and jump out to open the gate. Then I drive onto the long grass and park. Adam slowly pulls himself out of the passenger seat while I close the gate. *Really* need to get the landlord to fix that motor.

"I'm fine," Adam mumbles when I try to take his arm to help him up the front steps. He stumbles down the passage, using the walls for support, and then into his bedroom, where he promptly collapses onto his bed and doesn't say another word.

From: Alivia Howard <livi-gem@gmail.com>
Sent: Thur 20 Mar, 11:24 pm
To: Sarah Henley <s.henley@gmail.com>
Subject: Sad face

If you happen to see Jenna Mackenzie around, do me a favour and give her a good, hard slap for breaking Adam's heart. And if she's with the guy she decided to drop her panties for, you can slap him too.

I'M UP EARLY ON FRIDAY MORNING, PARTLY BECAUSE I have an early lecture, but mainly because I want to check on Adam. I put on my glasses and slippers and go into his bedroom.

He isn't there.

Seriously? Aren't people supposed to get hungover and sleep in late after they drink too much? I wander around the house until I find him in the lounge. He's dragged the couch across the room so it's sitting in front of the fireplace. The fireplace which—I see when standing on tiptoe and looking over the back of the couch—has a fire in it. We've had wood sitting in the grate for several weeks now, waiting for our first winter fire. I thought it would be at least another month before we lit it, though.

Without saying anything, I leave the lounge and head to the kitchen to make one mug of coffee and one mug of tea.

I carry them back to the lounge, place them on the floor between the couch and the fireplace, and sit down. I pull my legs up and cross them. "I've been thinking," I say. "I haven't missed any lectures yet, and you probably haven't either. Which makes us terrible students, because bunking lectures is all part of the experience, right? So … today seems like a good day to bunk lectures."

Adam nods slowly. "I think you may be right."

"I'm also a little confused to find you out of bed so early. Have you been burning love letters or something?"

"No. I just wanted to sit in front of a fire."

After a minute or two, he reaches forward and picks up his coffee. I pick up my tea. "Do you want to talk about it?" I say carefully.

He slowly swirls his coffee. "I just can't believe she'd do this. I never would have thought her capable of this kind of … betrayal. I can understand her breaking up with me. Not wanting to be with me anymore. But to go behind my back and do what she did with that guy, and then not say anything about it for *months*—pretending everything was fine—I just … never saw that coming.

"On the other hand, I was gone for so long, perhaps you could call me an idiot for *not* seeing it coming."

I shake my head. "You are not an idiot, Adam. If she couldn't stay faithful to you then she should have broken up with you before doing anything with anyone else."

He looks at me. "It happened in October last year. And not just once. That's when it *started*. Then she felt guilty just before I got back in December, so she ended things with the other guy. Made him promise not to say anything. Figured she and I could do the long distance thing for one more year. But seeing you in my jersey was apparently a good enough reason for her to start hooking up with that dude behind my back again, until last night when she finally found the guts to come clean about everything and break up with me."

"Oh, crap, I'm so sorry about the jersey thing. I had NO idea she'd get so upset about—"

"NO. You are NOT the one who's supposed to be apologising in this situation. She's the one who did the cheating. She's the one who broke my heart."

I rest my hand on Adam's knee. "Want me to beat her up?"

He makes a noise that sounds almost like a laugh. "Now that might actually be entertaining."

"Good thing she's on the other side of the country or I'd have kicked her ass already."

"Thanks, Liv." Adam pats my hand, then takes a long swig of coffee. He swallows. "I still feel as though I should be walking around with a label on my back that says Broken Hearted Loser."

I tap the side of my mug with my fingernail. "Mmm. I know what that's like. It'll pass with time."

Adam frowns. "Since when do you know what that's like? Has that Jackson dude already hurt you?"

"No, no, no. Everything's cool with Jackson."

"But … the only other boyfriend you've had was that

orchestra guy. And didn't you break up with him?"

"Yes. I'm not talking about him either."

"There was someone else?"

"Oh, you want to hear the story now?" I place a hand on my hip and give him my unimpressed look. "Because when I was getting ready to tell you and Sarah about it before Christmas, you weren't interested."

Adam's confused expression makes it clear he's completely forgotten telling me to keep my swooning-over-foreign-boys stories for when he's not around. "Well," he says, "I guess I've changed my mind."

"Ooh, good, a story. Sarah isn't the only one who can do this." I place my mug on the floor and clear my throat. "A long time ago in a galaxy far, far—"

"No. You do not get to rip off *Star Wars* in this story."

"Fine. Not so long ago in a land far, far away—"

"Seriously?"

"Just crush all my creativity," I say with a sigh. "And Germany *is* far away, in case you've forgotten." I cross my legs and hug one of the cushions against my chest. "Okay fine. Here's what happened. The family I was staying with in Germany had four kids. The four-year-old boy and the six-year-old girl were the two I was there to take care of, and they were *serious* brats. There was also a thirteen-year-old, but she was so quiet she hardly ever said anything. Kinda like Luke. Whoever took care of her when she was young must have had it easy. And then there was—" I pause for dramatic effect "—Carl."

Adam groans. "I think I remember why I didn't want to hear this story."

"I promise I'll keep the swooning to a minimum."

"Thanks."

"So anyway, he was pretty much gorgeous. Blond like the rest of his family, but with these really intense dark eyes. Total fairy-tale prince."

"Was he?" Adam asks. "A prince, I mean. Like an actual prince."

"Oh, I don't know. I don't think so. I think his dad might have been, and his mother had some other noble title. So I don't know what that made him, but in my mind, he was always … my prince."

"Oh my goodness," Adam says, shaking his head. "I don't think I need to hear this."

"Hey, shh. No more interrupting." I squeeze my cushion and continue. "We didn't really interact that much. He was nineteen and not all that interested in hanging out with his little brother and sister. But one morning after I'd been there about a month, we both ended up on a bench outside. The Brats wanted to play out there, even though it was freezing, and Carl had just had an argument with his parents and come outside, he said, to clear his head. We ended up having a long conversation, and after that, things felt different between us. Like there was some kind of connection, you know?"

"Um, I guess."

"Months passed like that. Smiles from a distance, brief

conversations whenever our paths crossed, the occasional almost-flirting. And then one night, while his parents were holding some function that involved plenty of pompous people in fancy gowns and suits, we bumped into each other in the library. The Brats were finally asleep, and I'd snuck in there to look for a new book to read—although, as I soon found out, there wasn't much on those shelves that actually interested me. Carl was bored with all his parents' friends, so he escaped to the library to get away from them. There was a window seat and a full moon and a forbidden kiss and … oh." I sink back against the couch. "It was such a perfect fairy-tale moment."

"Hey, no swooning," Adam reminds me.

"Right. Yes. So our relationship was a secret because we didn't think his parents would approve of him dating the girl they'd hired to look after their children. We met up in secluded parts of the grounds where we knew no one would see us, and sometimes I'd have to go days without seeing him. We didn't send texts because he didn't want anyone seeing them on his phone, and after I sent him a few emails, he said that was dangerous too, because they also showed up on his phone. So I created a new email address for him that he'd have to go online to check, made up a ridiculously long, random password no one would ever guess, wrote it inside the back of a book, and gave the book to him as a gift."

"So, no passing love letters to one another like back in the old days, huh?"

"Nope. None of that. We arranged our meetings via email, and it was thrilling meeting up in secret every few days. Anyway, when it got to about a month before I was due to come back home, I asked him about the future of our relationship. I said that surely once I was no longer employed by his parents, it would be okay to date publicly. I even told him I'd been looking into studying in Germany so we could stay together."

Adam gives me a knowing look. "I'm guessing this is the part of the story where you acquired the Broken Hearted Loser label."

"You guess correctly. Carl said he needed to think about it, and the next time we met up, he had the book with him. The one I'd written the password in. He used a whole lot of words to essentially tell me that I'd never be good enough for his family or friends, that they'd never accept me, and that our relationship had reached its end. He gave the book back to me, and that was that. A week later, I saw him escorting another girl around the property, showing off his grand home to her. When I took The Brats out for the day, the driver told me she was some duchess's daughter."

"Wow," Adam says. "What a royal ass."

"Indeed. It may not be as bad as cheating on someone, like Jenna did to you, but man did I feel rejected and worthless after that."

"I can imagine." He frowns. "Wait, I don't need to imagine that. I'm feeling it already."

I lift my mug from the floor and hold it up. "Here's to moving on."

"To moving on," Adam says, knocking his mug against mine. "Hopefully soon."

"Yes. Now let's stay in our pyjamas all day and eat junk food and see how many episodes of *The Big Bang Theory* we can watch."

I HURRY INTO MY FIRST PERIOD LECTURE ON MONDAY TO find Allegra sitting alone on the other side of the lecture theatre, far away from Charlotte, Amber and Courtney. Jackson isn't here yet, so I walk around to where Allegra is sitting and drop into the chair beside her. She gives me a half-hearted smile, then slouches down in her chair and draws doodles on the inside cover of her notebook.

Oookay. I've never seen Allegra so quiet. She's definitely more *allegretto* than *allegro* today. No, that doesn't fit either. She isn't even a little bit lively. I pull my notes and pens out of my bag while searching my brain for the Italian musical term for 'subdued.' *Sotto*. That's the one. Allegra is definitely *sotto* today.

"Where've you been all weekend?" she asks. "And Friday. You missed every single lecture."

"Yes, um, Adam needed me." He spent most of his nonworking weekend hours at the piano, cycling through every depressing Satie composition he knows. And when he was working, I hung out in a corner at Jazzy Beanbag, consolidating all the notes for my various courses and making sure Adam didn't start yelling at anyone about his demon ex-girlfriend.

Allegra nods, but doesn't say anything else.

I lean closer to her. "What's wrong?"

She bites her lip, taps her pen against the page, then glances across at our other three friends. "Charlotte and Damien are officially a couple now."

My eyes follow Allegra's line of sight to where Charlotte is tossing her perfect brown curls over her shoulder. "Damien? The guy from Smuts? The one you have a crush on?"

Allegra grips her pen tightly and draws over and over and over the star doodle on her notebook cover until I'm worried she's going to push the nib right through the cardboard. "She *knows* how I feel about him," she says between clenched teeth. "And I've never seen them together, which means she's been doing all her flirting when I haven't been around. Intentionally sabotaging any hope I might have had with him."

I lay my hand on her arm. "I'm really sorry. That sucks."

"How could she do this? Isn't there supposed to be some kind of girlfriend honour code? Now we can never be friends again, even if she and Damien don't last. And why are Amber and Courtney siding with *her*? Don't they care about me at all?"

"You know what?" I say. "This all sounds like silly high school drama. You shouldn't worry about it. If any of the three of them had even a scrap of maturity, they would have *spoken* to you about all of this like adults. So … just … hold your head high and show them how mature you are."

"Mature? *Mature?*" Allegra looks at me as though she doesn't know the meaning of the word. "Mature isn't going to change the fact that she took my guy, Livi!"

Right. Maturity obviously wasn't the best line to go with.

Allegra drops her pen and crosses her arms. "He's too serious for me anyway. She can have him."

I want to roll my eyes, but that probably wouldn't be well received. "Allegra, I'm sure there's someone out there's who perfect for—"

"Only two weeks to go till the end of the quarter," Professor Batch booms from the front of the lecture theatre, "and we've got lots to cover, so let's not waste any more time."

I pick up my pen and get ready to take notes, but only after glancing around to see where Jackson is.

He still hasn't arrived.

Jackson never showed up. Which would have been fine if I hadn't seen him chilling on Jammie steps five minutes after first period ended as Allegra and I were walking to Stats. I was about to wave and run over to him when I realised he was sitting in between two girls. No, not sitting. Reclining in sexy Norse god fashion while laughing at whatever the two girls were saying. I'm not ashamed to admit to the gleeful satisfaction I felt when, about three seconds after I stopped to gape at him, the clouds parted and some of that Cape Town rain I've heard so much about dumped itself on top of UCT, putting a quick end to the two girls' shameless flirting.

Allegra shrieked, grabbed my arm, and dragged me into the nearest building. And that was the last I saw of Jackson all day.

Now, after getting drenched while finding my way to my car, then fighting with afternoon traffic on slippery roads, I stomp into my room and throw my bag onto the armchair in the corner. I don't want to wet my duvet with my soaked clothes, so I sit at my desk while checking my phone for the fifty-seventh time.

No message from Jackson.

Ugh, what is up with him? Is he annoyed with me for telling him I couldn't see him this past weekend because I needed to help out a friend? I didn't mention the friend was a guy, so he can't be upset about that. Maybe he's playing the hard-to-get game. Or maybe what I saw this morning is the way he always acts around other girls when I'm not there.

With a sigh, I push my wheeled chair away from my desk and travel out of my room, across the passage, and into Adam's room. "Hey," I say. "How are you doing?"

His computer screen goes black, and he swings around

to face me with a guilty expression on his face.

I narrow my eyes at him. "You weren't looking at porn, were you?"

He gives me a blank stare. "Seriously, Livi? I wouldn't even know how to find porn. And if I were going to search for it, I'd probably close my door first."

I spin my chair in circles a few times, then drop my feet to come to a stop. "So why do you look guilty?"

Adam groans. "I was on Jenna's Facebook page."

I sigh. "Probably not the best idea, huh?"

"No."

"But at least you're not playing Satie's *Gymnopédies* anymore, so that's good, right?"

Adam shrugs. "I suppose. You know, I never fully appreciated the instructions to play that music 'painfully' until now."

I nod. "Yes. It was pretty painful listening to it on neverending repeat this weekend."

Adam throws a dirty sock at me, but he's smiling, so I know I haven't offended him. "You need to phone your dad," he says. "Tell him what you told me last night."

I spin around on my chair again. "How do you know I haven't phoned him already?"

"If you had, you would have told me about it."

"Fine, fine, fine. I'll go call him now." I propel my chair backwards, aiming for the open doorway. One of the wheels catches against the doorframe, the flimsy chair topples over, and I find myself lying in a pile of dirty laundry by the door.

Adam shakes his head. "How have you made it to age

nineteen without seriously injuring yourself?"

I pick myself up and turn my chair back onto its wheeled legs. "I always make sure there's something soft to land on when I'm about to perform an act of supreme clumsiness."

Adam points to my bedroom. "Phone."

I point to his computer. "Porn!"

"What?"

"Sorry, I thought we were shouting out random—Okay, okay, I'm going!" I duck out of the way of the flying cushion before pushing my chair back to my room. I shut the door and pick my phone up from the bed. A moment later, I'm spinning slowly in my chair in the middle of the room waiting for dad to answer. He said I could call any time, but I didn't really believe the part where he said he'd answer no matter what. If he's in an important meeting, he wouldn't—

"Hi, Livi."

"Oh, uh, hi. Hi, Dad."

"I'm glad you called. Did you just speak to Mom?"

"No. Why?" I wrap a strand of hair around my finger.

"Oh. Well, I spoke to her earlier. She agreed that some counselling might be good for us. She, uh, hasn't said if she'll be coming home, but counselling is a good start."

"Okay." I'm surprised to hear that Mom spoke to Dad. I thought she'd ignore him for a lot longer. "Um, I actually wanted to ask you something."

"Of course. What is it?"

I stop spinning and stand up. "Well, uh ..." *Just say it.* "I want to meet her. Andrea. I want to meet my half-sister."

"Oh. I ... didn't think you'd want that. I thought you'd

be so angry you'd never want to meet either of them."

I begin pacing. "I am angry, Dad. I'm angry with you. And I'm angry with the woman who decided to have an affair with a married man. But that *mistake* you ended up having? It's not her fault. She didn't do anything wrong. And now that I know she exists, my curiosity is never going to go away. I'm always going to be wondering about her. So yes. I want to meet her."

My little speech is greeted with a long pause. Eventually Dad says, "Livi, I really don't think that's a good idea."

"It doesn't matter what you think."

"It does, actually. Have you thought about how this will make your mother feel?"

"Oh, great move, Dad. Use Mom against me. This doesn't have to have anything to do with you or Mom. Just tell me how I can contact her, and I'll get on with it my—"

"Alivia!" he shouts. "I am trying to keep our family together, and you are making that very difficult."

"*I'm* making it difficult? *Me?* No, Dad, you're the one who made it difficult seventeen years ago when you COULDN'T KEEP YOUR DAMN PANTS ON!"

I end the call and throw my phone across the room at the bed. My hands are shaking. I can't believe I just said that to my own father. If he calls back right away and demands I apologise for being so disrespectful, I wouldn't be surprised.

He's the one at fault here, I remind myself. *He's the one who messed up big time and is trying desperately to hold all the pieces together now that everything is blowing up in his face. All you did was lose your temper.*

I flop onto the bed—who cares about damp clothes—
just as my phone pings. *Oh, great. Now I'm text fighting with my
father?*

It isn't Dad, though. It's Jackson.

Jackson: Hey, my sexy bunny. Sorry I didn't see you
today. I was catching up with some friends from school.
They're med students, so they're not often on Upper
Campus. Missed you.

Huh. Friends from school. I suppose that could explain
why he was being so friendly with those two girls. I try to
remain aloof in my response, though.

Livi: No problem. I was busy anyway. Lots of work to get
through before the vac.

Jackson: Tell me about it. Next two weeks are gonna
suck.

Jackson: There's a party in Camps Bay next Friday. I
know you said you might be flying home that evening,
but if you're not you must come. Gonna be epic.

Livi: Decided I'm not going home anymore. So I'll be
there.

From: Alivia Howard <livi-gem@gmail.com>
Sent: Mon 24 Mar, 5:31 pm
To: Carl <cpsb21@yahoo.com>
Subject: Dear Carl

I used to hear you fighting with your dad all the time. You wouldn't think so, would you, with it being such a huge castle, but I guess you guys fought a lot. Sometimes I'd listen and think, well at least your dad pays attention to you. My dad doesn't really care all that much what I do. But now that I'm fighting with my own father ... well, it sucks.

"O. M. G. Is this *you*, Livi?"

I turn away from my mirror and look across the room. Crapazoid. Allegra's got hold of my high school yearbook. Why didn't I think to hide that before she got here? "Uh, which page are you on? Because there was this other girl who looked a lot like me but—"

"It *is* you! Oh my Gucci, you cute little orchestra girl. What instrument did you play? Was it one of the cool ones? Oh, wait." She taps a finger on her chin. "I don't think orchestras have any cool instruments, do they? Not, like, guitars and drums and stuff. My brother tried to play the violin for a bit. Horrid, screechy thing. I've never heard anything so awful in my life." She looks up and places a hand on her hip. "Isn't it weird how different things are popular at different schools? Like, at my school, the orchestra was where all the sad loser kids ended up."

"Uh … it was like that at my school too," I admit. I could have lied, but she's got the yearbook in her hands, so she's most likely about to find every other nerdy picture of me in there. Fortunately, there's no picture of me holding a violin. Allegra doesn't need to know I play that 'horrid, screechy thing.' Or *played*, rather than *play*, since I haven't removed it from its case since I got to Cape Town. I took it with me to Germany and played whenever I had free time, but now the softening calluses on the fingertips of my left hand are a testament to my lack of practise.

"Really? Huh." She looks between the yearbook picture and me, her eyes moving back and forth several times. "You've really transformed, Livi. I mean, I know most people do when they leave school, but you've *really* transformed. Like a butterfly from a caterpillar," she says with a large grin, clearly pleased with her comparison. "Anyway, hurry up at the mirror. I've still got to do my make-up."

I return to the mirror inside my cupboard door, and Allegra drapes herself across my armchair with my yearbook in her hands. She's flying home to Empangeni tomorrow afternoon, which means we're going to the Camps Bay party together. "Did you bring that new eyeshadow?"

"Uh huh." She points to the make-up bag on my bed.

"Thanks." I rummage through the bag until I find the new smoky eyeshadow Allegra bought today after we were set free from our last lecture for the quarter. "Oh, did I tell you Jackson finally referred to me as his girlfriend today when introducing me to someone?"

"FINALLY!" Allegra lowers the yearbook and beams at me. "I mean, we all knew you guys were heading that way, but at least it's official now."

"I know." I let out a happy sigh before returning to the mirror.

"Oh, wow," Allegra says. I don't look. Whatever incriminating photo she's found this time, I don't want to know about it. "I didn't notice this cushion before. It's awesome."

Cushion? I peer around my cupboard door and see her holding the Marauder's Map cushion. AND SHE THINKS IT'S AWESOME! I try to remain cool and uninterested as I say, "Oh, you like Harry Potter?"

"Yes. Well, I've grown out of it now, but I was totally obsessed back when I was, like, fourteen. I would have *loved* this cushion."

"So … when you were obsessed, did you read all the books?"

"Oh, yes, of course." She turns back to the yearbook and flips through another few pages. "Believe it or not, I actually used to read more than just magazines."

She used to read more than just magazines? Fantastic! Maybe she used to watch more than just trashy chick flicks and shallow TV dramas. Finishing off my make-up with a final application of mascara, I say, "How do you feel about *Star Trek*?"

"Um … is that the one with lightsabers and that little green guy with the pointy ears?"

"No, that's *Star Wars*."

"Okay, great, 'cause that little green dude was creepy."

"You've … seen *Star Wars*?" Because if so, my mind has just officially been blown.

"Yes, my brother's a fan, so I probably saw most of the movies when we were growing up. I'd definitely say I prefer the other one. *Star Trek*, right?"

"Yes." I indicate that she can use the mirror now, and she jumps up to take my place. "So … you've seen *Star Trek* as well? Like, the series?"

"Oh, no, not that ancient crap. But I had to check out the movies. I mean, hello, Chris Pine. Drool-worthy."

I perch on the edge of my bed and slip my feet into my heels. This is incredible. Who would have thought that my super popular, super beautiful friend would know about all this stuff. "And what's your take on superheroes?" I ask.

She turns back to me, her eyes suddenly wide. "Thor—" she points her make-up sponge at me "—is hot." We both start laughing. "What is this, anyway?" she asks. "Some kind of interrogation?"

I shake my head, still laughing. "It's just … I thought all these things were seriously uncool. I was teased at school because of how excited I got about the interactive tribble toy my friends gave me for my fourteenth birthday. And once one of the cool kids caught me doing the Vulcan salute and saying 'Live long and prosper,' and I was labelled 'alien dork' for at least a month. Oh, and I had Spiderman socks in primary school, and all the girls teased me because I was apparently wearing boys' socks. So, you know, I thought I had to hide the fact that I like all this stuff."

Allegra lets out a dramatic sigh. "Kids are mean. They'll tease you about anything. Being cool is all about confidence, really. Anyway, nerdy stuff is in these days. I mean, no one actually wants to *be* a nerd. Can you *imagine* the horror?" She doubles over with laughter, then straightens suddenly, her eyes going wide as they flick to the year book and back to me. "Right. I guess you can. Anyway, with all the movies these days—superheroes, kiddie wizards, Star-this and Star-that, X-Men, Y-Men, Z-Men, and who knows what else—this stuff has become popular. I mean, widely popular. Not just popular amongst the nerds."

I lean back on my hands. "One more question. What did you think of *Firefly*?"

She presses her lipstick-covered lips together, then pouts at herself in the mirror. "*Firefly*? Never heard of it."

I smile to myself. "I guess that one was only popular amongst the nerds."

Someone knocks at the door, and I cross the room to open it.

"Hey," Adam says, his eyes moving down my body before quickly looking away. "Uh, sorry. I didn't know you were getting ready to go out."

"Hey there, cute guy with the glasses," Allegra says, practising her flip-the-hair-over-the-shoulder move. With a sultry half-smile, she says, "I heard you're back on the market."

Adam looks at me, his cheeks reddening. They can't possibly be as red as mine, though. *Change the subject, change the subject.* "Um, you wanted to ask me something?"

"Oh, yes, I'm working at Jazzy Beanbag tonight, but there's a new band, *The Electric Goat*, that's gonna be there. Hugo said they're pretty good, so I thought you might want to come along and listen. Um, but you obviously already have plans."

"Yes. I'm sorry. But thank you."

"Oh!" Allegra says, her wide eyes and excited tone suggesting she's just come up with a brilliant plan. "What time do you finish working? You should come join us later. This is the kind of party you could never get into on your own, but if you're with *us*, everyone will think you're part of the in-crowd."

"Allegra," I mutter. Doesn't she know how rude she's being?

"What? Come on, it would be awesome. Adam can transform just like you did." She nudges me, then winks at Adam. "You know, the caterpillar to butterfly thing." Flipping flip, why does she like that stupid metaphor so much?

Adam clears his throat. "What party is this?"

"It's in Camps Bay," Allegra tells him. "You probably don't know Royson Graves, but it's his parents' place. They're away, so, you know, party time!"

"Uh huh. Sorry, but I think I'm going to be working really late tonight." He turns to me. "Can I talk to you for a moment, Livi? Out there?" He motions to the passage with his head.

Yes. Please. Before Allegra says anything else embarrassing.

I follow Adam to the lounge. "I'm so sorry about that," I say. "She has no filter sometimes. She honestly thinks she'd be helping you out by getting you into that party. She just has no idea how to say it without sounding ..."

"Offensive?"

"Yes."

"She was pretty rude, but that's not what I'm worried about. This party tonight ... I heard some people talking about it. About what's going to be happening there. I really don't think you should go."

I give him a reassuring smile. "Remember when you were worried about me going to that club? And it all turned out fine?"

"But this feels ... different."

"Look, even if there is dodgy stuff going on, it doesn't mean I have to take part in any of it. I'm not that kind of person, remember?"

"Really?" Adam looks doubtful. "You've changed, Liv. Sometimes I think you'll do anything if it means the 'right' people accept you."

I take a step backwards. "Okay, now you're the one being offensive."

"Am I? You wear these tight, revealing clothes you never used to wear, and this heavy make-up that makes you look like someone else entirely. You tell your friends I'm 'back on the market' like a piece of meat on special—"

"I did *not* say it like that, okay. I just mentioned to Allegra that—

"—and you *never* play your music anymore. What happened to the girl who told me she'd die if she could never create music again? The girl who agreed with me that music is wound so tightly around our souls it would never stop calling to us?"

"I don't know what to tell you, Adam, other than that *this is me.* No one is forcing me to be this way. I like these clothes, I like my make-up and my hair, and the music—" I swallow past the hollowness, past the sick feeling in the pit of my stomach. "Maybe the music never meant as much to me as it did to you."

I turn to go, but he catches my arm. "I didn't mean for this to be another fight," he says with a sigh. "I just wanted to tell you that I'm worried about you."

I look at his fingers wrapped loosely around my arm. "Thanks." I pull free. "But you don't need to be."

"Oh. My. Groot," I murmur as Allegra and I climb out of her car and stare up at the palatial Camps Bay home.

Allegra looks at me. "What's Groot? Oh, is that the new clothing line we saw at YDE?" She frowns. "No, wait, that was ..." She shakes her head. "Never mind. So not important right now. This house. THIS. HOUSE. Oh my EVERYTHING."

'Oh my everything' sums it up pretty well. I'm so in awe

of this house I can't even laugh at Allegra for mistaking my *Guardians of the Galaxy* reference for a clothing line. Nestled into the hillside rising behind Camps Bay, with a spectacular panoramic view of the ocean and surrounding mountains, it's the kind of house that gets featured in glossy magazines along with a price tag at least five times the average person's income for their entire working career. "Thank goodness we didn't come in my car," I whisper to Allegra as a group of people walk past us to the entrance.

She laughs. "I know, right? Wow. Freaking wow. We are eternally in Logan's debt."

Logan the Legend is the one who actually knows Royson Graves, so it was Logan who told Jackson and the rest of my group of friends to come along. We're apparently part of a select few freshmen who've been invited. Charlotte couldn't come, though, much to Allegra's delight. She had a flight home this afternoon—and was apparently *horribly* disappointed to be missing out on this epic party.

"When's Jackson getting here?" Allegra asks.

"Oh, in an hour or two I think. He had some stuff to do."

"Cool, well let's get inside. I don't want to miss another second."

We do our sexy walks across the driveway and into the house, where the vibe is similar to The Banana Pearl, but a thousand times classier. All the beautiful people are here, mingling with drinks in their hands, or—as we move further into the house—dancing to music that's loud enough to really feel the beat but not so loud I'm worried my ears will be permanently damaged. With classes behind me and a week of holiday ahead of me, I'm feeling happy and confident and ready to DANCE.

"Hey!" Amber and Courtney call out and wave from the balcony where they're sitting on two white-cushioned loungers surrounded by a bunch of guys I don't know. Two weeks ago, they were apparently 'on Charlotte's side' and not talking to Allegra, but Allegra's been using her confidence and supreme socialite skills—as well as me and my connection to Logan—to show them that to be friends with Allegra is to be on the fun side of the island. It didn't take long for them to come running back.

Allegra smiles and flips her hair, but doesn't stop to say anything as we saunter past Amber and Courtney. Because, of course, it's all about letting them know that *they* need *her* and not the other way around. It makes me want to shake my head and laugh, because she clearly didn't hear anything I said about maturity.

"Let's dance," I say to her. I slide between the moving bodies, raise my arms, and sway my hips to the beat. I don't know what Adam was so worried about. Other people can do whatever the heck they want, but this is what I'm here for. Losing myself in the rhythm, the beat, the sound. All I need now are Jackson's hands on my hips as the music winds around us, tangling us together, and this party will be perfect.

An hour or so and one or two drinks later, I notice a girl

walking between the dancers holding what looks like a small silver platter. She leans closer to some of them, speaking into their ears. Others call her over. When she finally gets near enough for me to see what's on the platter, warning bells go off in my head.

Dozens of small, coloured pills.

WITH A STRAINED SMILE, I CONTINUE SWAYING MY HIPS and lean closer to Allegra. "Is that what I think it is?" I say, glancing towards the girl with the platter.

Allegra puts on her playful half-smile and says, "You bet it is."

The word 'ecstasy' runs through my head, but it probably has some cool street name I don't know, so I say nothing, opting instead for a forced giggle.

Allegra moves past me, her shoulders and head bobbing up and down in time to the music. "Shall I get us some?"

"Oh yeah," I say with a laugh. "I'd *love* to try some."

"Awesome. I'll be right back."

"No, wait." I grab her arm and pull her back. Someone gives me an odd look, so I smile, let go of Allegra, and start dancing again. "I was joking. I don't ... do that kinda thing."

"Oh, come on. Don't be such a goody-goody. Experimentation is totally normal. You're not about to become some hardcore addict."

I raise my arms, throw my head back, and change swaying tempo as the music morphs into something else. "I don't need it," I say, widening my smile so she can see how much fun I'm having *without* drugs.

Allegra shrugs and gives me a smug look. "Whatever. I'll convince you later."

Okay, so that was probably the part Adam was concerned about, but, like I told him, I'm not that kind of person.

The music continues, another drink finds its way into my hand, and before long, the sexy guy I'm lucky enough to call my boyfriend moves through the crowd towards me and slides his hands around my waist. "My sexy bunny," he breathes into my ear, just loud enough for me to hear. His lips move down my neck and across my collar bone, and even though I'm really warm, a shiver passes through me.

I don't know how long we spend locked together on the dance floor, but I'm relieved when Jackson finally leads me away, through several more rooms of dancers, and to a corner that could almost be considered private. His dancing was starting to feel a tad inappropriate, and I was on the verge of jokingly reminding him just how many people could see us.

"I've missed my sexy bunny," he says, his thumb trailing along my jaw.

I bite my lip and give him a sultry smile. "Well, I'm all yours now."

His eyes move to my mouth, and then his lips are on mine and he's pressing me against the wall and our tongues are twisting together and I'm warm in places I've never been warm before. His fingers rake through my hair, trail over my shoulders, and then he's squeezing my left breast. Which is a whole lot more than I was expecting, and feels super awkward in a crowded room of dancers.

"Whoa, hold on there," I say through my laughter, removing his hand as his lips press kisses against my neck. I feel his breath against my skin as he chuckles.

His hands slide down to my waist—an area that isn't off-limits—and his mouth moves back to mine. I return his kisses with just as much passion, slowly forgetting about the room and the dancers and the music until it's just Jackson and me and his lips and my lips. His hand slides down between us, reaches the edge of my short dress, and pulls up.

"Whoa, hey."

His fingers slide up my leg and brush over my panties.

"Hey!" I push him away from me.

"Don't worry, bunny," he says with a smile. "Nobody's gonna see." He covers me with his body, and his hand is back there, rubbing against—

"I said stop!" I shove harder this time, and he stumbles away from me. He stands there, breathing hard and looking confused. Maybe he's had too much to drink and doesn't know what he's doing. Maybe we both need to find a balcony and get some air.

"What's wrong?" he asks, stepping closer to run a hand down my arm. I look around to see if anyone noticed his gigantic inappropriateness a moment ago. Apparently not. "Don't worry, Livi," he says, his confusion replaced with a knowing smile. "It's dark in here. You don't have to worry about anyone seeing." And then he's smothering me, both hands gripping my thighs, his hot breath in my ear as he says, "Or we could find a bedroom if you want to—"

"STOP! Get OFF me!" I push as hard as if my life depends upon it. Jackson stumbles backwards into a small glass table standing against the wall. He goes down along with the table and the expensive-looking ceramic bowl that was sitting on top of it. Glass shatters and someone screams and Jackson's on the floor and everyone's staring at us and the music pounds but no one's dancing and Jackson's yelling obscenities and I'm shaking and shocked and scared and ...

I run. Through the people and out of the room and up some stairs and into a bathroom. I slam the door shut and lean against it, breathing hard. What did I just do? What did *he* just do? How dare he think he could touch me like that? Perhaps I gave him the wrong signals, but he should have backed off after I first pushed him away. He should have. This *isn't* my fault.

Isn't it? says a small, needling voice at the back of my mind, reminding me of my short dress and my sexy smiles and my flirty glances.

"No!" I may want to look sexy, but that doesn't mean I'm ready for ... whatever Jackson was planning to do. And he should have respected that.

I glare at my reflection, which begins to wobble as tears fill my eyes. I take a deep breath and blink them away. I need to get out of here. Out of this bathroom and out of this house.

I walk down the stairs on shaking legs. I hurry through room after room, lost for a while until I find the wide open space Allegra and I were first dancing in. The music's still playing, drinks are flowing, an empty silver platter sits on a side table, and everyone's having a wild time.

"Livi!" Allegra hurries over to me and pushes my purse—which I'd completely forgotten about until this moment—into my hands. "What the hell happened? People are saying you totally flipped out. That you, like, attacked Jackson."

"What? No, he—"

"I saw his hands. They were bleeding."

"Listen, Allegra. It was an accident. We were in a corner, and he was ... he was trying to ..."

Allegra's eyes widen. "Did he hurt you?"

"No, but he—"

"Then what the hell, Livi? You don't attack your boyfriend just for making out with you in a dark corner."

"It *wasn't* just making out. It was—" I stop and take a deep breath. I don't want to do this here. I don't want to *be* here. "Can we please go home?"

"Go home? Livi, the party's just starting."

"Okay, but ... I just ... I think the party's over for me."

Allegra takes my hand. "Come on, let's go dance again.

Just forget about Jackson and enjoy the dancing. And look what I got for you!" She opens her purse and produces a pink pill with a butterfly indentation stamped onto it. "You'll definitely have fun after you take this."

I shake my head. "No. That isn't going to help."

"Livi, just try it. I've also got one. We'll take it together, and I promise it won't be scary or—"

"No! Aren't you listening? I really need to go home."

Allegra looks around at the people throwing concerned glances our way. She tugs me to the edge of the room. "You are embarrassing me, Livi. You need to stop being weird, okay? Just chill. Now, I'm going to give you this." She holds the pill up. "And you can either—"

I lose track of what she's saying as I start to feel lightheaded. Sweaty, nauseous, shaky. Flashing lights mix with images I don't want to see. Jackson and his hands, Allegra and her hyena laughter. Drinking and flirting and drugs and—I DON'T WANT THIS.

"NO!" I push dizzily past her. "I'm done with this. I'm done with all of this." The walls seem to be tilting, but I manage to find my way outside. I lean against a car in the driveway and slowly take in gulps of cold air. The nausea subsides, but I can't rid myself of the feeling that I've just lost my friend. My friend who feeds me drugs when I'm upset and won't take me seriously when I try to tell her about a guy forcing himself on me. So it's probably a good thing she'll never want to speak to me again.

My hands shake as I run them through my hair. How am I supposed to get home? I've never called a taxi before, and they probably cost more money than I have on me. Allegra told me about a new taxi app earlier, but I can't remember the name, so that option's out. And no way am I calling Adam. Not after he told me not to come in the first place. Luke? Maybe he's free.

I pull my phone out and find his number. "Don't cry," I murmur to myself as I listen to the ringing. "Don't cry, don't cry, don't cry."

Voice mail.

My lip shudders. Tears well up. I stare at Adam's name on my phone. I stare at it until the screen goes dark as I try to figure out what to say to him. I unlock the phone and press my thumb over his name. I listen to the ringing, ringing, ringing while half of me desperately hopes he'll pick up and the other half hopes he doesn't.

He doesn't. Another voice mail.

This time the tears spill over onto my cheeks. I blink through them and check the time on my phone. It's just before midnight, so Adam's probably still at work. He did say he'd be finishing late tonight.

Maybe I'll just have to wait out here until he looks at his phone. But it's getting cold, and tiny drops of rain are beginning to fall. I back up until I'm standing beneath the shelter of the entrance. I rub my hands up and down my arms. I don't want to go back inside, not even to wait. I DO NOT want to come anywhere near this house ever—

"Oh, I'm so sorry," a voice says as someone bumps into me. I scoot out of the way and see a guy with his arm around a girl. Another couple walks out of the house behind them.

"Oh, that's okay. Um, hang on." I'm about to die of embarrassment inside, but I'm so desperate, I have to ask. "Where are you guys heading? I kinda need a lift."

"Uh, Claremont," the guy says.

"Gotta get to the next party," his date adds with a giggle.

"Any chance you can drive by Rondebosch on the way?" I ask.

The guy looks around at his friends for confirmation. The other guy shrugs. "Yeah, I think we're sorta going that way."

"Awesome. Thank you so much." *Thank you thank you thank you.*

I climb into the back seat beside one of the couples, relief filling me with warmth as we drive away. I tilt my head back against the headrest, only to jerk it forward as music blasts suddenly from the speakers. The girl beside me laughs, then gets back to draping herself over the guy I assume is her boyfriend. The music pounds, the couple won't stop making out, and the driver pushes the car faster and faster and faster through the rain until I'm almost certain I'm not going to make it home alive.

"Hey, Rick," the girl beside me yells above the music. She unwinds herself from her boyfriend and leans forward with her phone in one hand. "Can you stop and pick up Jody from Tugwell?"

Rick, whose driver's licence should be confiscated before he kills a whole lot of people, nods.

I cling to the car door and close my eyes.

When we finally screech to a halt, I open my eyes and look out at the tall towers of Tugwell Hall. "Hey, chick in the back seat," Rick says. "This close enough?"

"Oh, um …" I lean forward. "Is it possible for you to drive just a little further down Main Road?" That still won't get me all the way home, but at least I'll be a bit closer.

"Yeah, I guess I could."

"Rick, there isn't going to be enough space," the girl beside me complains. "Alice is coming with Jody, so there'll already be four of us squashed in the back here."

"Well, where the hell are they? You said we're here, right?"

"Yes. They're on their way."

Rick taps his fingers on the steering wheel. "I don't see them." The car jerks forward and speeds off down the wet road and through a red traffic light.

"Rick!" the girl screeches.

Rick slams on the brakes outside the Pick 'n Pay. "Okay, out you get," he says to me.

"Um, thank you." I fumble with the seatbelt and the door handle. I've barely slammed the door shut when the car takes off, kicking water up from the wet road. Two seconds later, the car speeds past me back towards Tugwell.

I look down at the muddy water splashed across my feet. The satin fabric of my high-heeled shoes is probably ruined. *Who the hell cares?* I tell myself. *You have bigger problems right now.* I glance around briefly before clutching my purse tightly beneath my arm and hurrying along the sidewalk. All kinds of horrible things can happen to a girl walking alone in the middle of the night. I've heard the stories. I heard one just a few days ago about a girl walking somewhere near campus who ended up stabbed and in hospital because somebody wanted her cell phone and—

Stop. Don't think about that. Just walk.

The rain, which was a light drizzle up until now, begins to fall faster. Shivers raise the hairs on my skin. I wrap my bare arms around myself and hurry as quickly as I can in these stupid shoes. I'm damp and cold and tired, and I can't tell anymore if the drops running down my face are rain or tears or both. How much longer till I reach home? Two minutes? Maybe a bit—

Are those footsteps behind me?

Frack! Please let there not be anyone there. Please please please.

It can't be footsteps. I wouldn't hear them over the rain, would I? But I don't want to look behind me. I need to move faster. I need to run.

My heeled feet pound the uneven sidewalk. Sobs escape my lips. I'm only four houses away from my own now, but I keep expecting to feel a hand on my arm, or someone grabbing my waist, or—

"Oh!" My right ankle twists as the heel of my shoe snaps. My flailing hands grasp at the air, catching onto the diamond shapes of a wire fence. I half-fall awkwardly onto my left knee, but it's my right ankle that's screaming at me. I look over my shoulder, but I don't see anyone there. Did I imagine the footsteps?

I kick my shoes off, grab my fallen purse, and use the

fence to pull myself up. I hobble the rest of the way on bare feet, wincing and shivering and sniffing. I tug the gate open and slide it shut behind me, then stumble over to the broken motor and flip the switch off manual. I do *not* want whoever's out there to walk through this gate as easily as I did. I don't know if I imagined those footsteps, but I'm not taking a chance.

I pull myself up the front steps and lean against the door, keeping my weight off my throbbing ankle as I remove my keys from my purse. I can't see properly and my fingers are shaking and I can't get the key into the lock and I'm about to start banging my fists on the door to wake Luke up—but then the key slides in. The door's unlocked. I'm inside. The door's closed.

I'm safe.

I collapse against the door, covering my eyes with my hand as I shake with silent tears.

And then I hear something I didn't expect to hear: Voices. And laughter. Freaking heck, who the hell is chilling in our lounge? Luke doesn't ever invite people over, and Adam's still at work. Isn't he? No. That's definitely Adam's laugh I just heard.

DAMMIT! Why is he home? And why did he have to bring people with him? Why *now*? I can't get anywhere in this house without walking past the lounge door, and whoever is in there does *not* need to see me like this. A hobbling, shoeless, dripping wet mess.

Maybe if I can get past quietly and quickly enough, they won't notice me. *Right. Quietly and quickly. With a twisted ankle.*

I try anyway. I tell myself not to look up as I pass the door, but my eyes flick upwards anyway, just long enough to see Adam, his friend Hugo, the petite drummer girl from *The Flying Monkey Train*, and another girl I don't recognise. Then I'm past the doorway. It only took about a second, but a lull in conversation tells me I was spotted.

"Livi?" Adam calls out, his voice suddenly anxious.

Crap. I hobble faster. My ankle screams some more. I make it to my room and slam the door shut.

A second later, Adam taps against it. "Livi, are you okay?"

"I'm fine," I shout.

"Are you sure? You, uh, didn't really look fine."

I press my lips together and decide not to answer. I don't think I can say anything without my voice coming out wobbly.

"Livi?"

Just go away, just go away.

"Liv, please. What happened?"

I don't want to talk about it.

"Alivia, come on. You're scaring me." And he does sound scared. Helpless. Which is how I feel. "I'm coming in," he says.

The door opens, but I can't meet his eyes. I stare at the floor. At my dirty, wet feet. At the graze I didn't realise was on my knee. I wish he wasn't seeing this. I wish he wasn't standing there knowing he's been right all along.

"Liv," Adam breathes. "What happened?"

"Say it," I whisper.

"What?"

"Say it!" I shout, still looking down. "Say that you told me so. Say that I should never have gone. Say that you were right."

"I—I don't—Livi, are you hurt? Did someone … do something to you?"

I shake my head and wrap my arms around myself. "No. He didn't." He may have *tried*, but Adam doesn't need to know that much. "And he won't ever get the chance to *do anything* to me because I don't plan to go near him ever again."

Silence from Adam. Then he backs out of my room and walks away. I feel relieved, but empty. I hear the bathroom tap turning on, and moments later, Adam returns to my room with a towel. He tentatively places it over my shoulders. I take hold of the edges and pull it around me.

"You, um, look cold," he says. "I thought maybe you'd want to bath. I'll run the water, then you can go, uh, when you're ready. But maybe you should put ice on your ankle first. I'll get some."

He hurries away, leaving me trying to remember if I said anything about my ankle. Maybe he saw me hobbling. Maybe my right foot looks fatter than my left foot.

By the time Adam returns with ice blocks wrapped in a tea towel, I'm sitting on the floor. "I know you don't want to feel ice when you're already so cold," he says, "but it'll help."

"Your friends," I whisper as he fits the ice pack around my ankle. "I'm so embarrassed."

Adam forces a laugh. "Don't worry about them. They didn't really see much."

"I'm sorry I ruined your date."

"My—what?" Adam looks alarmed.

"You said Hugo liked that drummer girl. And there's another girl here. I thought maybe … a double date."

"Oh. No, no, no. We finished up earlier than we expected at Jazzy Beanbag because *The Electric Goat* turned out to be awful. So we came back here for a bit, but just as, like, a friend thing. Anyway, they're on their way now. So … I'll go finish running the bath. Then when you're done, I'll be in my room. If you want to talk. Or if you want to chill and watch series. Or if you just want to go to bed, that's fine too."

"Adam?" I catch his hand as he stands to leave. "Thank you."

From: Alivia Howard <livi-gem@gmail.com>
Sent: Sat 5 Apr, 1:26 am
To: Carl <cpsb21@yahoo.com>
Subject: Dear Carl

I miss you. If I asked, would you come and rescue me?

21

From: Alivia Howard <livi-gem@gmail.com>
Sent: Sat 5 Apr, 15:17 pm
To: Sarah Henley <s.henley@gmail.com>
Subject: This is my moping face

Dear Sarah

Thanks for your call this morning. I should have known Adam would send you an SOS on my behalf! Once again, I'm really sorry for not coming home this holiday. I just can't face my dad at the moment, and I think it might be better for him and my mom to have some time to work through things without me there. They have an appointment with a counsellor on Wednesday. My mom keeps threatening to not show up, but I think, in the end, she'll go.

I shall now do my best to follow your instruction to NOT MOPE. As you know, I've never been particularly good at moping, so NOT MOPING should be easy. No doubt I'll find a distraction soon enough ... Oh! Squirrel! (That was meant to be a distraction joke, but it's kinda funny because Cape Town actually does have a lot of squirrels. Are you laughing? You're not laughing? Okay. I chuckled. A real chuckle. But then, I'm not in the healthiest state of mind right now, so that could have been a crazy chuckle.)

My new problem: I now have a total of zero girlfriends in this city, which means that if I'm looking for a distraction, I may be forced to drag Adam to the mall with me for some retail therapy. Or perhaps not. The mall is where I'm most likely to come across Allegra, who, being the wonderful person that she is, may try to feed drugs to me again.

How did I manage to lose my friends, my boyfriend, and my popularity status in one night? (I'm not entirely certain about the popularity status, but I think it probably shattered into hundreds of pieces along with the glass table I pushed Jackson into.)

Wait, I think that paragraph counts as moping ...

Adam just came in and said I should go to the gym with him and Luke. Apparently endorphins will make me happy. Ugh, I'd rather pull my toenails out than exercise. No, wait, that sounds really painful. I don't hate exercise that much.

Okay, I'm going to gym.

Missing you lots, my friend.

xx Livi (not xx L, which is like XXL. How did I never notice that before?)

From: Alivia Howard <livi-gem@gmail.com>
Sent: Sun 6 Apr, 13:21 pm
To: Sarah Henley <s.henley@gmail.com>
Subject: The gym bunnies on the bus go 'ow, ow, ow'

Okay, so I officially joined the gym. I must have been high on endorphins at the time, because when my alarm went off at 7:15 am this morning so I'd be at gym in time for an 8 am abs class, I couldn't remember why I thought any of this exercise stuff was a good idea.

1. It was way too early to think about getting up.
2. My arms were aching from all the weights and machines I used yesterday.
3. I have a twisted ankle! Why didn't I wait till that's better before joining the gym? Now the only exercises I can do involve abs and arms.

I recited my list to Adam, who didn't seem to care and dragged me out of bed anyway. Then when we got to gym and I told him I was too late for my class and would just get a smoothie and sit on a couch while I waited for him, he laughed in my face and made me exercise with him.

SIT-UPS
Adam: 130
Livi: 20

CRUNCHES
Adam: 150
Livi: 30

PLANK
Adam: 90 seconds
Livi: "What the freak is a plank?"

Yeah … so … I'm pathetic.

xx

P.S. I remembered that Allegra and Co. are all at home for the holidays, so the mall is safe. Adam doesn't know it yet, but he is assisting me with Expedition Retail Therapy in about an hour.

———————————————————————————

From: Alivia Howard <livi-gem@gmail.com>
Sent: Mon 7 Apr, 9:08 am
To: Adam Anderson <ADA007@gmail.com>
Subject: Most epic funny cats

www.youtube.com/watch?v=WXUoZkBoGg

This one. Seriously. It's the funniest by far. Did you hear me fall off my chair just now? Because I did. That's how funny this is.

From: Adam Anderson <ADA007@gmail.com>
Sent: Mon 7 Apr, 9:10 am
To: Alivia Howard <livi-gem@gmail.com>
Subject: Get off your lazy bum

Why are you sending me emails when you live about three metres away from me? If you find a funny video, get off your lazy bum and come over here and show me!

P.S. You are ten minutes late for the *Star Wars* marathon.

From: Alivia Howard <livi-gem@gmail.com>
Sent: Mon 7 Apr, 9:11 am
To: Adam Anderson <ADA007@gmail.com>
Subject: Re: Get off your lazy bum

My bum is not lazy. Did you see it last night? I was rocking those kneeling rear leg raises.

P.S. Cat videos are more entertaining than *Star Wars*.

From: Adam Anderson <ADA007@gmail.com>
Sent: Mon 7 Apr, 9:12 am
To: Alivia Howard <livi-gem@gmail.com>
Subject: Sigh

File under *Inappropriate Things Livi Says*: "Did you see my bum last night?"

From: Alivia Howard <livi-gem@gmail.com>
Sent: Mon 7 Apr, 9:14 am
To: Adam Anderson <ADA007@gmail.com>
Subject: I do not say that many inappropriate things

Really? You have a mental file labelled *Inappropriate Things Livi Says*? I would have thought it more likely you'd have a mental file labelled *Things Livi's Walked Into*.

From: Alivia Howard <livi-gem@gmail.com>
Sent: Tue 8 Apr, 20:45 pm
To: Sarah Henley <s.henley@gmail.com>
Subject: Am I a snooty wine drinker?

Adam has this friend at Jazzy Beanbag, Hugo, who really likes this drummer girl from one of the bands that plays there regularly. So Adam decided to help him out by casually mentioning last night that the four of us should check out this food and wine festival happening in Franschhoek this week. Pixie said she doesn't like wine, but she'd be happy to come along for the food part (and no, Pixie is not her real name, but everyone calls her that because she's so small).

So it was all going well. Adam and I were secretly watching the two of them and awarding Hugo points every time he was brave enough to do something like hold her hand or compliment her or casually drape his arm around her shoulder. It was cute. And Hugo was doing really well.

So we'd been tasting all this food and wine, and we'd just sat down at a table under the trees somewhere so I could give my aching ankle a rest, when Pixie looked at Adam, groaned, and said, "Can you please get your girlfriend to stop being a snooty know-it-all about the wine? I don't think I can take it any longer."

Well. Excuse me for enjoying the taste of wine. Excuse me for wanting to share my enjoyment by telling Adam and Hugo everything they should be able to smell and taste and then seeing if they can smell and taste it. Which, by the way, was a fun game until Miss Pixie decided she couldn't 'take it any longer.' Maybe if she'd been drinking wine since she was fifteen she'd also appreciate how fabulous it is. But no. She had to make things awkward.

Anyway, I didn't say any of that. I said, "Snooty?" And Adam blurted out, "She's not my girlfriend." And Pixie looked at us with this what's-wrong-with-you-guys expression and said, "So why is your arm around her shoulders?" Instead of playing it cool and saying, "We're friends. Friends do that. What's your problem?" Adam whipped his arm away as fast as if my shoulders were on fire. I hadn't even realised it was there because, you know, it's ADAM, and we've put our arms around each other many times without it meaning anything. AND THEN he proceeded to keep at least two metres away from me for the rest of the day, which made whispering about Hugo and Pixie impossible. And Pixie kept sighing every time I said anything to her, as if I'd become this major annoyance in her life.

So today sucked.

I miss you.

xx

____

From: Alivia Howard <livi-gem@gmail.com>
Sent: Wed 9 Apr, 21:30 pm
To: Sarah Henley <s.henley@gmail.com>
Subject: Livi Hearts Exercise

I know. I KNOW. You probably saw the subject line and thought my email had been hacked, but it was not! This endorphin thing is working out well for me. And Adam too. He isn't sad about Jenna and I'm not sad about Jackson. Not that you can really compare a two-and-a-half year relationship to one that lasted about three weeks, but still.

Sit-ups: 35
Crunches: 45
Plank: 25 seconds

It's nowhere near as impressive as what Adam did today (no wonder he got over Jenna in only a few weeks. With all the exercise he's been doing, he's probably got bazillions of happy little endorphins whizzing around his body), but I still think it's a brag-worthy achievement.

Luke usually comes to gym with us, but he goes off and does his own thing, which is pretty much his modus operandi for everything in life. He's going to East London tomorrow to visit his girlfriend for a few days, so Adam and I will have the house to ourselves. Which, now that I think about it, is what it feels like most of the time.

xx

P.S. Mom said the session with Dad and the counsellor went quite well this morning. She's still staying with my grandparents and she isn't ready to make any major life decisions yet, but I'm just relieved nobody's mentioned the D-word.

From: Alivia Howard <livi-gem@gmail.com>
Sent: Thu 10 Apr, 15:53 pm
To: Sarah Henley <s.henley@gmail.com>
Subject: My flaming face

It finally happened. The thing I've been fearing since I moved in here at the beginning of the year: I walked in on a naked guy in our bathroom. And that naked guy was the guy I've been friends with since we were thirteen.

AWKWARD.

So here's what happened. Our bathroom has this damp problem. Well, it has many problems (just ask my mother), but the major one is the lack of ventilation which means the steam doesn't go anywhere and the walls and ceiling are always damp and mould is starting to grow. So we've taken to showering with the door ajar to assist with ventilation. We all do this. We all know about it. And I've never had a problem identifying when the bathroom is in use or not.

Until today.

Adam and I had just got back from gym, so obviously we needed to shower. I told him to go first. I made a snack and took it to my room to do some Facebook browsing. I don't know how long I spent doing that, but by the time I realised I was cold and still needed to shower, I assumed Adam MUST be done in the bathroom. I passed his bedroom, where the door was half closed and music was playing. Which meant he was in there, right? Wrong. I pushed the bathroom door open and—

Holy naked buttocks.

He said "Whoa!" and I said "Whoa!" and then he started TURNING AROUND, at which point I managed to squeeze my eyes shut and stumble out of there.

Now I'm hiding in my bedroom trying not to think about the fact that my best friend has a sexy butt. I just heard him go back to his room. Do you think it's safe for me to shower now?

I pull on my comfy jeans and my hoodie with the White Tree of Gondor on the front, then comb my wet hair. These items of clothing have made a reappearance at the front of my wardrobe since I abandoned the party last Friday night and decided Cool wasn't worth chasing anymore. I'm not sure if I'd be brave enough to wear them on campus, but for now, I'm enjoying not having to suck my tummy in every waking moment of the day.

I retrieve my slippers from under my bed—feeling a familiar stab of guilt when I see my violin collecting dust under there—and slide them on before shuffling across the passage to Adam's room. His door is ajar, but there is NO WAY I'm pushing it open without knocking first. I tap the door frame and wait.

"Come in." I slide the door open with my slippered foot—*naked butt image, get OUT of my head*—and walk in. Adam is sitting on his bed sorting through a pile of sheet music and refusing to look up at me. "Hugo called just now to apologise for Pixie's rudeness yesterday. Apparently he doesn't find her quite so attractive anymore and is reconsidering having a crush on her. I suggested that perhaps she was just having a bad day, but he said that since he's started hanging out with her rather than simply admiring her from afar, he's noticed how moody she is."

"Okay. Adam?"

"And he added that he really enjoyed all the wine and appreciated you sharing your knowledge in an entirely non-snooty way." More shuffling of sheet music. "So I guess we can do that again sometime, but without Pixie."

"Adam."

"Oh, and he mentioned the new band that's playing tonight. He said they're good, but I'm not sure I trust his judgement after *The Electric Goat* turned out to be so—"

"Adam!" Finally, he stops talking. "I know what you're doing."

"What am I doing?"

"Trying to avoid talking about the bathroom moment."

"Yes. And I will continue to avoid talking about that moment for the rest of my life. Ah, here's the one I was looking for." He slides several pages out of a flip file.

"I just wanted to say that I'm really sorry I walked in. I thought you were finished and in your bedroom. And I honestly didn't see much. Just—"

"Right, okay. Apology accepted. We can move on now."

"Cool. So … things aren't going to be weird?"

"Of course not. Why would things be weird?"

"You still won't make eye contact with me."

He sets the papers down on his lap and makes a point of meeting my eyes. "Happy now?"

I widen my eyes and stare back. "Super ecstatic."

A doorbell rings.

We frown at one another. "We have a doorbell?" I say.

"I guess we do."

"Rightio, then. I'll go see who it is." I swing around, knock my knee against the door frame, and limp down the passage while Adam shouts "Princess Clumsy" after me. I rub my knee and unlock the front door. I pull it open and find—

A girl. A little younger than me. Red hair. Small frame. Dad's eyes.

No way.

"Hi," she says. "Are you Livi?"
No way, no way, no way.
I grip the door frame for support as I nod slowly.
She smiles, swallows, and says, "I'm Andi."

"OKAY," ADAM SAYS. "SO THIS IS A LITTLE UNEXPECTED."

"Unexpected? *Unexpected?*" I stop pacing and stand in front of his bed, gesturing vaguely in the direction of the lounge. "My half-sister, who I did not even know existed until a few weeks ago, is sitting on our couch! Words cannot explain just how *unexpected* this is."

"I thought you wanted to meet her."

"I did. But I thought I'd have some time to mentally prepare myself. I wasn't expecting her to just show up with absolutely no warning."

"Hence my use of the word 'unexpected,'" Adam mutters.

"You—" I point at him "—are not helping."

"Well, I guess it's fortunate, then, that I'm about to leave for work."

"No!" I grab both his arms as he stands up. "Don't leave

me. Please don't leave me."

"Livi, it's going to be fine. It's not like I'm leaving you alone with the Chucky doll or something."

"WHY WOULD YOU SAY THAT? You know that movie scared the crap out of me."

"I'm sorry. I forgot." He pats my arm before picking up his keys from the desk.

"You did not forget. You're trying to get back at me for the naked butt moment."

He laughs. "Stop being ridiculous and just go and *talk* to her."

"But I don't know what to say."

"Livi." He places both hands on my shoulders and focuses his gaze on me. "You have a lifetime to catch up on. I'm sure you'll find something."

For some insane reason—possibly because my brain is looking for *any* distraction from the girl sitting on my couch—I can't help remembering Allegra saying that glasses make guys look cute. And maybe I've just never noticed it before, but Adam's glasses *do* make him look cute. And the eyes behind those glasses ... I never noticed how light they are. Kind of greyish green, but so *light*. As if they've been luminously lit up.

I'm staring. Crapazoid. How long have I been staring for? And why is Adam staring back at me with that weird sort of uncertainty, as if ...

I step back and look away, because apparently my legs have more of a brain than my brain does right now. "You, uh, you're right. There's plenty of stuff for us to talk about.

I just have to find the right place to start."

"Exactly." Adam scratches his head, causing his sticking-up hair to stick up a little more. "If you really don't want to be left here alone with her, you could always come to Jazzy Beanbag and do your chatting there."

"Yes! That's a great idea."

Adam disappears behind the bar, and Andrea—*Andi*, I correct myself silently—and I sit down at the table next to the red leg-shaped lamp. I glance up. She glances up. We both look away.

I run my finger along one of the scratches on the table. With an uncomfortable laugh, I say, "This is weird."

"I know." She tugs at her brightly coloured scarf. "I'm so sorry I just showed up. I was expecting you to slam the door in my face or scream at me about how my mom ruined your family or something. I still can't believe I'm sitting here with my … sister."

I look up. "Are you also an only child?"

She nods. "It's always just been me and my mom."

"Your mom," I murmur, not really wanting to think about that part of the equation.

"Yes. Oh my gosh, you must *hate* her." Andi covers her face with her hands and groans. I notice the dark green nail polish on her fingers and wonder what her favourite colour is. "I'm so sorry. I thought you'd hate me too because of her, but I really wanted to meet you, so I thought I'd risk coming here." She peeks through her fingers. "Thank you for not hating me."

I take a deep breath and say, "I wanted to. I tried to hate you. But the sensible part of my brain kept reminding me that none of this was your fault. And ... honestly ... I wanted to meet you too. I asked my dad—um, our dad—but he said no. How did you find me anyway?"

"Well, you see—" She breaks off as a waitress comes over to take our order. Andi asks for coffee, and I order hot chocolate.

"Hey, you're Livi, right?" the waitress says before leaving. "Adam's friend?"

"Uh, yes, that's me."

"I don't mean to put you in the middle of anything, or make you uncomfortable, but can you please tell Adam to just *talk* to me?"

"To talk to you?" With half my mind still focused on Andi and her story, I wonder if perhaps I've missed some important detail here. "You both work here, right?" I say to the waitress. "Can't you just walk up to him and start a conversation?"

She sighs. "I've been trying. But he's managed to avoid me for *three weeks*. I know he's embarrassed, but it really wasn't a big deal. He's an *amazingly* talented musician. I'd hate for him to give up his guitar lessons because of one drunken incident."

Say WHAT? Adam's taking guitar lessons? And there was a drunken incident with this woman who looks about a decade older than us? And I'm supposed to figure out what's going on with the half-sister I only just met sitting right here listening to all this?

I clear my throat and sit up a little straighter. "Whatever it is that happened, I don't think it's appropriate for you to be discussing it with your customers." Ugh, I sound exactly like my mother. Next thing I'll be calling the manager and making a scene.

"I—I'm so sorry. You're absolutely right." She hurries away before I can say anything else.

"That was strange," Andi says.

I shake my head, filing that brief interlude away for further examination at a later time. "Anyway. You were saying?"

"Oh yes. My mom's been refusing to tell me anything about my father for years. She kept saying it was just better that way. Then earlier this year I was looking for old school records in the top of a cupboard, and I found a biscuit tin with a bunch of random stuff in it. Movie tickets, a theatre ticket, a few letters, and ... a photo. Of my mom and a guy with red hair. I confronted her about it, and she couldn't exactly lie. It was pretty obvious who he was. I told her I wanted to contact him, and that's when she admitted that he was married. He had a wife and ... you."

I shift uncomfortably in my seat. "Did ... did she say if she was still in contact with him?"

"She said he sends money every month, but other than that ... nothing."

Well, at least Dad was telling the truth about that.

"Apparently he has a colleague who's friends with my mom," Andi says, "so that's how my mom knows he's still married and that he doesn't have any other children aside from you—well, and me, obviously—and that you came to UCT this year. She told me I needed to forget about him because he has his own family and we shouldn't mess with that, but … I couldn't stop thinking about him. And you. I found an email address for him online, and even though my mom said not to contact him, I eventually did. Which you already know, because that's why your family's falling apart now, and I'm so, so sorry for doing that. I never meant for—"

"Okay, you need to stop apologising. Yes, your email is what caused everything to blow up, but you can't apologise forever. And our parents are the ones who caused this mess in the first place, not you. They've just been hiding it all this time. Also," I add, "none of this explains how you arrived on my doorstep."

"Oh. Yes. Well, after my mom used a whole lot of shouting to tell me that my email had potentially ruined someone else's marriage—

"Like her adultery had nothing to do with that," I mutter.

"That's what I said!" Andi exclaims. "And I was grounded for it. Anyway, after that, I decided to contact you instead. A friend of mine—he was my neighbour—is at UCT now. So I asked him how I should go about finding a particular student. I mentioned your name, and he was like,

'This is crazy, but I actually know who she is.'"

"What?" I sit forward. "Who's your friend?"

"Damien Sanders."

"Damien Sanders?" I sit back as our waitress places our coffee and hot chocolate on the table and vanishes without making eye contact with either of us. "Damien, Damien … I don't think I know—Oh, wait, does he have a girlfriend named Charlotte?"

"Yes."

"Wow. That is super weird."

"So all Damien had to do was ask his girlfriend where you live, and it was that easy."

"You didn't think to maybe ask for my number and just *call* instead of coming all the way here?"

"Phone calls, texts and emails have a much greater chance of being ignored," Andi says, sliding her giant coffee cup closer and wrapping her hands around it. "This way, I ran the risk of you slamming a door in my face, but I was prepared to hang out on your front steps or outside your gate for as long as it took for you to pay attention to me."

"Jeez. You must have been really desperate for a sister."

"Well, yes," she says simply. "It was lonely growing up with just me. Wasn't it lonely for you?"

I pick up my hot chocolate and take a sip. It *was* lonely at times. But I don't know this girl well enough to admit that to her. "I'm surprised your mom let you fly across the country to see me."

"Oh, no, she doesn't know about this. I mean, she'll find

out when I get back on Saturday, but right now she thinks I've gone to Kruger for two nights with my friend Ashley's family."

"She—she doesn't know?"

Andi shakes her head. "Damien helped me get here."

"And ... where are you staying?" My mind flashes back to the small suitcase sitting in the lounge.

"That, uh, depends on how generous you're feeling," Andi says, purposefully avoiding my gaze.

"You were hoping to stay with *me*?"

She bites her nail, then says in a tiny voice, "Yes?"

My half-sister. In my house. For two nights.

This day could NOT get any weirder.

"Is that okay? If it's not, I can make another plan. Damien said he could help me find—"

"No, it's fine, it's—" I pause, just to make sure I really am okay with this. "It'll be fun. Like ... a sleepover. There's even a free bedroom in our house right now. I'm sure its usual occupant won't mind if we put some clean sheets on the bed for you."

She smiles. "Thank you."

"Hey, ladies." Adam stops by our table and leans against it. "How's it going over here?" I made him promise to check in with me after twenty minutes in case I needed to be rescued from my terrifying half-sibling.

"Everything's great," I say. "Andi's going to be staying with us for two nights."

"Oh, okay, cool." He smiles down at me and adds, "You see? I told you she wasn't scary."

Heat burns its way up my neck as Andi laughs and says, "You thought I was *scary?*"

"No."

"She may have compared you to the Chucky doll," Adam tells her.

Andi bends over her coffee, laughing even harder. "I think I'm supposed to be offended by that," she says between gasps of laughter. "If only I could take horror movies seriously."

I cross my arms and lean back in my chair with a huff. "I did not compare you to a terrifying doll. Adam is trying to embarrass me because I walked into the bathroom this morning and saw his SEXY, NAKED BUTT." I raise my voice on the last three words so everyone around us will hear.

Adam stares at me, shock morphing into amusement on his face. Wait, why is he *amused?* He's supposed to be *embarrassed.* "Well, it's official," he says with a grin. "Everyone inside Jazzy Beanbag now knows that you think my butt is sexy."

Crap in a hat. I said the word 'sexy,' didn't I. Adam smirks and heads back to the bar. I groan and drop my head onto the table.

"Are the two of you this entertaining all the time?" Andi asks.

My groan slowly changes to a laugh. Entertaining. That's one way of putting it. "Pretty much."

"Well," she says, "now I'm looking forward to staying with you even more."

From: Alivia Howard <livi-gem@gmail.com>
Sent: Sat 12 Apr, 7:16 am
To: Sarah Henley <s.henley@gmail.com>
Subject: Weirdness

That word keeps going through my head. Weird. I can't seem to stop thinking it. It's just so WEIRD that she's here! I keep looking for similarities between us. Things that mean she's not just another person, but connected to me by BLOOD.

We have the same colour hair and eyes, but our noses and mouths are different shapes.
We have similar builds, but she's a little taller than me.
I hate coffee; she loves it.
We're both quite chatty.
We both read sci fi and fantasy books.

I love *Star Trek*; she's not a fan.
We're both afraid of heights (which we discovered when we hiked up Lion's Head this morning. It is REALLY steep at the top!).
I like wine; she doesn't.
We're both musical! She plays the piano.

I know it's silly, but every time we find something we have in common, we get excited, as if it's because we're sisters rather than the more likely explanation—it's simply a coincidence.

I haven't told my parents she's here. Dad would get angry, and Mom would be hurt. I fully understand Mom's perspective. I mean, to her, Andi is living proof that her husband cheated on her. And when I think of that, I get angry all over again. Not at Andi, though. At Dad. So I'm trying to move on from that and focus instead on the person who's here. She's leaving this evening, but she's hoping to come to UCT next year, so there might be a lot more sister bonding in our future.

Sister bonding. The concept sounds so weird when I'm applying it to myself. Weird but cool! (And there's that word again!)

xx

I wave goodbye one last time before shutting the door and wandering towards Adam's bedroom. Damien offered to drive Andi to the airport, and I didn't have any objections. I prefer not to drive The Tin Man after dark.

"So," Adam says as I let myself fall backwards onto his bed. "You guys certainly managed to fit a lot of bonding into two days." He's busy adjusting the angle of his computer screen and getting the next episode of *The Big Bang Theory* ready to watch.

"So. Weird." I stare at the ceiling, trying to sort out my thoughts. "What my dad did was terrible. Cheating on my mom like that. He never should have done it. I *wish* he hadn't, because then there wouldn't be all this hurt between the two of them and between Dad and me. But at the same time … Andi is awesome. She's so honest about everything, and funny and sweet and intelligent and just … really great. But she's only here because Dad had an affair. If I wish that away, then I'm wishing her out of existence. How does that make sense?"

Adam switches on his lamp, turns the main light off, and flops onto the bed beside to me. "It doesn't. Life doesn't make sense. That's just the way it is."

"I suppose so. Thanks for driving us around and hanging out with us. Doing the tourist vibe. I was worried it might get awkward with just me and her."

"I think I cleared up the awkward atmosphere for good when I mentioned you found her scary."

"Mmm. Thanks again for that."

"You're welcome." He picks up the remote for his

computer and presses play.

"Hey, can I ask you something?

He presses pause. "Sure."

"Do you still miss Jenna?"

Adam rubs a hand over his hair. "Does it make me a bad person if I say no?"

"Why would that make you a bad person?"

"Because … I'm supposed to mourn over this long relationship we had for more than just a couple of weeks? I don't know. The truth is, we started growing apart a while ago. I was overseas for almost a whole year, and then after only a few weeks at home, I came here. When we were both at school, it felt like we had this incredible, amazing thing that would last forever, but in the past year and a bit … well, we haven't really had much of a relationship."

I nod. "I guess that makes sense."

"Can I ask you something now?"

"You may. And the answer is, 'No, I don't miss Jackson.' He may have had a bronzed, babe-magnet body and been an amazing kisser, but forcing me into a dark corner so he could attempt to violate me is NOT something I'm looking for in a boyfriend."

"He—that's what he did?" Adam twists to face me, his eyebrows drawing together in anger.

"I—oh. Too much info. Sorry. I forgot you're not Sarah."

The angry eyebrows rise. "You think of me the way you think of Sarah?" I'm trying to figure out how to answer that when he shakes his head. "Never mind. That's not what I mean. What I mean is, why did you pick such an ass for a boyfriend?"

"Wait, are you angry with *me* now?"

"Yes! Do you really think so little of yourself that you'd want to date someone like *that*?"

I stare at him, my mouth hanging open a little, as I try to figure out what caused this sudden Adam explosion. "Okay." I put my hands on his shoulders. "I have a feeling that's not the question you were originally going to ask. So I'm going to go to the kitchen and get snacks, because I forgot to do that on my way here, and you're going to calm down from your sudden, unreasonable, unnecessary anger. Okay?"

Before he can argue, I climb over him and run to the kitchen. *Hmm. Snacks, snacks* … There's a tub of baby tomatoes in the fridge, which Adam will enjoy—he's always been a healthy snacker—but I need something more than that. I find a bag of popcorn in the cupboard, grab my jar of peanut butter and a spoon, and hurry back to the bedroom with my collection. I climb over Adam as he finishes typing something on his phone and places it back onto his bedside table.

"Hugo says hi."

"Oh. Hi, Hugo." I hand Adam the tomatoes and popcorn while I unscrew the lid of the peanut butter jar.

"Oh, didn't I tell you I already got a snack for you?" Adam says.

"Hmm? No."

Adam pulls open the drawer in his bedside table and

removes a pink packet of chewy sweets. He tosses it onto the bed next to me. I pick it up, take one look at the name on the packet, and narrow my eyes at him. "Princess gums? Really?"

He smiles innocently. "Seemed like the perfect snack for you."

"Uh huh. Thanks." I give him my unimpressed face before adding the packet of pink, purple and white sweets to the snack collection. "ANYWAY. Did you remember what question you were going to ask before you went all Hulk on me and got strangely angry? Or are we going straight into watching *The Big Bang Theory*?"

"I was going to ask," Adam says, tearing the popcorn bag open, "why you don't play your violin anymore. You said you were too busy before, but you've had time since the holiday started, and I still haven't heard you play anything."

Horrid, screechy thing, Allegra's voice echoes in my mind as I rub my thumb over the disappearing calluses on my fingertips. *I've never heard anything so awful in my life.*

"Oh." I sink back against the cushions and stick a spoonful of peanut butter in my mouth, hoping it'll somehow assuage the guilt I experience every time I think of my beloved instrument cultivating dust bunnies under my bed. It doesn't work. "It's hard to explain," I say eventually. "I really miss it, and I feel guilty about not playing, but the longer I go without picking up an instrument, the more I try to avoid it. I know when I eventually do play again, I'll be rusty and it'll sound terrible and I'll feel like a horrible failure, so I'm trying to avoid that experience by not playing, but the longer I avoid it, the worse that experience will be."

"Livi?"

"Mmm?" I lick more peanut butter off the spoon.

"Stop overanalysing and just play the darn violin."

"I guess. Maybe tomorrow."

He throws a piece of popcorn at me and says, "Princess Procrastination."

I pick up the popcorn and put some peanut butter on it before crunching down on it. *Hmm. Not bad.* "That's actually quite tasty." I help myself to a handful of popcorn and get ready to coat each piece with peanut butter.

"Weirdo," Adam mutters. He balances the tub of tomatoes on his stomach, presses Play, and the episode begins.

"Hey," I say, and he presses pause once again. "I just remembered something. That waitress at Jazzy Beanbag." I turn to Adam with an accusing stare. "When I was there with Andi, she said something about you and an embarrassing incident and guitar lessons."

"Oh. Right." Adam rubs his thumb over the remote control's buttons.

"So? What was she talking about?"

Adam groans. "This is something I prefer not to talk about."

"I'm afraid that's not an option."

"Fine. That day Jenna broke up with me and I drank too much at Jazzy Beanbag, Mel was working. She came over to check on me and … I suddenly found myself kissing her."

I start laughing. "Most girls just want a decent tip, Adam,

not a slobbery kiss with the drunk dude in the corner."

"It was not slobbery, okay. And it wasn't exactly a conscious choice."

"Ha. I'm sure. And the guitar lesson part?"

Adam scratches his head. "Mel also happens to be my guitar teacher."

I smack his arm. "You started playing a new instrument, and you didn't tell me?"

He shrugs. "You were always busy and never around. I didn't think you'd be that interested."

"Rubbish. Of course I'm interested. Where is this guitar hiding, and how long have you been playing?"

"Since January. I saw a flyer stuck up at Jazzy Beanbag the first time I went there and thought it might be fun to learn another instrument. And the guitar isn't *hiding*, it just happens to live in my cupboard. It's Hugo's Dad's. I'm still saving up for my own."

"Adam! I want to hear you play."

He chews on a tomato and says, "I'm not that good."

"I don't believe that for a second. Music is your language. You probably learned how to read it before you could read words. Remember when you taught yourself to play that old cello lying around at school? And your uncle's saxophone?"

Adam gives me a noncommittal nod. "Still doesn't mean I'm going to play the guitar for you."

"Okay, fine. Will you at least talk to Mel about continuing your lessons? She was worried you'd end up wasting your talent."

"Nah, I'm over the lessons." Adam tosses the remote back and forth from one hand to the other. "I've been teaching myself ever since that embarrassing drunken kiss."

"YOU SEE! Music *is* your language. Please play something for me."

He looks at me, his eyes moving across my face before sliding back down to the remote in his hands. "I'm not ready."

I nod slowly. "Okay. Play for me when you're ready. For now, let's get this *Big Bang Theory* marathon started." I take the remote from him and hit play. The opening song starts playing, and images of history, science, and technology whizz by at high-speed. I settle back against the cushions to enjoy my peanut butter popcorn and some good laughs.

We're about five minutes in when I become aware of a noise outside growing louder and louder. A noise like wind howling through thousands of leaves. I slap my popcorn-free hand down on Adam's leg and say, "Can you hear that?"

He fumbles for the remote and presses pause—yet again. The noise from outside fills the room.

It isn't wind. It's rain. Rain pelting down so hard it sounds as if it's trying to break through the roof to attack us.

Adam looks at me, lowers his voice to a deep rumble, and says, "Winter is coming."

ADAM'S *GAME OF THRONES* REFERENCE MIGHT HAVE MADE me pack up laughing, but I no longer find it funny when I leave for campus on Monday morning and it's *still* raining. Winter is certainly getting a head start in the rain department. I considered using the weather as an excuse to avoid the friends who aren't my friends anymore, but in the end I decided to face the inevitable on day one rather than putting it off until tomorrow or the next day.

So here I am, shivering inside The Tin Man while waiting for a break in the rain so I can dash to lectures without getting drenched. I pull my phone out of my bag and type a message to Adam.

Livi: It seems silly that we don't share lifts to campus. Why don't we do that?

Adam: Because I leave about forty-five mins before you when traffic isn't as bad and I can still get a parking close to lectures. Or I leave even earlier than that and go to gym. Speaking of which, you should come with Luke and me now that you're a gym member.

Livi: How about I get a lift with you on rainy, non-gym days?

Adam: You just want me for my umbrella.

Livi: Busted.

Adam: Umbrellas don't work so well with sideways rain. Just run.

Livi: I'm wearing heels.

Adam: It's like you're asking me to say I told you so.

Livi: Ooh! No rain!

The break I've been waiting for arrives, and I shove my phone back into its pocket inside my bag, climb out of my car, and hurry up the hill. I'm looking good in my super skinny jeans, high-heeled boots, and the jacket I got during Expedition Retail Therapy at the beginning of the holiday. It turns out I'm not brave enough to wear any of my comfy clothes to varsity. Even though I'm no longer part of the cool crowd—or any crowd, for that matter—I still want to turn heads with my fabulous fashion sense.

I arrive outside my first period lecture theatre and peek inside. I scan for Jackson first, because he's the one I really, *really* don't want to see. He isn't here. Allegra, Courtney and Amber, however, are present. So is Charlotte, although she seems to have latched onto another group. The we-take-our-studies-seriously-but-look-gorgeous-while-doing-it group.

So. Where to sit, where to sit …

I wonder what would happen if I slid into the seat next to Allegra as if last Friday night were no big deal? Perhaps we'd have a little argument about how I ran off and didn't contact her for the whole holiday, but then we might laugh it off and things would get back to normal.

Do I really want that, though? The kind of normal where every conversation is as shallow as a puddle, no party is considered complete without the addition of a few recreational drugs, and couples are comfortable crossing lines I can only see myself on the other side of when I've found the guy I know I'll love for the rest of my life?

No. You don't want that. Even if it means sitting alone.

Crap. I really don't want to sit alone.

It's FINE. Just remember CONFIDENCE. You can be cool—on your own—as long as you're exuding confidence.

Confidence. Got it.

I saunter in, looking out for an empty seat. I've targeted the perfect spot, four rows from the back, when I notice the loner Indian girl in the back row, and suddenly my feet are carrying me quickly to the seat next to her.

Just. Can't. Sit. Alone.

"Hi," I say brightly as I sit down and drop my bag on the floor. I hold my hand out to her. "I'm Livi."

She stares at the hand as though it presents a health risk. She folds her arms tightly over her chest. "Did you get lost?" she asks.

"Wow." I lower my hand. "You're really friendly. Has anyone ever told you that?"

"Has anyone ever told you that you come to campus completely overdressed?"

My mouth hangs open for a while before I respond. "Okay. Not only unfriendly, but downright rude."

She gives me an icy smile. "I didn't come to university to make friends."

"Clearly. It appears you'd rather make unpleasant memories."

"I came here to work hard and graduate summa cum laude."

I remove my books and pens from my bag and lay them out neatly across the desk. "Looks like I chose the right person to sit next to, then."

"I don't think so. Why don't you—"

Our lecturer chooses that moment to launch into a new section, and whatever Rude Unfriendly Loner Girl was about to tell me is forgotten as she hastily picks up her pen and turns her full attention to the front of the room.

Salima, the label on her textbook says, which is helpful, since I'm pretty sure she wasn't about to introduce herself.

Salima is out of her chair and heading for the door before I've packed away any of my things. Great. So much for making a new friend. Allegra glances my way as she walks out with Courtney and Amber. I grab my phone, bring it to my ear, and laugh as I answer a non-existent phone call. Then I have to continue the fake phone call, feeling like a complete idiot, as other members of our class look my way before heading out of the lecture hall.

Ugh, I can't believe I just did that.

I slowly pack my things away as students file in for the next lecture. Maybe I should give my next class a miss. I think Adam's free now. I could meet him at the library or computer lab or … wherever it is he usually hangs out during his free periods. But if I miss classes, I've got no one to help me catch up on the work. Blast it. I hadn't considered that particular side-effect of friendlessness.

I take my time heading to the next lecture venue. Perhaps I'll slip into the seat beside Salima just as the lecture starts so she won't have time to say anything rude. At least I won't have to sit alone that way.

I'm almost at the door when someone heading the same way almost walks into me. I take a step to the side, catching my balance, and look up. Icy adrenaline kicks my heart into top gear. "Jackson?"

I stare at him. He stares back. "Well?" he says eventually, gesturing to the door. "Are you going in, or are you just going to stand there all day? Perhaps you'd like to push me into the door."

I cross my arms over my chest. "Perhaps I would. But I thought you might have something to say to me first. Something like an apology."

"Ha! An apology? If anyone should be apologising, it's you, after throwing me into a glass table. Have you seen my hands?" He shoves them in front of my face so I can see the half-healed scabbed cuts across his skin.

"That wasn't intentional, that was self-defence. You're the only one who did something wrong that night, and—"

"Oh really?" He looks at me with complete contempt. "And what exactly did I do wrong?"

"You …" I look down as someone hurries past us into the lecture. "You … tried to …"

"To what? Put my hands on you? Touch you? Yes, Livi, because I wanted you. And from all the signals you were giving me—from our making out, from your flirting—you wanted me too. So I only did what any guy would do, and suddenly you're freaking out like, I don't know, I'm trying to rape you or something."

I squeeze my eyes shut for a moment to hold the tears back. How did this end up being my fault? "I did want you, Jackson. But that … what you did … was seriously inappropriate."

"No it wasn't, Livi. That was normal."

"Not for me!"

"Oh, God, don't tell me you're one of those girls."

"One of what—"

"You want to *wait*. You don't want our relationship to be *physical* now. You probably think I'm The One, and you're expecting me to produce a ring before you'll go anywhere near a bed with me. Or the corner of a room, apparently."

I shake my head. I can't believe what a jerk this guy turned out to be. "Yes. I *do* want to wait. And there are plenty of people out there like me—girls *and* guys—who are happy to wait for the—"

"Ya, they're all a bunch of weirdos."

"—wait for the right person!" I yell at him. "When I get married one day, I don't want to have the ghosts of all the girls my husband's ever slept with in the bed with us, and he shouldn't have to deal with that from me either. And one more thing." I point my finger at him. "You are *so far* from being The One, it's not even funny."

I spin around and storm off, having no intention of going into that lecture or any other today. A light drizzle dampens my face as I hurry back to my car. I fling my bag inside and climb in, slamming the door shut. My fingers shake with anger all the way home. Adam's car is gone, and so is Luke's, so I drive into the empty garage.

I leave my bag in the doorway to my bedroom and throw myself onto the bed. What is wrong with me? I pick a hot prince and he turns out to be a jerk. I pick a hot regular guy and he turns out to be a jerk too. Is there such a thing as a decent guy who's also hot? Am I being *shallow* by wanting to love someone good-looking?

I probably am.

Frustration and loneliness and anger and hurt well up

inside me and squeeze themselves out in the form of tears. I just want to be liked. I want to fit in somewhere. Somewhere I don't have to worry about anyone making fun of me for who I am and the things I like. Is that too much to ask for?

Without really thinking about it, I roll over and kneel on the floor. I reach beneath my bed and pull out the violin case. The bottom drawer of my desk is packed with flip files of music, so I pull that open and take out a stack of files. I tuck them under my arm, pick up the violin case, and head to the lounge.

It's a ritual my hands haven't forgotten: Unclip the buckles, flip open the case, remove the violin, attach the shoulder rest, tighten the bow, slide the bow across the rosin several times. I fit the instrument against my neck, and already the tension, stress and overwhelming emotion begin to slip away as my mind prepares to focus on one thing only: the music.

I walk across to Adam's piano and play an A, then slowly draw my bow across the A string of the violin. It's horribly out of tune, but the simple act of creating sound from a string leaves my heart feeling like it's come home.

Why did I wait so long to do this?

I twist the relevant peg until the A string is in tune, then move to the D string, G string, and finally the E string, twisting the pegs and fine tuners while listening for the resonance of the perfect fifth intervals.

The violin is ready. I should probably play some scales or arpeggios to warm up, but real music is what I'm longing for. I position my fingers on the strings, close my eyes, and breathe in deeply. I forget the pile of music lying on the coffee table as my memory takes over and I bring the bow down to play the first note of *Somewhere Over the Rainbow*.

The music soars, and along with it, my heart. My pitch is off here and there, and my vibrato isn't quite what it used to be, but I'm lost in a land of wishing stars and lemon drops and dreams that really do come true. Slowly, bit by bit, as the music rises and falls, pieces of my soul I didn't even know were missing fit themselves back together.

With the last long, wavering note, I breathe out slowly. Content. Finally.

"I could listen to you play all day."

I blink and look around. Adam is leaning in the doorway, watching me with a smile. Was I so lost in my musical world that I didn't hear a car driving up outside the window, or the front door opening and closing? I must have been.

"You're so graceful," he says. "The way your arm moves with the bow. It's like you're not only a musician, but a dancer too."

I look down to hide my warm cheeks. "Makes you wonder how I can be so clumsy when I don't have a violin in my hands."

He laughs quietly. "What are you doing home already?"

I shrug and sigh. "Bad morning, I guess. What about you?"

"Second period free, and my third period lecturer is sick, so I thought I'd come home for a bit. Do you, uh, want some accompaniment?" He gestures to the piano.

I give him a wide smile. "That would make me happier than you can imagine."

Adam crosses the room and sits at the piano. "How about the G-string one you love?" he says with a smirk.

I roll my eyes and laugh. Adam can never mention Bach's *Air on the G String* without making a reference to underwear, which I'm sure was the last thing on Bach's mind when he was writing Suite No. 3 in D major. G-strings hadn't even been invented back then.

I look through my files until I find the right sheet music. I pull out the piano accompaniment and hand it to Adam. He places his hands over the keys. I get my bow ready. He looks at me. I nod and murmur, "Three and four and …"

The music begins.

DAY FIVE AFTER THE HOLIDAY. I HURRY INTO MY FIRST period lecture towards my new spot next to Salima Who Never Talks To Me, only to find that she isn't here. I've only recently begun paying attention to her, but I doubt she's ever missed a lecture before, and I'm pretty sure being late isn't part of her summa cum laude plans. I crane my neck as I search every other row in here, but I don't see Salima. Perhaps I scared her off for good when I sat next to her in yesterday afternoon's mathematics tutorial and read every question out loud while she ignored me and answered them on her own. I made no effort to hide the fact that I was looking at her answer page for 'assistance' with my problem-solving theories. She probably didn't like that.

The lecture begins.

Salima still isn't here.

Oddly enough, I'm starting to worry about her. It's clear

she doesn't like me, and if I didn't arrive at the last minute for every single lecture, she'd probably move away as soon as I sit my butt down next to her. But I can't help feeling that Rude Unfriendly Loner Girl isn't who she really is, and I'm determined to get her to talk to me. I think we could be friends. So it worries me that my potential friend, who thinks lectures are the most important part of every weekday, hasn't shown up yet.

It also means I'm sitting alone, which isn't great.

The lecturer starts shouting things from the front of the room, and I write down everything that shows up on the projector screen. Whenever he heads off on a boring tangent, I doodle music notes and treble clefs in the corner of my page before the next slide comes up and I carry on writing. Doodling means my eyes are stuck on my notebook rather than wandering a few rows forward to where Allegra, Courtney and Amber are sliding cell phones back and forth across the desk and quietly giggling at whatever's on them.

After about fifteen minutes, I notice movement from the corner of my eye. The long desk that spans from one side of the row to the other wobbles slightly as Salima hurries towards me and sits down, leaving one empty seat between us. Breathless, she hastily tucks her long black hair behind her ears, grabs a pen and pad of paper from her bag, and frowns at the screen. Her lips move silently. She writes something down, then frowns again.

I clear my throat. When she glances over at me, I raise an eyebrow and nudge my notebook towards her. *Time to make friends, Salima.* She eyes the notebook as if it may bite her, then relents and slides it closer. She quickly copies down everything she missed, then passes it back to me, hesitantly mouthing, *Thank you.*

Score! We are totally on our way to becoming best buddies.

The lecturer takes off on another boring tangent that ends up with him answering a complicated and pointless question posed by someone in the front row. He leans against the front desk as he gets deeper into a discussion with the student, and the rest of us shuffle around and start chattering, because we can't hear a thing the guys at the front are saying, and it doesn't really bother us.

I lean towards Salima and say, "I doubt you've ever been late for a lecture before."

For a moment, I think she might ignore me, but after taking down a few more notes, she says, "My stupid car. My parents insisted I live off campus so I wouldn't be distracted, but that means I have to fight through traffic every day, and when my car misbehaves, like today, then I wind up late. I've never been as late as I was today, though, so … thank you." She glances up quickly, then turns back to the page in front of her and writes something else down. What exactly, I have no idea, since nothing new has gone up on the projector screen in the last five minutes.

"Your parents sound like hard-asses," I say.

She looks up, startled, then laughs.

"Oh my hat. You *laughed.* I didn't even know you could *smile.*"

She laughs again, then looks quickly to the front of the

room to see if she's missing anything.

"Don't worry," I tell her. "I'm sure that boring discussion is going to go on for at least another three minutes."

She gives me a smile. A SMILE. "I'm sorry I was so rude to you on Monday. I know who your group of friends is, and I assumed you were sitting next to me as a joke. But you actually seem like a nice person, Livi. I'm sorry we can't be friends."

Can't be friends? I'm confused for a moment until I realise she's joking. "Oh right," I say with an eye-roll. "Because you didn't come to university to make friends."

"Exactly."

Wait. She's not joking. "You—you were being serious about that?"

She nods. "Hard-ass parents, remember? It took me two years to convince them to let me move across the country for university. Our deal is that I get above ninety percent for every assignment, test and exam, or I'll have to move back to Durban. Maintaining those kinds of results means lots of work. Hence, no time for friends."

"I—that's—*ninety percent?*" Before I can form a coherent response, the next slide comes up and the lecture continues. Salima begins scribbling words down at lightning speed—I think she writes down every word the lecturer *says*, as well as what's on the screen—while I compose a note to her.

You're also from Durban? Cool! Me too! What school were you at? We should hang out some time. DON'T tell me you

*don't have time for friends. You probably get 100% for
everything, so you can afford to slip a few % if it means having
a tiny bit of an actual LIFE. And I don't mean clubs and
drinking and drugs and hair salon dates. Trust me, that stuff is
overrated. I mean movies and wine tasting and Xbox and
chilling at this cool music cafe by my house. What's your phone
number?*

At the end of the lecture, we pack up our things and Salima turns to me. "Thank you for helping me catch up at the beginning. And I'm sorry again for being rude. You're welcome to sit with me in the future, as long as you don't distract me while the lecture is happening."

"Wow. How magnanimous of you. You're welcome to read this note I wrote you, but only if you respond immediately."

She frowns, takes the folded paper I'm holding out to her, and reads it. Her eyes scan my words before looking up. "I don't drink. My parents wouldn't allow my brother to get an Xbox, so I don't know how to play games on it. And my phone won't let me add new contacts."

"Are you kidding me? Your phone won't let you add new contacts? That's the worst lie I've ever heard."

"I'm not lying." She pulls her phone out of her bag and holds it up. "It's an old phone—my parents didn't want me distracted by a new one with, as they say, all the bells and whistles—and it won't let me add contacts or take photos or use the hash key."

I eye the phone suspiciously. "I wouldn't be surprised if

your parents got someone to disable those functions before giving it to you."

She laughs and puts the phone away. "Neither would I. But I'm living on a strict allowance, and I don't have extra cash to get a new phone. And I don't really need one," she adds, heading for the door.

"You know, my friend Adam could probably fix that phone for you," I say as I follow her outside. "He's a total genius with all things tech. And music too, but I think most people know him for the tech stuff. He's doing computer science here."

Salima frowns at me. "Is that Adam Anderson, by any chance?"

"Yes! You know him?"

She nods, and even though it's difficult to tell with her darker skin, I'm pretty sure she's blushing. "Yes. I'm taking a computer science course as an elective. Just for fun."

"Oh my goodness. Somebody needs to show you what fun actually means."

She smacks my arm, but I can tell she's trying not to smile.

"Why do they make us do maths as part of a Marketing degree?" I whine. "Seriously. I am never going to use these mattress things in real life."

Adam looks up from across the table at Jazzy Beanbag.

We had dinner here earlier and now he's doing some complicated coding thing on the laptop he just bought from someone on Gumtree while I try to understand the newest section in my mathematics course. "Mattress things?" he asks.

"Yes." I hold up my notes to show him the heading I wrote down based on Professor Muzenda's garbled words before he spent the entire lecture scribbling numbers and brackets hastily across the board. I barely managed to keep up with note taking, let alone brain processing. "See? Mattresses."

Adam makes his trying-really-hard-not-to-laugh face. "I think you mean 'matrices.'" He spells it out for me while I write it down.

"*Oh.*" I tilt my head to the side while examining the word. "That's what he was saying?"

"Oh my goodness, Liv."

"What? He's foreign. I only understand about twenty percent of what he says."

"Does that mean you'll only be getting twenty percent for your exam?"

"I hope not. But what am I supposed to do? I can't make his accent disappear."

"I don't know. Ask one of the tutors for help?"

I smile and flutter my eyelashes. "Want to be my tutor?"

"Uh ..." Adam swallows. "I guess I could."

"Relax. I'm not such a terrible student. It shouldn't be that difficult for you to help me."

Adam mutters something before turning back to his coding.

"What was that?"

"NOTHING," he says, which probably means he was making fun of my mathematics ability. "Oh. Livi." He looks around his work area, disoriented for a moment, then reaches under the table for his laptop bag. "Livi, Livi, Livi. I can't believe I forgot to tell you."

"What? What's wrong?"

"I was surfing YouTube and I found this *amazing* group. A pianist and a cellist. They do these incredible covers and mash-ups. I don't know how I haven't come across them before."

I smile to myself. Given Adam's level of excitement, I should have known it had something to do with music.

"Here." Adam plugs a pair of headphones into his laptop and hands them to me across the table. I adjust them before placing them over my ears. "Ready?" Adam asks. I nod, and he presses a button on his laptop.

I close my eyes as the music begins, shutting out all distractions so I can concentrate. It's familiar, but I've never heard it played on only a cello and a piano, so it takes me a while to think of the name. *I know it, I know it, I know it. It's from* ... The Mission. *Yes, that's it.* I smile to myself when I get the name. And then again, when I recognise the hymn layered over the music. Clever. They go perfectly together. I keep my eyes closed, only opening them when the final mournful tones of the cello have faded to silence.

"Beautiful," I say to Adam, who's watching me with a

small smile on his lips. I pull the headphones off and hand them back. "Can you send me the link to their YouTube channel? I want to listen to more of their stuff."

"Already sent," Adam says, winding the cord around the headphones and returning them to his bag.

"Thanks." I pick up one of my highlighters. "And now, back to the boring stuff." I add some more colour to my notes, but I can't concentrate for long. I lean back with a sigh. "I can't believe we're *studying* on a Saturday night."

"Missing the cool crowd?" Adam says absently, clicking away on the laptop keys.

"Definitely not. They can keep their parties to themselves. I kinda miss the dancing, but that's about it."

"You can dance here," Adam says. "Go stand by the stage and shake your behind to the beats of the …" He tilts back on his chair to read the flyer stuck to the window. "*Dofkop Donkies.*"

"You know—" I tap my chin with my highlighter "—I'm not usually a fan of Afrikaans music, but these songs are quite catchy."

"They need a better name for their band, though."

"Definitely."

"Like … *Die Koeksisters.*"

I laugh. "Brilliant, but I think they may take exception to that, considering they're all *guys.*"

"Hmm. *Kortbroek Laaitjies?*" he suggests.

"*Die Jean Pant?*" Hugo says, dropping into the chair next to me.

"Ha! Yes. That." I point at Hugo. "Awesome name for

an Afrikaans band. Oh, hey, aren't you meant to be working?"

"Yes, but the lady over there just yelled at me because I told her we can't make chicken noodle soup without the chicken, so I thought I'd hide here for a few minutes while she cools down."

"Customers are weird," Adam says, shaking his head.

"Tell me about it." Hugo turns to me and says, "So. Open mic night tomorrow, Livi. You coming? Ow!" He groans in pain and glares at Adam. "Dude, what the hell?"

"Don't pressure Livi."

Hugo lets out a pained moan-laugh. "That is so not why you kicked me."

I look back and forth between them, pretty sure I've missed something. "Yes, I'll probably be here. But if you were hoping I'll get up on stage and sing, you're going to be disappointed."

He smirks at me. "If everything works out, no one will be going home disappointed tomorrow night."

"What do you—"

"Hugo, you should probably start hunting for chicken-less chicken noodle soup before that woman gets you fired," Adam says loudly.

"Yeah, yeah." Hugo stands. "You kids enjoy your *homework*."

"Hey, we're studying in *style*," Adam calls after Hugo. He picks up his rum and coke. "Aren't we, Livi."

"Absolutely." I lift my wine and clink it against his glass.

"And we have the next season of *The Big Bang Theory* to

look forward to when we get back."

"Ooh, yes. Whatever will we do when we've watched every episode available?"

"Hmm. *Firefly? Star Trek? Stargate SG-1?*"

"Or *Stargate Atlantis* or *Stargate Universe*."

"Or *Battlestar Galactica*."

"Basically," I say, "we have a lot of 'star' options. I think we'll be fine."

"We'll definitely be fine." Adam pushes his glasses up and starts typing again.

"Ooh, want to hear something funny?" I say, looking for any distraction from my work and suddenly remembering my conversation with Salima yesterday.

"No." Adam continues tapping away. "I'd rather you tell me something really depressing so I'll end up crying."

"Okay, so I made a new friend—this girl from Durban who's in most of my classes—and it turns out she knows you. *And* she totally blushed when I spoke about you. I think she has a crush on you."

Adam looks up, suddenly a whole lot more interested in me than his coding. "Oh. What's her name?"

"Salima. She's doing one of your computer science courses as an elective."

"Oh, yes, I know her. She doesn't interact much with anyone else, but we had to do a tutorial together once."

"Well, you obviously made an impression."

Adam nods. "Maybe I did. Hmm. She's pretty."

I shrug. "I guess she is." I wink at him. "Maybe you should ask her out."

He leans back and runs a hand through his hair, ruffling it up. "You think I should ask another girl out?"

"Um, yes. I mean, unless it's too soon after Jenna."

"No, no, that's …" The tops of his ears turn red. "I think I've moved on."

"Okay." I pick up a pen and tap it against my notebook. This conversation feels weird all of a sudden.

"So … you'd be fine with me dating someone else?"

"Sure," I say, although I'm starting to think it might not be fine. I give my brain a few moments to imagine it—Adam's door shut with him and another girl behind it. Giggling and … other stuff—before deciding that it's definitely not fine. Flip, that would actually be really awkward. What if she stayed over? I'd have to smile and be all friendly in the morning, and I could never go into his room without wondering what they did in there. I'd never be able to just hang out with him watching TV series because this other girl wouldn't understand and she'd get jealous.

Other girl? This is *Salima* we're talking about. She's probably sworn off boys until she's graduated, got a job, and been promoted at least once.

"You know, she might be anti-dating, now that I think about," I say. "Her parents are super controlling slave drivers."

Adam laughs. "Well, there's no harm in trying, right?"

"Right." I smile, but I have the weirdest feeling that it isn't right. In fact, for reasons I don't want to examine too closely, it somehow feels very, very wrong.

AFTER FIVE EPISODES OF *THE BIG BANG THEORY*, I SHOULD be ready to fall asleep, but my tired brain keeps trying to figure out what's wrong with the idea of Adam dating someone. I didn't have a problem when it was Jenna, but perhaps that's because she was on the other side of the country, not in the room across the passage threatening my friendship with Adam.

Maybe that's what I'm worried about. Our friendship and how it will change once he has a girlfriend to spend all his free time with. But I wasn't exactly concerned about our friendship when I was chasing after Jackson, so I need to stop being selfish and let Adam do the same thing. With a girl. Not with Jackson, obviously. *Ugh, stupid brain. The things you come up with when you're tired.*

I turn over yet again and pull the duvet up to my neck. Where was I? Oh yes. I'm being selfish. *STOP BEING*

SELFISH, ALIVIA. Let Adam be happy with whomever he wants to be happy with.

Thanks to the maps app on my phone, I'm almost at the block of flats Salima mentioned she lives in. She never gave me her phone number, so this visit is unannounced, but it's probably easier to talk her into taking a night off in person than it would be over the phone.

Oh, who am I kidding. There is *no* possible scenario in which it will be easy for me to convince her to take a night off.

After instructing myself to let Adam be happy with whomever he wants to be happy with, I decided to give him a chance to do just that by bringing Salima to Jazzy Beanbag for open mic night tonight. I'm almost completely certain she'll say no if he asks her out, regardless of how she feels about him, and I'm trying really hard not to be relieved by that thought.

I WILL NOT BE SELFISH!

I park as close as I can get to the block of flats and walk across the road to the pedestrian entrance with the keypad. I raise my finger and—*Hang on.* She never actually mentioned which number she's in. *Shoot.* I didn't really think this through properly. I bite my lip and stare up at the building. She did say she lives at the very top, because that means fewer people walking past her flat and disturbing her—her parents' logic—but that still doesn't help me with what number to punch into the keypad.

Click.

The noise comes from the locking mechanism of the gate just as a young guy hurries out of the building and down the path towards me. I push the gate open, smile at him as he passes, and walk through. *I'm in! Yes!* Once inside the building, I wait for the lift, then hit the button for the highest floor. I sing softly to myself—a song that was just on the radio—as the lift creaks slowly all the way to the top of the building. I hope there aren't too many flats up there. And I hope they have windows I can somehow see into, so I don't have to knock on every door. Come to think of it, though, how am I supposed to recognise the inside of her flat even if I can—

"Livi?" The lift doors are open and Salima is standing in front of me, a handbag over her shoulder and a set of keys in her hand.

"Um. Hi?" I give her a small wave.

She leans into the lift, grabs my arm, and pulls me out. "What are you doing here? I didn't tell you where I live."

"You did actually mention the name of this place," I say. "Also, I am totally not a stalker. I just wanted to ask if you want to hang out this evening at Jazzy Beanbag—it's this really chilled cafe—and I don't have your number, so I couldn't phone you, and this block is only, like, five minutes from where I live."

She blinks. "You want me to go out somewhere with you?"

"Yes."

"It's a school night," she says automatically, then shakes her head. "I mean, you know, a varsity night. We have classes in the morning."

I cross my arms. "Looks like you were already on your way out somewhere."

A puff of air escapes her lips. "I was just going to get some dinner. I don't have time to cook anything because I'm too busy studying."

"Weeeeell, how about you get dinner with me?"

"You're starting to sound like a stalker."

"I just want to be friends!"

"You're coming across as desperate."

"Perhaps I just really want to be friends with *you*. You should be flattered."

"I told you I don't need any friends, Livi. My parents warned me about people like you. People who would try to tempt me away from my studies. People who could end up ruining me."

I groan. "I swear I am not out to ruin you, Salima. I thought it would be fun to relax for the evening at Jazzy Beanbag, eat some good food, clap for all the awful singers brave enough to get on stage for open mic night, and go to bed early enough to be fresh for lectures in the morning. Oh, and Adam will be there. He can fix your phone and you guys can … chat."

Salima purses her lips.

"Okay, how about this? You go back into your hermit hole now and work really hard, then meet me at Jazzy

Beanbag at, say, 8 pm. Look it up. It's easy to find. We'll order some food, and once we're done eating, you can leave. See? Early school night."

She narrows her eyes. "I sense you're making fun of me."

"Only a little," I say. "And it doesn't count, since we're friends."

Her eyes widen. "We are not friends."

I walk back into the lift—there obviously aren't too many people coming and going on a Sunday evening, since the doors never closed—and hit the number zero. "See you there, *friend*." I smile and wave as the doors close.

"Why do you keep looking out the window?" Hugo asks. "You're making me anxious."

I'm sitting at a table with Adam, Hugo, and another drummer girl Hugo appears to have a crush on but who is, fortunately, not Pixie. "I'm waiting for a friend," I say.

Adam looks around. He's been distracted all evening by the people up on stage, but apparently this is important enough to pay attention to. "Who?" he asks.

"My hot date. Biker dude with tattoos. He's bringing his electric guitar for open mic night."

Adam loses some of the colour in his cheeks.

"You know I'm joking, right? I'm waiting for Salima. So actually," I add with a smile, "it could be *your* hot date we're waiting for."

Adam sighs and turns back to face the stage while Hugo shakes his head and laughs. "Come on, man. Livi organised a date for you. You should be happy." His words are followed closely by a muffled groan of pain, which I'm guessing is a result of Adam kicking him under the table again.

"You guys need to grow up," Drummer Girl says, but she's smiling, so I take it she's not as moody as Pixie.

"I'm going to wait outside," I say, standing up. Salima should have been here fifteen minutes ago. Perhaps she's bailed on me. I *knew* I should have coaxed her phone number out of her.

I pace the sidewalk, rubbing my hands up and down my arms to try and get rid of the goosebumps. It's warm inside Jazzy Beanbag, and I left my jersey hanging over the back of my chair. I'm about to head back inside to fetch it when a car door slams and I turn around to see Salima walking towards me.

"You're late," I say.

She stops as her gaze travels down and up again. "Don't you ever dress sensibly, Livi?"

"Stop judging." I look down at my short dress. "Okay, so it's not exactly appropriate for a winter's-almost-here night, but I've got long boots on. And it's warm in there." I point defensively behind me.

"I'm sure." She sniffs and walks past me. "If you get sick, it's your own fault."

"You sound like my mom," I grumble.

"And I'm only staying until nine. Bed time is nine thirty."

"Now you *really* sound like my mom." I hurry after her. Warm air rushes over me as we enter Jazzy Beanbag, a welcome relief from the chill outside. "Over there," I say, pointing to Hugo and Drummer Girl, whose name I should have found out before I put myself in a situation where I have to introduce her to someone. Adam's gone—probably to the bar to get another drink. He seems to be throwing the rum and coke back a little faster tonight than normal.

Hugo introduces himself and his date Lainey, saving me from having to embarrass myself. I sit down, and Salima takes Adam's vacated seat next to me. She removes her jacket, arranges it neatly on her lap, then she looks up and squints at the stage. "Is that Adam?"

I look across the room, and my breath escapes me in a whoosh of air. It is Adam on the stage. And he's standing in front of a microphone holding a guitar.

WAIT. A MICROPHONE? ADAM DOESN'T SING. HE CAN probably play any instrument on the planet, but he doesn't *sing*. Not even in the shower or in the car when the radio's turned up loud. The microphone must be for the guitar.

Focus, Livi. ADAM IS ON THE FREAKING STAGE.

He adjusts the guitar strap around his neck, then fiddles with the microphone, bringing it up to the right height in front of his mouth. HIS MOUTH! He's going to be singing. I'm almost certain of it, and I suddenly feel insanely nervous for him. What if he messes up and embarrasses himself? What if he sounds awful? What if people boo him? It doesn't happen often, but there was an intoxicated guy up there just now who sounded so terrible he earned himself a whole chorus of boos.

Adam shuffles closer to the microphone, swallows, licks his lips, and refuses to look up at his audience. Nervousness is written all over him. CRAP! *Don't mess up, don't mess up, don't mess up.*

I watch him take a few deep breaths, and then his fingers begin moving over the strings. Plucking slowly, deliberately, perfectly. A beautiful, sweet melody I want to close my eyes and lose myself in, but I don't want to miss the way his fingers move across the strings because I'm already convinced beyond a doubt that his hands were made to play this instrument.

And then he starts singing—

—and all my remaining fears fly out the window.

My limbs go weak and the little hairs all over my body rise and I'm pretty sure I've stopped breathing and *his voice.* HIS VOICE. Deep and warm and soothing and just the tiniest bit husky. It gives me shivers and heats my blood at the same time.

HOW DID I NOT KNOW HE COULD SING LIKE THIS?

His words tumble past my ears, failing to make sense. Something about the wrong girl being the right girl, a kiss under the stars, and falling over and over again. Finally I recognise it. It's a pop song I've heard many times on the radio, upbeat and catchy, but the way Adam sings it is completely different. Slow and soulful, like a love letter whispered in the night from a Romeo to his Juliet.

I want someone to sing to me like this. I want *him* to sing to me like this. I wish there was no one else here but the two of us. One spotlight on him, and one on me. His fingers doing a slow dance across the strings, and his captivating voice melting my heart. I wish he'd look up, and our eyes would meet, and I'd know that every word from his mouth was—

"Holy crap, he's AMAZING," Lainey says, startling me from my reverie. I take a gasp of air, as if I've been underwater without realising it, and I remember that I'm not the only one in the audience, and that it's my best friend up there, and that it would be totally weird if he were singing to *me*.

A few beats of silence follow the end of his song before Jazzy Beanbag fills with applause and wolf whistles and a scream or two. My weak legs remember how to move, and I jump to my feet along with at least half the room. Adam sets his guitar down at the back of the stage, then jumps down the stairs and makes his way to our table, smiling awkwardly and thanking the people who clap him on the back as they congratulate him.

I act without thinking and throw my arms around his neck when he reaches our table. "Adam! You were incredible!" I squeeze him tight before letting go. "Why didn't you ever tell me you could sing?"

He shrugs, leaning across the table to high-five Hugo. "Too shy, I guess. Instruments are my thing, not singing."

"Not singing? Adam, are you *insane*? You could sing all day and I'd never get tired of it."

"Same here," Lainey says, which earns her a frown from Hugo. "Seriously, Adam, if you're looking to join a band, I'd be happy to give our lead singer the boot. You're miles better than he is, not to mention way less annoying."

Adam lets out a nervous laugh and sits in the empty chair between Lainey and Salima. "Thanks, guys. And thanks for the offer, Lainey, but I don't plan to venture beyond open mic night. Oh, and hey, Salima." He gives her an awkward half-wave. "Cool that you could join us."

She giggles. GIGGLES. I want to look at her and say, "Seriously?" but I manage to restrain myself.

I call a waitress over and order myself another glass of wine. I'm still feeling a little unsettled by my desire to have Adam serenade me with a love song, and I'm almost certain wine can fix that. "Oh, and you and I still need to order some food, right?" I say to Salima before the waitress leaves.

"Oh, no, I actually ate something at home while I was working."

"Cheater," I say, before leaning back and asking the waitress to bring me a burger. "What happened to us having dinner together, Salima?"

"You just never know how long these places take to prepare food, and it isn't good for you to eat right before going to bed."

"Yeah, yeah." I pat her arm. "I see it as a triumph that I got you to come here at all. We can work on dinner next time."

Before she can argue about there being a 'next time,' I change the subject to something Salima and Adam have in common—computers—and get Adam to tell Salima about his new laptop. The two of them converse awkwardly, while Hugo and Lainey chatter on the other side of the table, and I'm left feeling rather spare. It isn't for long, though. I'm halfway through my burger when Salima taps her watch and says, "Time for me to go, I'm afraid."

"Oh, okay. Uh, shall I walk you outside?" Adam says.

"Thank you."

They head to the door, and Hugo leans over and says, "Strict schedule, I see."

I nod, swallow a mouthful of burger, and add, "Hard-ass parents."

Adam takes far longer than necessary outside, and my burger's almost finished when he gets back. "Get a goodnight kiss?" Hugo teases with a wide grin.

The last bit of burger sitting on my plate suddenly becomes a whole lot less appetising. Probably because half my brain is still imagining that kiss under the stars from the song Adam sung and wishing I was the recipient, not—

Whoa. Wine. The imagination section of my brain needs more wine.

Two hours later, it's just Adam, Hugo and me left at the table, and I've had a teeny bit too much to drink. Not so much that I won't remember anything in the morning, but enough to feel warm and floaty and to find all the rubbish the guys are talking about unbearably hilarious.

"You're supposed to try and get through the night without having to pee when you're camping," I tell Hugo. "Don't you know that?"

"Such a camping novice," Adam adds with a laugh.

"I had to go!" Hugo says, far too loudly. "It wasn't my fault the toilets were up a hill on the other side of a forest. And it was almost completely dark, and then this *howl* happened, and this big shape was bashing around the trees, so of course I ran back to the tent shrieking like a girl."

My stomach aches as more laughter bubbles from my lips. "You should have just … dug a hole," I gasp.

"Oh, classy, Livi, really classy."

"That's me." I raise my glass and down the last mouthful. "Class personified."

"Hey, I think they're getting ready to close up," Adam says, looking around. "We should probably get home. Lectures in the morning."

"Oh, lectures, yaaaaay," I sing as I stand and spin in a circle on one foot. I don't fall over, which I consider to be quite an achievement.

"Wow, you sure are enthusiastic about Monday morning classes," Hugo says as I pull my jersey on.

"It was a sarcastic 'yay.'"

"And the spinning?"

"Clearly it was a sarcastic spin too, Hugo," Adam says. "Didn't you catch that?"

Hugo raises his eyebrows. "Are you guys okay to walk home? I mean, you know which way is home, right?"

"Hey, are you okay to *drive*, Mr Scaredy Pants?" I ask, poking his chest repeatedly. "You've had just as much to drink as we have."

"No way." Hugo grabs my poking finger to make me

stop. "I think your vision must be impaired, because there are way more empty glasses on your side of the table than on mine."

"Well, hello. There were two of us on our side of the table, and only one on your side."

He rolls his eyes. "I was talking per person. Obviously."

"*Obviously.*"

"Obviously," Adam mutters, giving me a *Duh* look.

Hugo's eyes move from me to Adam and back. "I think I should drive you guys home."

"But it's so faaaaar out of your way," I say as we walk to the door. "Don't be ridiculous. Of course we can walk."

"We can walk," Adam adds. "We'll be fine."

"Oh, we forgot to pay!" I say, spinning around as the door closes behind us.

"Relax, Liv." Adam pulls me back and puts an arm around me. "We paid twenty minutes ago."

"Oh yes. I remember that." I remember taking money out of my purse after Hugo told me how much I owed. My brain was taking far too long adding up the numbers.

"So, you said you'll be fine, huh?" Hugo says doubtfully.

"Yes, dude, stop worrying." Adam slaps his friend on the shoulder and pushes him towards his car.

Hugo climbs inside, shaking his head. "Let me know when you're home, otherwise I'll be back here in half an hour searching the sidewalks for passed-out bodies." He shuts his door. Adam lets go of me and sneaks around the back of the car, bending down as he goes.

"Hey, don't let the big, scary creatures get you," I call to

Hugo through the window.

On the other side of the car, Adam jumps up, bangs on the passenger window, and roars. Hugo flinches, swears, and yells something I can't make out because I'm now doubled over with laughter.

"Hilarious," Hugo shouts, shaking his head and starting his car. "If you pass out, you're on your own." And with a final wave, he takes off.

I'm shivering now, and Adam slings an arm around my shoulders again as we walk down the street. "Did you see his face?" I say, still laughing. "I wish I'd had my phone out so I could have got a photo. I so would have stuck that up on the pinboard behind the bar at Jazzy B."

"Oh, it's Jazzy B now, is it? Too much effort to get that last syllable out?"

"WAY too much effort." I sweep my arm through the air for emphasis. "And I feel so cool saying Jazzy B. Oh!" I add, suddenly remembering the song. "And I *am* cool because I'm with *you* and you're the latest Jazzy B singing SENSATION!" I belt out the last word so the whole neighbourhood can hear it.

Adam claps a hand over my mouth and laughs into my neck. "You're trying to get us arrested, aren't you. I've figured out your plan."

"YES!" I shout the moment he drops his hand from my mouth. "An arrest record will do WONDERS for my street cred. Just think how cool I'll be when—Ooh, pole, look out!"

Adam swerves us to the side and walks us around the

pole. "Come on, Liv. Like I'd really let my clumsy princess walk into a pole. I—" His words are cut off as he trips over a section of the sidewalk pushed up by a tree root. He stumbles away from me and catches himself against the tree.

"HA!" I point at him as I double over, shaking with silent laughter. "Who's … a clumsy princess … now, huh?"

"Oh, you are so going to pay for that," he says, pushing away from the tree and lurching forward like a zombie

I laugh as I run along the sidewalk towards our house. When I get there, I grab onto the rusted gate and look back, breathing in deep gulps of chilled night air. "I made it!" I shout back to Adam. "I'm safe!"

"And who says the gate is safe?" he calls back, then lowers his voice to a deep growl. "Nowhere is safe."

I tip my head back and drape my hand over my forehead, miming a fainting motion—just as rivers of water begin tumbling down from the sky. I squeal and push the gate open enough for me to get through. I run across the garden and up to the shelter of the verandah, Adam close behind me.

"A little warning would have been nice," Adam yells at the sky before removing his keys from his pocket.

We get inside, and I lean against the wall and close my eyes. "Ugh, I'm so tired."

"Me too." He locks the door and tilts his head back against it. "So," he says after a moment. "*Big Bang Theory?*"

I open my eyes and give him a sleepy smile. "Of course." I unzip and remove my boots so I won't make any noise on the wooden floor and wake Luke, then tiptoe to the bathroom, my wet dress sticking to my legs.

One brief shower and one warm pair of winter PJs later, I sway into Adam's room and tumble onto his bed. "I am going to sleep so well tonight."

Adam, who looks like he just fell asleep in his desk chair, stirs and opens his eyes. "Oh. Um. I can't remember which episode we watched last."

"Me neither." I crawl to the other side of the bed and pull a blanket over myself. "Whatever. Doesn't matter."

"I guess not." Adam picks an episode and starts it—adjusting the volume so it isn't too loud—then turns off the main light and joins me on the bed.

"If I fall asleep," I say, "wake me so I can leave. I'd hate to drool on you."

"Mmm. That would be gross."

"So gross."

The little people on the screen say something funny, and the studio audience laughs.

"Adam?"

"Mmm?"

My eyelids droop as the cogs in my brain struggle to turn. "I forgot what I was going to say."

"Mmm."

"Oh yes. I like listening to the rain."

"That's nice."

"It is nice."

"Livi?"

"Mmm?"

"Shh."

LIGHT BRUSHES MY EYELIDS AND GENTLY URGES ME FROM dreamland and back to the world of the living. I half open one eyelid and peek out, closing it again almost immediately. Too early. Too bright. My body feels stiff and achy, as if I've been curled tightly in one position for too long. I moan and try to stretch my legs out, but—

I freeze.

My eyes spring open.

And I realise several things at once.

One, something warm is pressed along the length of my body. Two, the blanket wrapped around me isn't mine. And three, I don't remember getting into my own bed last night.

HOLY FREAKING CRAP. I spent the night in Adam's bed. I've *never* spent the night in any guy's bed before, and now I'm in my best friend's bed, pressed up against him, his darned beautiful voice still playing at the back of my mind,

AND I JUST MOANED OUT LOUD!

So. Damn. Awkward.

Okay. Just breathe. This doesn't have to be weird. It's not like his arm is around me. THAT would have been weird. But no. I'm pretty sure I can't feel an arm around me. So we're basically just lying next to each other. Nothing wrong with that. This is fine. This is really fine.

I try to move again, and that's when I discover that one of Adam's legs is on top of one of mine, tangled up in the blanket wrapped around me.

THIS IS SO NOT FINE!

Heat spreads from the point of contact and zings all the way up my leg and into the rest of my body. Warmth and nerves and excitement—excitement?—coalesce into a feeling I actually kind of like, and suddenly I wonder what it would be like if Adam's arm *was* around me—

STOP! WHAT ARE YOU THINKING?

I need to get out of this bed right now. I hold my breath as I slowly slide my leg out from beneath his. I sit up and carefully unwrap the blanket from my upper body, leaving the bottom of it tangled around Adam's legs. The mattress moves beneath me as I get onto my hands and knees—*don't wake up, don't wake up, don't wake up*—and climb over him. I keep my eyes on his face to make sure he doesn't wake up, although that might not have been the best plan, because looking at his sleeping face leaves me with the strangest desire to kiss—

NO! Just keep moving!

Okay. I'm off the bed. I tiptoe across the room and open

the door—which swings into an empty laundry basket, which topples over and rolls across the floor. DAMMIT! I scamper across the passage, into my room, and shut my door.

And then I fall onto my bed in a heap of giggles. I grab my cell phone off the bedside table and—Oh SHOOT. Is that the time? No wonder it's so bright outside. I've already missed two lectures. Oh well, since I'm late already, I may as well take an extra minute or two to send a message to Sarah.

Livi: Oh my fluffy PJs. I just spent the night in Adam's bed. UNINTENTIONALLY, of course. But I think I liked it. I mean, I didn't know it was happening until I woke up. But then I liked that it had happened. I liked feeling him right next to me. I liked—oh my gosh what is WRONG with me?

Then I chuck my phone into my varsity bag, grab my towel from the back of my door, and peek out into the passage. There's no way Adam slept through all the noise I made on my way out, and he's just as late as I am, so he's probably also about to make a beeline for the bathroom. And I do NOT want to meet him halfway there. Or halfway back. Or anywhere in this house.

Crumbs, this is going to be awkward.

Miraculously, I make it out of the house without bumping into Adam. Perhaps he never woke up and is still peacefully sleeping through all his lectures. Doubtful. It's far more likely he knows exactly what happened and was hiding in his bedroom until I left.

I wonder if he'll say anything about it later. Maybe he's completely embarrassed and wishes it hadn't happened. I mean, I'm embarrassed too—sort of—but I'd be lying to myself if I said I wish it hadn't happened. Adam, on the other hand, is supposed to be asking Salima out, right? Or any other girl. But not me. Because we're friends. He's known me since I was a pimply, brace-faced thirteen-year-old, and I've probably never crossed his mind as potential dating material.

Ugh, Livi, just concentrate on the road!

I have to park miles away from Upper Campus and wait for a Jammie Shuttle to take me up the hill, so I get to my third lecture five minutes before it ends. I don't bother going inside. I take my phone out and stare at the screen, willing Sarah to reply to me. Then I look down and realise I'm still wearing slippers.

I close my eyes and groan. Slippers? REALLY? How on earth did I leave the house without noticing that? I look up and find students spilling from the lecture theatre. Salima should be out soon. She seems to like being one of the first students to arrive at each lecture. Maybe to get in the zone or something. That's probably why she looks so annoyed whenever I show up.

I take an involuntary step backwards as Allegra, Courtney

and Amber exit the doors. I don't want them to see me in my slippers, and the moment I realise that, I hate myself for feeling embarrassed in front of them. I look down and silently chant, *Keep moving, keep moving.*

"Oh, Livi," Courtney says, and I look up. My chanting was useless, apparently, because they're not moving. The three of them are standing in front of me. Courtney looks to Allegra, then back at me. "We actually wanted to talk to you."

"Yes," Allegra says. She motions to Courtney, as if telling her to continue.

"We've seen you sitting alone in lectures," Courtney says, "and we figured it must be kinda sad and embarrassing for you. So even though you were really weird at that party in Camps Bay and totally freaked out, we were talking about how cool you actually are, and how the weirdness was probably just a once-off thing, and we figured we should let you back into the group."

I stare at the four of them as something strange happens. Like a fairy-tale curse lifting, my embarrassment vanishes. I'm left wondering why I ever felt the need to change myself in order to impress these girls. I start laughing then, because there really doesn't seem to be any other way for me to respond. "Thank you," I say once my laughter has subsided, "for making it so easy for me to say no."

"No?" Amber repeats.

"You guys clearly haven't noticed, but I actually haven't been sitting alone. I've been sitting with Salima—formerly known as the loner Indian girl. She's kinda weird in her own way, just like me. And guess what? The weirdness isn't a once-off thing. The weirdness is HERE TO STAY." I test out my opera voice on the last three words, just to illustrate my point about the weirdness. All three girls look more than a little alarmed. "Anyway," I continue, "was there something else you wanted to say?"

Amber's gaze moves to my feet, then back up to my face. "Nice slippers," she says, in a tone that actually means, *You retard, why the freak are you wearing slippers on campus?*

Oh yes. The slippers. Funny how I went from feeling embarrassed to not giving a rat's buttocks in less than two minutes. I give Amber my sweetest smile and say, "Thank you. All the celebrities are doing it." I turn on my slippered heel and saunter off, my smile still in place as I imagine Amber whipping out her phone to check for photos of celebrities wearing slippers in public.

Only when I get to my next lecture do I remember that I haven't seen Salima yet. She dashes in about twenty seconds later, muttering under her breath. "More car troubles?" I ask.

"No, thank goodness. I stayed behind in the last lecture to tell the professor I don't agree with something he said. He gave me a condescending look, told me I must have misunderstood what he said, and proceeded to repeat the exact argument I'd just given him." She sits down in a huff. "So I told him, 'Yes, that's what I said,' and he said, 'Great, so there's no problem then.'" She slaps her textbook onto the desk. "Infuriating man."

"Profs, hey," I say with a shake of my head. "Real

buttheads." I reach into my bag and pull out a packet of princess gums. I haven't told Adam, but I actually like them. I tear the packet open, offer it to Salima—who shakes her head with a horrified look—and remove a purple handbag-shaped sweet. Yum. Probably not the best idea to fill myself with sugar in place of breakfast, but hey. Whatever.

The lecture begins, and we're not even halfway through the first slide when my phone starts buzzing in my bag. Salima glares at me, and I quickly fish the phone out and reject Sarah's call.

Livi: Sorry! In a lecture.

Sarah: So ... you slept with Adam ;-)

Livi: Ha ha. Not like THAT. But thanks for putting the image in my head. As if maths isn't hard enough already without imagining Adam's naked butt when I should be seeing numbers.

Sarah: Ew!

Livi: YOU started this line of conversation!

Sarah: *backtracking*

Livi: So I'm freaking out.

Sarah: Because you suddenly find one of your best friends attractive?

Livi: Well, I wouldn't go so far as to say THAT. I mean, he's cute in those glasses, and I love that I can be myself around him, and he makes me laugh, and we both speak music jargon and nerd jargon, and WOW have you heard him SING? Spoiler alert: he's INCREDIBLE. And I guess I DO think about him quite a lot. I love the way his hands move over the piano keys or

Livi: Okay. Yes. I find him attractive.

Sarah: So why are you freaking out?

Livi: Hello! Because it's ADAM! I'm not supposed to find him attractive. He's supposed to be my goofy friend who looks at me disapprovingly when I wear inappropriate clothes to varsity.

Sarah: What clothes are you wearing to varsity?

Livi: Don't get sidetracked.

Sarah: Send me pictures.

Livi: YOU'RE GETTING SIDETRACKED!

Sarah: Sorry! You should talk to Adam. Maybe he feels the same way about you.

Livi: Oh yes. That must be why we were talking about this girl he thinks is pretty and is planning to ask out. She's also really smart—just like him. I'm sure I'm way too dumb for him to be interested in me in THAT WAY.

Sarah: You are not dumb. Just talk to him.

Livi: Ugh. That sounds so sensible and grown-up. And potentially SUPER awkward if he's like, 'No, sorry, I've never thought of you in that way. The idea grosses me out.'

Sarah: TALK TO HIM!

So, I decide to do the exact opposite of what Sarah says, and I don't talk to Adam about spending the night in his bed. Things feel kind of weird between us—forced, uncomfortable—and I can tell he's avoiding me when he switches his gym routine from early morning to evening, slap bang in the middle of our usual dinner time. So it's clear *he* doesn't want to talk about it, which must mean he wants to pretend it never happened.

Cool. I can do that. Let's pretend it never happened.

Friday arrives, and I've managed to convince Salima to come over and watch a movie. According to her parents, movies are an evil distraction, but I'm determined to show her otherwise.

I park in the long grass in front of the house and lug my shopping bags up the steps and into the house. It was supposed to be a quick stop for just a few movie snacks, but

I wound up with three bags full of junk food. Preparation for future movie nights, I told myself.

I start packing everything away into the cupboards as Adam walks in wearing his sweaty gym clothes and fixes himself a protein something-or-other shake. "You sure you got enough chocolate slabs there?" he asks.

I look up, but his eyes remain fixed on the scoops of powder he's tossing into the shaker. "I don't know. I may have to go back for more. This will probably only get me through half the movie."

"Movie?" Adam asks, still not looking at me.

"Yes. Salima's coming over this evening."

"Oh." Adam finally looks up at me. Only for a second, though, and then he's staring at the shaker in his hand. "Um, I asked Hugo to come over and play Xbox, since neither of us are working tonight. But, I guess—"

"You can watch with us," I suggest. "It won't be late. You know Salima likes to get to bed early. Then Hugo can stay afterwards and you guys can play Xbox."

"Okay." He tosses the closed shaker back and forth between his hands. "You can play too, if you want."

"Okay. Cool." I put away the last few items and close the cupboards, and when I turn around, Adam is gone. Darn this awkwardness. I'm hoping it won't be too long before things are back to normal between us.

The doorbell rings.

I immediately think of Andi, because she's the only other person who's ever used our doorbell, but she wouldn't show up again unannounced. We have each other's phone numbers now. It could be Salima, but that would mean she's an hour early. Unlikely, considering she had to 'get work done.'

I walk to the front door and open it to find—a fashionably dressed golden haired blonde.

"Allegra?"

"Um, hi," she says. When I gape at her and say nothing, she adds, "Can I come in?"

"I … suppose so." I step back, and she walks past me into the lounge.

I follow her and lean in the lounge doorway, watching her twist her hands together. "So. What's this about?"

"Um …" She bites her lip. "Okay, so, my mom's white and my dad's Indian."

"Okaaay."

"And I spent the first twelve years of my life in a largely Afrikaans town."

I tilt my head and squint at her. "I'm still not entirely sure where you're going with this."

"So I know what it's like to be teased. To not fit in. To not be accepted for who you are. To be called horrible names that play over and over in your head, even when the other kids aren't shouting them. To want to do *anything* just to be accepted. So when we moved to Empangeni and I started high school, I decided things would be different. I was going to be confident. I was going to be popular. All the girls would want to be me, and all the guys would want to be with me." She looks at her hands and lifts one shoulder. "And it worked. I never went back to being that kid that other people made fun of."

"So … what are you trying to say? That you and I are alike? We were both teased and rejected, and now we'll do anything to fit in? Because I don't think we're alike. You might do anything to fit in, but I have a line I'm not willing to cross. And the moment I figured that out, that's when you and I stopped being friends."

"No. That's not what I'm saying. I'm trying to tell you—" She stops and takes a deep breath. "I'm trying to get you to understand why I held onto this popularity thing for so long. Why I did just about anything to stay at the top of the social ladder."

I take a few steps into the lounge. "I may be wrong, but it kinda sounds like you're talking in past tense."

She nods, staring at her hands once more. "It just … it doesn't seem so important anymore."

"Right," I say slowly. I still don't get what this whole confession is about.

As if she can read my mind, she says, "Okay, here's the thing. I—I miss you, Livi."

"You miss me?"

"Yes! You're fun, Livi. I liked hanging out with you. You actually say intelligent stuff. Amber and Courtney … well, it gets boring. So yeah. I want us to be friends again. Even if it means losing all the rest of that popularity crap, because honestly, it's not that important now that we're not in high school anymore. People grow up. They do what they want to do, and nobody else really cares. And those who do look at you funny for doing something or not doing something, well so what? Their opinion doesn't matter."

"Really? Their opinion doesn't matter?" I cross my arms. "You seemed to care a great deal about everyone else's opinion when you were pushing drugs into my hands. Or when you didn't believe that my boyfriend was forcing himself on me."

"Oh, hell, I'm so sorry, Livi." Allegra covers her face with her hands. "I'm so, so sorry. I thought you'd freaked out just because Jackson was kissing you in front of other people. That's what I heard him say when he came past with his hands bleeding. I didn't realise he was forcing himself on you. And I'd already had too much to drink so I wasn't thinking properly, and everyone else was taking these pills and looking like they were having such a good time, and you were so upset, and I just wanted us to be happy and have fun." She drops her hands and looks at me with wide eyes. "And then this guy collapsed and an ambulance arrived and rushed him off to hospital, and people were saying afterwards that he almost died—"

"What?"

"I know! It scared the crap out of me. And then last weekend I drank way too much and I woke up in Logan's bed and I couldn't remember a damn thing, and—"

"What?" My hand flies to my mouth. "Did he—"

"No, he didn't do anything. I mean, I couldn't remember, but I could tell, you know, that nothing …" She trails off awkwardly. "But I just kept thinking, what if it hadn't been him? What if it had been some other guy I didn't know who *did* want to do something to me? Or what if I'd been the person who collapsed at that party and almost died? I just … I don't want that to be part of my life." She sits on the edge of the couch and presses her shaking hands together. "I want … real friends. People I'm not always trying to impress or outdo. People I can be … real with. And I kinda thought—I mean I hoped—" she looks up at me "—that you might be one of those people."

I take a breath and let it out slowly as I sit on the coffee table. "You really want that?"

"Yes."

"Even if it means people might say mean things because you're hanging out with me and Salima?"

She rolls her eyes. "Like I said, I don't really care about that anymore. People must just grow up and get over themselves."

"Okay. Well, this is me: Musician, *Star Trek* fan, peanut butter binger, virgin, movie music aficionado, hater of fashion magazines, and lover of most fantasy and sci fi worlds."

Allegra laughs. "Well, I think you know me already. I haven't exactly been hiding who I am—other than my mixed-race parentage. I like buying new clothes and having my nails done, I'll enter any competition I find in a magazine, I'm still in search of my soulmate, I'm secretly a Harry Potter fan, even though I told you I'd grown out of that, and I'm not ashamed to say that the only novels I currently read are of the chick lit variety."

"Well, as long as you're not ashamed of it," I say with a laugh. "So. Doesn't sound like we have all that much in common."

Allegra purses her lips. "We both like dancing."

"Oh yes. And singing," I add, remembering all the times her neighbours in res had to knock on her door and ask us to keep it down.

"And, despite the fact that conversations about boys tend to get boring after a while, we're both still in search of love."

"True." My mind turns immediately to Adam, and I have to force my thoughts back to the present.

"So," Allegra says.

"So. Want to stay and watch a movie tonight?"

"Yeah, that sounds cool."

"Great."

She stands up. "Can we, like, hug now or something?"

"It does feel like the appropriate time for a hug." We both laugh as we wrap our arms around each other.

"Okay, please tell me we're watching a chick flick."

"*Star Wars*, actually," I say, managing to keep a straight face despite her horrified expression. "I know how much you love the creepy little green dude."

AWKWARD. THAT'S THE ONLY WAY TO DESCRIBE THIS movie night. I'm sandwiched between Adam and Hugo, Salima is on Adam's other side, and Allegra on Hugo's. Adam's got his arms crossed tightly over his chest, as if trying to avoid physical contact with the girls on either side of him, and Allegra's leaning all over Hugo, who's now leaning on me as he tries to put some space between the two of them. All five of us are pretending to be fully engrossed in the chick flick Allegra picked out, which—oh, fabulous— is about to move into a sex scene I TOTALLY forgot about when I agreed to this movie.

"More popcorn?" I blurt out, jumping to my feet just as Adam leans forward and says, "Another drink, anyone?"

I meet his eyes for a second before he looks away, and I have to work hard not to laugh. Clearly Adam's seen this movie before—and he knows what's coming. I skip off to the kitchen to make popcorn while Adam takes drink requests. He joins me after a few moments, carrying empty glasses in his hands.

I place a bag of unpopped popcorn in the microwave as Adam takes clean glasses from the cupboard. I lean against the table as the popping begins, waiting for Adam to say something.

He says nothing.

"That was getting way too awkward," I say, attempting to lighten the atmosphere between us. "Let's hide in here until the sex scene is over."

Adam laughs as he pours Sprite into a glass, but it isn't his normal laugh, and I can see the tops of his ears turning red. Great. I think I just made the awkwardness worse. He fills a glass with water—probably for Salima—and adds it to the collection of drinks while managing to look everywhere except at me.

"Oh my heck." I drop into a chair. "I can't take this anymore." I point at him. "You. Chair. Now. Prepare for confrontation."

"W-what?" He seems too startled to sit, but he's finally looking at me, so that's good.

"We slept in the same bed for a night. SO WHAT. Yes, it was kinda weird, and your leg was on my leg, and we were sorta spooning, and I moaned 'cause I thought I was in my own bed stretching out, but NO BIG DEAL, right? So let's stop tiptoeing around each other and just get back to normal. Okay?"

His ears are burning even more now, and his cheeks appear to be joining the blush party. It's actually pretty darn cute, which is probably why I'm now wondering what it would be like to kiss him, even though most of my brain knows it isn't worth risking our friendship just to find out.

Friendship. That's the most important thing here. I don't want to lose that.

"Please?" I say. "I don't want things to be weird. I miss just hanging out."

He half-smiles. "It's only been five days, Liv."

"And what a TERRIBLE five days they were."

He lets out a long, slow breath. "Okay. You're right. We're just two friends who happened to fall asleep next to each other. It really doesn't have to be weird."

"Exactly. Oh! The popcorn!" The pops have slowed down to about-to-burn speed, so I jump up and hit the stop button on the microwave. I open the bag and empty the popcorn into a bowl, looking out for burnt bits. I sniff. No burning-popcorn smell. Excellent. "Do you think it's safe for us to go out there?" I say, hugging the bowl to my chest.

"I think so. Hugo just laughed." We head down the passage, me with the popcorn bowl and Adam practising his waiter skills with a tray of glasses. He nudges my arm with his elbow. "It was kinda funny when you moaned."

I press my lips together to keep from laughing. "If you mention my moaning to anyone, I will bring up the naked butt moment."

He fakes a terrified expression. "My lips are sealed."

I try not to imagine his lips—or his butt—as we squeeze back into our places on the couch.

Resume awkwardness.

Salima is the first to leave after the movie finishes. "That," she says, pointing towards my house as we stand beside her car, "is why I don't watch movies. It's all ridiculous romance stuff designed to tempt me into wanting a relationship with a boy who'll only end up distracting me from my studies." Then she leaves before I can explain that lots of movies aren't about ridiculous romance stuff.

The next to leave is Hugo, who gives some lame excuse about needing to pick up Lainey from somewhere when Adam reminds him they're meant to be playing Xbox now. We all know the real reason he's so eager to get out of here, though—Allegra. I want to smack her for being so snuggly with Hugo when he clearly wasn't interested, but I decide to save that until Hugo's left the house.

The door closes behind him, and I get ready to—

"I don't think he likes me," Allegra says immediately. "Did you get that vibe from him? I was just trying to be friendly and he kept shrinking away from me."

Adam rolls his eyes and heads back into the lounge with a sigh.

"Allegra," I say slowly. "You were being a little bit *too* friendly. I think you may have scared him."

"Oh."

"Yes. Anyway, do you want to stay a bit and play Xbox?"

She hesitates, then says, "Okay, so this is the part where I'd usually make up an excuse about a prior engagement I have that's way more fun and cool, but since we're doing the *real* friends thing … is it okay for me to say that I hate the idea of playing on an Xbox and I just want to lie on my bed and watch another chick flick?"

I smile. "It's definitely okay."

"Cool. Well, I'm off then." She grabs her handbag from inside the lounge doorway, and I open the front door for her. "Bye!" she sings as she runs down the steps.

I shut the door, then slowly wander back into the lounge. "So," I say to Adam. "Let's *not* do that again." I shiver—damn, that gust of air from outside was freezing—and rub my hands up and down my arms.

"Agreed," Adam says. He lifts his crumpled jersey from the arm of the couch and throws it at me before crouching in front of the fireplace and arranging a few logs of wood. "You girls can have your chick flicks, and Hugo can come over whenever Allegra *isn't* around."

Biting back the urge to say, "Ooh, the forbidden jersey," I curl up on the couch and pull the jersey on over my head. "I don't think Salima will ever watch another chick flick. That sex scene probably scarred her for life."

Adam shakes his head with a chuckle as he lights the fire. "You still think I should ask her out?"

"Oh." I rub my finger over a small patch on my knee that looks like it was a crumb of chocolate before it got squished into my jeans. "Well, it's up to you. I'm pretty sure she'll say no, though."

"Yes, I'm also pretty sure. I asked her last weekend if she's dating anyone, and she very firmly told me she doesn't plan to date while studying."

"You—oh." I force my expression into neutral. Wouldn't want to look too gleeful about Salima not being interested in dating Adam.

"Yes, so I'm guessing she's uncomfortable around *all* guys, and that it didn't mean anything when you mentioned my name to her and she blushed."

"Right. But, I mean, I'm sure there are other girls you could ask out. If you wanted to, of course."

"Yeah, I guess." He dusts his hands off and walks back to the couch. "I'm not really good at that stuff, though. Not like you."

I'm distracted for a moment by the sound of the rain starting up once more, but then I focus on what Adam said. "What stuff?"

"Well, you know, flirting and all that. I'd probably stumble over some embarrassing pick-up line, and I'd never see the girl again. I don't imagine you'd have that problem."

"Oh yes," I say with a laugh. "I am SUPER skilled in the flirting department. That must be how I ended up flashing half of Clifton when I was trying to be sexy."

"You—when—" The tips of his ears start going red again, but he laughs, and this time it's a real laugh. "You see? You can say that kind of thing without getting the slightest bit embarrassed. I can't."

"Of course you can." I throw one of the couch cushions at him. "You just need to practise. Come on. Hit me with your worst pick-up lines, and we'll laugh about them until you're not embarrassed anymore."

He sighs, but he seems to be considering it. "Okay, I've got one."

"Ooh, wait, wait. I'm not ready." I sit up and cross one leg over the other. "Okay, I'm sitting at the bar in Jazzy Beanbag, all alone, sipping on my drink, and you come up to me and say …"

"Hey there." His voice is low and sexy. "Is your name Wi-fi? Because I'm feeling a connection."

I fall back on the couch laughing. "That is so cheesy."

"Also," Adam continues, not breaking character, "I was wondering if your father's a boxer, because you're a total knockout."

I sit up, trying desperately to stop laughing. "Why thank you. You know, I'm not a photographer or anything, but I can picture you and me together."

Adam chuckles, then moves a little closer on the couch. He rubs a section of his T-shirt sleeve between his thumb and forefinger. "Feel that? That's marriage material, baby."

"Oh really?" I manage to say through my giggles. "You might want to keep marriage references till the third or fourth date. Wouldn't want to scare the girl away."

"Would this scare her?" Adam asks. He grabs my hand, holds it to his chest, and stares adoringly up at the ceiling as he says, "Our love is like dividing by zero. It cannot be defined."

I roll over, laughter erupting uncontrollably from me. "You cheesy maths nerd. You see? You can totally do this pick-up line thing."

Adam tosses a cushion at me. "Yes, because this is a ridiculous game, not the real thing."

"Okay, okay, be serious." I sit up and flatten my hands against my cheeks. "No laughing. Give me a real one."

Adam closes his eyes, sucks his cheeks in, and breathes deeply. "Okay." He opens his eyes. "Yoda one for me."

Giggles attack me again. "I said a *real* one, silly."

He stands up and holds his hand out to me. "Wanna dance? I can really put your inertia in motion."

"Ooh, dancing. That's a good one." I take his hand and let him pull me up. "Only if you know what you're doing, though."

"What's to know?" Adam says, putting one hand beneath my shoulder blade and holding my other hand up. "Just sway back and forth and add a few twirls and spins here and there."

"Man, this girl isn't going to know what's hit her," I joke, trying to keep myself laughing so I don't think about the romantic mood lighting and the soft pattering of rain and the fluttering in my chest.

Adam spins me out and pulls me back. "You," he says, ignoring the fact that I almost tripped over his feet when I curled back into his chest, "are hotter than the bottom of my laptop."

"Okay, that's quite funny." I twirl beneath his arm and—after losing our imaginary beat while trying to figure out where to put my arms—we end up in the same position as when we started. "Because I picked up your laptop at Jazzy Beanbag last weekend, and I almost burnt my fingers."

"Finally. A line you actually like." Our side-to-side swaying slows, and Adam seems to be making up for not looking at me all week, because now he won't *stop* staring into my eyes. "There's an eighth wonder in the world," he says, "and I'm looking at it."

I groan. "Are we heading back to cheesy land?"

Adam nods and smiles. "I think I need a map, because I'm getting lost in your eyes."

I try to laugh, but it comes out way too breathy. The atmosphere between us has changed, and I'm not sure how, but I *know* he isn't talking to some imaginary future girl anymore. He's talking to me.

He pulls me closer so that my cheek is against his shoulder and his lips are by my ear, and he softly says, "You must be a fourth or a fifth, because you're perfect." Then, without warning, he dips me down low and holds me there. "And even if there were no gravity on earth, Livi, I'd still fall for you."

And then he kisses me.

SHIVERS ZING ALONG MY ARMS, AND A FIRE IGNITES INSIDE me. I want to stay in this moment forever, suspended in Adam's arms, his lips pressed against mine. But then he swoops me back up, and I'm breathless and dizzy, and I'd probably fall over if he didn't catch me.

"Liv," he whispers, his hands moving to either side of my face. The way he says my name makes the fire blaze brighter inside my chest. I grab hold of his T-shirt and pull him closer. His fingers slide through my hair, and his lips graze over mine, gently, leaving tingles wherever they go.

Closer. I want to be closer.

My arms are around his neck now, and his hands are sliding down my sides and wrapping around my waist. We're pressed together, no space between us, and I can feel the wild thudding of my heart and his breath against my lips and his hands fisting in the jersey at the small of my back.

He moves backwards, and the next thing I'm aware of is the couch right behind him, knocking into the back of his knees, and me falling ungracefully on top of him as he goes down. My chin bumps his glasses, and we both end up laughing. But then I pull my knees up so I'm straddling him, and his hands find their way around my waist again, pulling me against him, and all the laughter is sucked from the room as I lower my lips to his. I run my tongue over his bottom lip, smiling against his mouth when I feel his breath quicken even more. Our tongues slide over each other, causing a heat explosion in my chest. His hands slip beneath the jersey, beneath my T-shirt, and an embarrassing moan escapes my lips as his fingers tentatively trace the skin just above my jeans.

His lips move away from mine, kissing my chin, my jaw, my neck. "I have … a confession," he whispers, his lips tickling me as they move against my skin. "I knew you were still next to me when I fell asleep last Sunday night. But I wanted you there, so I didn't wake you." He kisses my lips again. "And also—" he cups my face with both hands and waits for me to open my eyes and look at him "—I think it's incredibly sexy when you wear my clothes."

A smile grows slowly on my face. "No way. We had a major fight because I was wearing your jersey."

He closes his eyes and groans, which he probably doesn't realise sends my blood pumping even faster through my body. "That was mainly because I felt so guilty when I realised I *liked* seeing you in it."

"Well, you know …" I place my hands on either side of

him and lean forward until our faces are so close we're almost touching, and then I stop, because I like how it makes my heart race faster and his breath come quicker and the heat inside me burn hotter. "I don't exactly need it on right now," I whisper.

He swallows. "That's okay. Doesn't change how sexy you are in it."

I lean back. "Are you sure? It doesn't, perhaps, look a little more sexy like this?" I grasp the edges of the jersey and slowly, ever so slowly, pull it up. A memory of the bikini incident flashes through my mind, and I almost start giggling, but darn it, I WILL get the sexy move right this time. The jersey slowly comes over my head, and I drop it on the floor behind me as my hair falls around my shoulders.

I don't have time to gauge Adam's reaction before he's pulling my face closer and kissing me again, but I'm guessing I got the sexy move right this time. His fingers travel slowly down my arms, leaving a trail of goosebumps across my skin. Cold and hot. Ice and fire. I think I'm melting against him …

The doorbell rings.

I pull away from Adam so quickly I lose my balance and topple backwards, but he grabs my arm, and I end up landing on my side on the couch next to him. I scramble to a sitting position. "What the freak? Who would be here so late?"

"I … I don't know." He grabs a cushion. "Can you … see who it is?"

"What?" He wants *me* to open the door when we have no idea what kind of psycho could be standing on our verandah? "Why me?"

"Uh …" He looks at the cushion on his lap, his face turning red.

"Oh." I stand up, slapping my hand over my mouth to stop the giggles.

"Yeah, yeah, it's hilarious having guy problems. Just look out the window, okay?"

I move the curtain aside, peer out, and see Hugo's car parked outside our gate. I groan and pull the curtain shut.

"What is it?" Adam asks, standing up but still holding the cushion in front of him.

I take a deep breath to push the laughter down, smooth my hair back, and say, "You need to talk to Hugo about his exceptionally bad timing."

I walk to the front door and pull it open.

"Livi, hey. Uh, Adam's still around, right?"

"Yes." I step back, rubbing my neck self-consciously. I shut the door, then I run down the passage and into my room. I jump onto the bed, bury my face in a pillow, and squeal. When I can't breathe anymore and have to surface for air, I grab my phone. I think about calling Sarah, or sending her a message, but then I put the phone down. I want to keep this deliciously wonderful feeling to myself for just a bit longer. And I want Hugo to leave ASAP so I can have Adam to myself again.

When half an hour has gone by without Hugo leaving, and I'm bored of hugging my pillow and staring happily at nothing, I head to the bathroom to get my night-time routine done. Shower, teeth, contact lenses.

Now I'm SUPER sexy in my winter PJs, slippers and glasses—and Hugo's still here. So I get my phone out to send Adam a message, hoping his phone is in the lounge and not his bedroom. I want to type something cute and flirtatious, but I can't think of the right thing, so I end up staring at the screen until, a few minutes later, a message pops up with Adam's name on it.

Adam: I'm so sorry. Hugo might be here a while. Lainey drama.

Livi: Lainey drama? So they're officially together now?

Adam: No. That's part of the drama.

Livi: I miss you.

Adam: That's crazy. You just saw me ;)

Livi: It's not crazy.

Adam: It is. And you know what's crazier? I miss you more.

Livi: OH MY GOSH I just realised something.

Adam: What?

Livi: Adam Anderson kissed me ;)

Adam: I think I also just realised something …

Adam: I kissed Livi Howard, and she kissed me back ;)

Livi: *blushing*

Adam: Ok Hugo's starting to look at me funny. Should probably stop flirt-texting. Sleep tight, my princess.

Livi: xx

I wake up early. It's Saturday, and I'd usually sleep in, but my heart is bursting with happiness and I can't stay in bed a minute longer. I tiptoe to Adam's door, quietly open it, and look inside. He's fast asleep, and even though I want more than anything to slide under the covers and snuggle against him, I don't want to wake him up. I got up for a bathroom visit at 2:51 am, and Adam and Hugo were still talking in the lounge. I don't know when Adam eventually got to bed, but I'm guessing he needs his sleep.

Since I've got so much happy energy buzzing around my body, I decide to go to gym. I do a spinning class, and I'm feeling so energised, I don't even cheat. We get to the half-hour point—the point at which I usually feel like collapsing in a sweaty heap on the floor—the instructor tells us to turn the resistance up, and I TURN IT UP. My legs are like wobbly pudding when I get off the bike, and I have to cling to the rail when climbing down the stairs to the change room, but I sing to myself the whole way there, right up until the point I realise I didn't pack clean panties.

"Darn," I mutter to myself. Option one: shower here and put sweaty panties back on. Ew. Option two: shower at home. I pack everything back into my bag and zip it up. I'm definitely showering at home. I stop on my way out and order a smoothie, then sit on the edge of a couch drinking it and watch the news on one of the big TV screens. No point in rushing home when I'm almost certain Adam is still sleeping.

I stop at the shop and grab some stuff for a surprise lunch for Adam—I'm thinking an indoor picnic in front of the fireplace—since he'll be at work this evening, so I can't very well surprise him with dinner. Well, not that I can really surprise him with anything, since we live in the same house, but I'll make a plan.

By the time I get home, I'm shivering right to the core of my being. I'm still in my skimpy gym outfit, and the chilly air sweeping down from the mountain has long since dried the sweat on my body. Consuming half a litre of iced fruit before I left the gym didn't help either.

I carry my gym bag and shopping up to the door, fumble with my bunch of keys, and—

The door swings open, revealing Adam on the other side of it. Wet hair ruffled up, cheeks pink—probably from the hot shower he just had—and those glasses I love so much. I almost drop my bags and leap into his arms, but something in his expression stops me.

"Adam?"

"Your prince is here to rescue you," he says in a strange voice.

"W-what?"

"He even arrived on a white horse." Adam gestures behind me, and I look over my shoulder and see a sleek white car with tinted windows parked on the other side of the street.

"Um … what's going on?"

"You should be happy, Liv," Adam says. "This is what you've always wanted, isn't it? To be accepted by the right people." He lifts a shoulder. "Can't get more right than royalty, can you?"

"What … I don't …"

He walks past me down the stairs, then stops and looks back. "Oh, and Hugo's looking for a new place to live from next semester. I thought your room would be perfect. So you should probably start looking for a new home. Shouldn't be a problem for you, though. No doubt you'll be in a castle somewhere."

"Adam, what are you—"

He turns away without another word. I run into the house, into the lounge, and—

"*Carl?*" My feet freeze to the ground and my brain backfires.

Carl. In Cape Town. In my house.

Not computing.

I blink, trying to get rid of the image of him sitting on the couch.

It doesn't work. My German not-quite-a-real-prince prince, with his white-blond hair and those uncommonly dark eyes I used to dream about, jumps up from the couch and rushes over to me. His expression is joyful, hopeful, but all I can feel is my horror-filled stomach plummeting to my feet. "*What are you doing here?*"

"I got your messages."

"My—what? Wait." I run back outside, shouting for Adam, because this is all a stupid mistake, and if I could just talk to him … "Adam!" I yell. I reach the gate and look both ways down the road, but I don't see him. Maybe he ran, or maybe he developed a superpower and flew right out of here. Either way, he's gone.

32

Steaming hot water cascades over my head. It rids me of my shivering, but it does nothing to ease the shock of finding Carl here or the terror that I've just seriously messed up with Adam.

After realising he was gone, I ran back into the house, told Carl to give me ten minutes, then headed straight for the bathroom. I must have been in here at least twenty minutes by now, though. The hot water's probably about to run out. I twist the taps off, grab my towel, and rub my skin dry with far more force than necessary. Ugh! Why did Carl have to show up NOW and ruin everything?

I freeze as I hear the tinkle of piano keys. Did Adam come—

No. That's not Adam. Adam plays a thousand times better than that. Carl is the one at the piano, and I want to tear his fingers away from the keys. How dare he touch that beautiful piano that isn't his?

I get back to the lounge as I'm pulling a scarf tightly around my neck. Carl's still playing simple piano melodies, and each tone grates at my nerves. "Don't do that," I say, barely managing to keep myself from pushing him off the piano stool and onto the floor.

He swivels around and stands up. "My Alivia," he says, coming towards me. He always called me by my full name, and I used to love that, but now it makes me want to scream.

"Tell me again," I say, stepping back so he knows not to pull me into an embrace, "what you're doing here."

"Your messages. I—"

"What messages?"

"The emails. The ones you've been writing all year."

"Emails? Those emails weren't for *you*. They weren't for anyone."

His brow furrows. "But ... you sent them to my account."

"Yes—but—it was more like a Dear Diary thing. I was just ... sending my thoughts out there so they didn't have to be in my head anymore. I didn't know you were actually going to read any of those emails. You gave the password back to me, remember? When you broke up with me? I didn't think you could get into that email account anymore."

"Alivia." He smiles at me. A smile that tells me to stop being silly. A smile I want to slap. "Returning that password was symbolic. I had it memorised, of course."

"You—it—that password was sixteen random

characters! Why would you memorise that?"

He shrugs. "It wasn't too difficult. And thank goodness I did." He steps closer and takes both my hands in his. "My Alivia," he breathes, and damn that accent that always made me want to swoon at his feet. "I couldn't stop thinking about you. You were in my head, driving me crazy with your laugh and your beautiful smile and the memories of our secret kisses. Finally, last week, when I could take it no longer, I went back to that email account, daring to hope that I might find something there. And I did."

I close my eyes and groan. Why the heck did I ever think it was a good idea to use emails as a diary?

"You made me laugh with your stories, but my heart ached to see that you had found someone else to be with. And then, I am ashamed to admit, it soared when you told me it hadn't worked out with him. Alivia." He brushes his thumb along my jaw, and maybe it's his sexy accent or those mesmerising dark eyes, but I can't look away. "You told me you missed me. And that was when I knew I had to come."

I squeeze my eyes shut and find the strength to push Carl away. "No. You didn't have to come." I open my eyes and glare at him. "Why would you come all this way without saying anything to me first? And what about your *parents*? What about the *shame* you'd have to live through if everyone knew you loved me?"

"I'm so sorry I said those things to you. I'm so, so sorry I hurt you. I realised how wrong I was, that I couldn't live without you, and I told my parents. I told them everything. I told them they couldn't stop me—"

"Oh, great, I'm sure that went down really well."

"It did," Carl says, and, unlike me, he isn't being sarcastic. "Alivia, they like you. Don't you remember that?"

"Yes, I actually do remember that. I remember pointing it out to you, and you said, 'They like you taking care of their children, not marrying one of them.'"

He grasps my hand again, his eyes pleading with me. "I was wrong. I was so wrong. I thought they couldn't be open-minded, but they can. All this nobility stuff—the titles and everything—it doesn't mean that much anymore. There are those who want to hang on to it, and I thought my parents were like that, but ... they just want their children to be happy. And you, Alivia, make me happy."

This is all wrong. All mixed up. Why couldn't he tell me these things last year when I wanted to hear them?

"Remember all the things we whispered to each other late at night," Carl says. "Our glittering fairy-tale future. We can have that, Alivia. We can have it all."

I could have it all.

But then I think of Adam. I think of the TV episode marathons late at night. Our silly 'Guess the Composer' game. Playing music together and laughing over jokes only we understand. I love the way his hair sticks up even when he tries to get it to behave, and how his ears turn red when he's embarrassed. I love every princess name he's ever called me. He's the one I run to when things go wrong. The one I want to tell when something exciting happens.

How could I possibly *have it all* if I couldn't have any of that? If I couldn't have *him*?

"I'm sorry, Carl. I'm sorry you had to come all this way to hear this, but … you and I … it isn't going to happen."

"But … you said you missed me. And last year—all the things we spoke about—"

"Yes, that was last year. I was far from home and lonely and swept up in the whole secret romance thing. I would have given you my heart, but fortunately you were sensible enough to end things. I didn't think of it like that at the time, but I know now it was the right thing."

"No, Alivia, that's what I'm trying to tell you. It *wasn't* the right—"

"It was. I'm not the right person for you, and you're not the right person for me. The right person for me is … someone who's been in front of me the whole time."

Contempt fills Carl's eyes as he steps away from me. "That idiot you wrote about in your emails?"

"No. Someone I've known for much longer than that. Someone I … can't picture my life without."

Carl shakes his head and looks out the window. "I can't believe this," he mutters.

"I'm so sorry. You really should have contacted me before coming out—"

"Do you know how embarrassing it will be to go back to my parents and tell them this? After I begged them to let me have you?"

I raise an eyebrow. "*Have* me?"

His fingers tap a fast rhythm against his leg. A sign—if I remember correctly from watching him interacting with his parents—that he's about to lose his temper. "I think I should leave."

"Probably a good idea."

"My parents are expecting to see us both back at the hotel, but I suppose they'll just have to be disappointed."

"They—they're here?"

"Yes. Family holiday. Don't you remember me telling you about it last year?"

"So … you didn't come all this way just for me."

He makes an irritated sound and marches to the door. "Goodbye, Alivia."

"Wait, Carl?" He looks back. "That guy who was here. Did you … did you tell him about my emails to you?"

"Yes."

Ugh, no!

"He didn't believe me. Looked at me as if I were crazy and said I must be making things up—"

Oh, thank goodness.

"—so I took out my phone and showed him the emails."

"You WHAT?"

"Oh, I'm sorry," he says, not looking the least bit apologetic. "Is he the one you love? What a shame. I do hope I didn't mess things up for the two of you."

33

Adam doesn't answer his phone. Hugo answers his, but he hasn't heard anything from Adam. I knock on Luke's door to see if he might possibly know anything, but he isn't there. I know Adam has other friends—they've been over here a few times to play Xbox—but darn it, I don't know how to contact any of them.

I wander pointlessly from room to room, telling myself not to panic. This really isn't a huge deal. It's just a misunderstanding, and once I've explained it to Adam, everything will be fine. Right?

I try to play my violin. I try to get to that place where the music is the only thing that fills my mind.

I can't.

I can't stop seeing that look on Adam's face. *Can't get more right than royalty, can you?* But I can! *Adam* is the right one. But what if he doesn't believe me? Where will I go if he makes me move out? What if he doesn't even want to be *friends* anymore?

My phone rings, and I bellyflop onto the couch in my haste to get to it. Hugo's name appears on the screen.

"Hello?" I gasp before the phone even gets to my ear.

"Hey, Livi. So, uh, Adam's probably going to slaughter me for telling you this, but …"

"What? Whatwhatwhat?"

"I called him and he didn't answer. But he sent me a message just now saying he went for a walk and ended up at Rhodes Mem."

"Rhodes Mem? Like, way up at the top there behind the university?"

"Yes."

"Thanks, Hugo."

That's certainly a long walk. I grab my bag and keys and jump into my car. Then I have to stop at the end of the street and type 'Rhodes Memorial' into my phone's maps app because even though I kind of know where it is, I'm more likely to end up in Muizenberg than behind the university if I trust my own direction sense.

I get to Rhodes Mem in less than ten minutes. I park my car in the half-full parking lot, jump out, and look around. I was going to come up here during orientation at the beginning of the year, but Charlotte said it was boring and that we should rather hang out at Smuts where the view of the city is just as good and the view of the guys a *whole* lot better.

I've decided Charlotte is wrong. It's beautiful, this grand monument sitting on the lower slopes of Devil's Peak with its stairs and its pillars and its bronze horseman looking out over Cape Town. If I weren't so desperate to find Adam, I'd love to take the time to admire the architecture and the view.

But I am. *Very* desperate. And no matter where I turn or how many times I climb up and down the stairs and around the pillars, I can't find Adam anywhere. Somebody mentions a restaurant, and I hurriedly make my way behind the memorial to find it. But I scan every table, and still I don't see him.

He's nowhere.

I head back outside and sit down on the steps between the horseman and one of the bronze lions. I call Adam again, but his phone simply rings and rings until it switches over to voice mail. I end the call. I don't want to explain this misunderstanding in a message Adam may or may not listen to. I want to do it in person where I can be certain he knows *he* is the one I want, not the German guy who told me I'd never be good enough for his family or friends.

I stare at the city for a while, running through all the things I wish I hadn't done since I got here. I wish I hadn't made the wrong friends and dated the wrong guy and used an abandoned email address—that apparently wasn't so abandoned after all—as my online diary. Most of all, I wish it hadn't taken me so long to figure out how important Adam is to me.

When I've tortured myself enough with regrets, I walk back to my car and drive home. Adam isn't there.

I lie on my bed and eventually fall asleep.

It's dark when I wake up. I lie still for a while, listening for any noise in the house, but all is silent. I lean over and grab my phone from beside my bed. No message from Adam. No call. I take note of the time before dropping the phone onto my bed with a groan. It hasn't even been twenty-four hours since our electrifying, passion-filled kiss, and I've already messed things up.

Wait. Saturday night. Adam has a shift at Jazzy Beanbag. And he can't ask Hugo to swap with him, because Hugo's also working tonight. They were talking about it last night before we put that horrible chick flick on. *Yes!* I finally know where to find him.

I spend a few minutes in front of the mirror neatening my hair and putting some make-up on—I want to look nice for Adam—before heading out to the road. On second thoughts, perhaps driving is a better idea. Who knows what time I'll be leaving Jazzy Beanbag, and if I'll be on my own or not. As I've already discovered, walking the streets alone at night isn't the wisest thing to do.

I wait outside the door at Jazzy Beanbag for at least two full minutes trying to calm my nerves before going inside. I look around at the tables—students with their drinks, a couple sharing a snack basket, a group of ladies giggling over their salads and wine—but there's no Adam.

SERIOUSLY?

He must have swapped shifts with someone else. Maybe that guitar teacher lady. What was her name? Mel, I think. I don't see her anywhere either, though. Oh, crap, what if he's *with* Mel right now? I know she's older and everything—at least late twenties or early thirties—but maybe Adam likes that. Maybe after Jenna he decided he wanted someone more mature. Someone more mature than Jenna *and* me. Maybe *that's* why he seemed awkward every time I mentioned him asking a girl out, because he's already having a secret relationship with—

"Oh, hey, Livi." Startled, I look to my right and find Hugo stuffing a notepad into the front of his apron as he walks over to me.

"Hi. Is Adam here?"

"Uh …" Hugo's eyes move to the door behind the bar that leads to the kitchen. "He is. But … I'm sorry, Livi. He doesn't want to talk to you."

"So he's hiding back there in the kitchen?"

"Well, not hiding. Just avoiding you."

Which sounds like hiding to me, but I can't exactly judge him since I'm the one at fault here. "But … he has to come out eventually, right? I mean, he has tables to serve."

"And what are you going to do then? Interrupt him while he's taking someone's order? Chase him down on his way back to the kitchen?"

"If I have to."

Hugo hesitates, then says, "Probably not the best idea to make a big scene with the guy you're trying to apologise to." He squeezes my arm, then turns and walks to the bar.

Fine. *Fine.* If Adam doesn't want to come out here to listen to my apology, I'll make sure he can hear it no matter where he is. I huddle in a corner until the band on stage—Lainey's band—is finished playing their current song. Then I hurry over to Lainey's side of the stage and stand on tiptoe to whisper my plan to her. She seems doubtful, but when I start begging, she rolls her eyes and waves the lead singer over. He's clearly annoyed that I'm interrupting, but after I tell him my sad story, he gives in.

A minute later, I'm standing at the front of the stage behind a microphone with half the room staring at me expectantly and Hugo mouthing a horrified, *What the hell are you doing?* from the table he's supposed to be taking orders from.

I nod to the guitarist, who starts strumming the music for a recent popular song I've sung in the shower more times than I can remember. It's about a guy apologising to a girl for all the things he's made more important than her after she leaves him and he realises he made a big mistake taking her for granted. It doesn't exactly fit this situation, but it's close enough.

I swallow and grip the microphone with my sweaty right hand. My voice isn't terrible, but I don't enjoy singing solo in front of other people. I close my eyes and remind myself that this isn't about me, it's about Adam. And then I begin singing.

My voice is wobbly and weak, and I almost let go of the mic and run, but I focus my thoughts on Adam. This is for him, and if he accepts my apology, this embarrassing performance will be worth it. I remind myself to breathe the way my choir teacher taught me to breathe, and after another few lines, my voice evens out and grows in strength. I reach the chorus, which is easier to sing, and finally I'm brave enough to open my eyes.

I scan the audience as I continue singing, but Adam isn't anywhere. I know he can hear me, though. Why isn't he coming out?

Another verse.

The chorus again.

And still Adam hasn't shown himself.

I squeeze my eyes shut and belt out the bridge, pouring my heart into every word. Then it's the final repeat of the chorus, slowing down into the last two lines. I hold the final note as the guitarist's final strum reverberates through the room.

Then quiet.

As the clapping begins, I dare to open my eyes. My gaze combs the room, over the tables, the customers, the waiters—but I see no Adam.

I stumble away from the microphone in shock. I honestly didn't believe for a second that he'd leave me hanging here. He was supposed to run up onto the stage and take me in his arms and kiss me. Or walk out from behind the bar so I could jump down, run over to him, and apologise over and over again as he forgives me. Or, at the very least, stand behind everyone else where only I can see him, a smile growing slowly on his face as he realises this song is for *him*.

But he isn't here.

WHY ISN'T HE HERE?

TEARS SPILL FROM MY EYES AS THE DOOR TO JAZZY Beanbag swings shut behind me. Cool air soothes my burning cheeks, but the rest of my body feels the icy cold of rejection.

"So you come here," a voice says to my left, "and make a great big public declaration of love. Everybody claps for you, giving you the attention you so eagerly desire, and I'm supposed to fall back into your arms?"

I look down the sidewalk and see Adam leaning against one of Jazzy Beanbag's windows, his arms folded over his chest. "Adam. No, that's not—it was for *you*. I was saying sorry."

"And everybody else needed to hear that?"

"Well, no, but you wouldn't talk to me, so—"

"Because I wasn't ready to hear whatever your excuse is, Livi. But that didn't matter to you, did it. No, you'd rather belt your apologies out to a crowd of strangers for a round of applause than wait until I'm ready to talk to you."

"I … I didn't …" I look down at my feet as another few tears course down my cheeks.

"Well," Adam says, "since you worked so hard to get my attention, what is it you'd like to say?"

I sniff, swallow, and look up at him. "It's all a silly mistake, Adam. The messages Carl said I sent him—the ones he showed you—they weren't for him. They were just … it was just …" I try to figure out the best way to explain it, but there doesn't seem to be any good way. "It sounds dumb, but that was like my online diary. I didn't think he could get into that email account anymore, so I didn't think he'd ever read those messages. It was my Dear Diary. Just … my thoughts and feelings about … stuff."

"Really?" Adam doesn't look convinced. "If that's all it was, why didn't you use a *book* like any other girl?"

"I—I don't know. I just … opened up my email one day and … I don't know."

Adam shakes his head. "Maybe you believe yourself when you say you don't know, but I don't."

"I …" I run my hands through my hair and tug at it. Maybe I do know. Maybe I just never admitted it to myself. "Okay," I say, starting to pace. "Okay. Maybe at first I was doing it because, at the back of my mind, in that place where people keep their secret fantasies, I thought that perhaps somehow he'd see those emails and realise he made a mistake letting me go. And then he'd come along and sweep me off my feet and far away to a foreign castle where I'd live happily ever after like … like a princess." I whisper the last few words because they sound like a betrayal. 'Princess' is Adam's name for me, no one else's. "But I didn't really believe that," I continue quickly, "and after a while, it was just like writing in a diary. That's all it was, I promise."

"'Dear Carl,'" Adam recites, "'I miss you. If I asked, would you come and rescue me?' Yeah, that really sounds like you were talking to a diary, Liv."

I slump against the window with a groan. That one? Carl had to show him *that specific one?* "Yes, okay, I wanted to be rescued then. I'd just had drugs forced on me and my boyfriend groping me. I was dropped on the side of the road in the dark and the rain, and then I was running for my life because I thought someone was chasing me. I was feeling more miserable than I'd ever felt before, and I just wanted to GET. AWAY. It wasn't *him* I was missing. More just … the idea of someone who cared enough to come and rescue me from everything."

"And it didn't matter that *I* was right here taking care of you?"

"Of course it mattered! And after I wrote those words and clicked send, they were gone from my thoughts, just like everything else I ever wrote to that email address. Type. Send. Gone. That's what every one of those emails was about, I *swear*. And if you don't believe me … well, I don't really have anything else to say."

Adam stares at me for a long time. The seconds tick slowly by until eventually he says, "Okay. Let's say I believe you."

Yes. Please. One step in the right direction.

"That isn't the only problem."

"It—it isn't?"

"Livi …" He seems to be grasping for words like I was a few minutes ago. Eventually his hands fall to his sides and he says, "I don't know if I can ever be enough for you. I'll never be the hot guy. I'll never be the popular guy. I'll never be the rich guy. I'm just me, Livi. That's all I have to offer you."

"And that's all I want!" I step closer to him. "Just you."

"The thing is … I don't know if it is. The first thing you did when you got to Cape Town was change everything about yourself so you could fit in with the popular people. You hid your violin and the books and DVDs you love. You wore clothes I've *never* seen you wear before, and you changed your hair colour because your friend said it would make you hotter. Then when things went south and you decided the glamorous life might not be so great after all, suddenly I was good enough for you to hang out with again. Fast forward a few weeks: Allegra shows up, and now the two of you are *besties* again, and we're watching horrible chick flicks when I *know* you'd rather be watching something else. What's next? Are you going to abandon Salima because she doesn't fit Allegra's definition of cool? Are you going to be out every night of the week again, stopping by my room occasionally when you have nothing better to do?"

"No! It's not like that. She—Allegra told me all this stuff about herself that I didn't know. She said she's not interested in that popularity crap anymore. She wants real friends. She knows who I really am, I know who she really is, and we're happy with that. We're … it's not gonna be like it was before when I was out all the time."

"Really?"

"Really." I move closer to him and try to take his hand, but he steps away.

"I just … I don't know, Livi. I want to say yes to you. I want to *be* with you. But I can't help thinking that this is more of an … in-the-moment thing for you. That in a month or two you'll end up bored and want to go chasing after some hot, popular guy you saw in a club or on a beach, and then I'll be the one left with a broken heart. Because you know that place at the back of people's minds where they keep their secret fantasies? That's where I kept you, Livi. And if I finally get to make that a reality, I want it to last."

After one final pause, he steps around me and pushes through the door into Jazzy Beanbag, leaving me stunned and unable to move. "Is that a 'no,' then?" I whisper to the night.

I close my eyes and let tears tumble down my face. Adam's words replay in my mind even though I don't want to hear them again. I can't believe he thinks I'm that shallow. That fickle. After all this time, doesn't he know me better than that? Doesn't he know how much he means to me?

A message dings in my pocket, and I swiftly pull my phone out, even though the logical part of my brain *knows* it can't possibly be a message from Adam. It's from my mother, telling me to let her know when she can call again. I exit my messages and see that I missed a call from her twenty minutes ago. I tap the three numbers that will take me to my voice mail and bring the phone to my ear.

"Livi, darling, I have some exciting news. Dad and I will be arriving in Cape Town early tomorrow morning. I'll try you again just now so I can give you more details. We can't wait to see you."

35

From: Alivia Howard <livi-gem@gmail.com>
Sent: Mon 28 Mar, 0:39 am
To: Sarah Henley <s.henley@gmail.com>
Subject: Trying to think of something wacky, but I'm just not feeling it

Dear Sarah

My parents swooped in this morning for an impromptu visit. I've been selfish and preoccupied lately, and I kinda haven't been paying attention to what's going on between them. Things seem to be—as surprising as it sounds—much better. They hold hands a lot, which they've never done before, and when they laugh they sound genuinely happy. Apparently they've dealt with a lot of stuff over the past few weeks. Dad's affair was just the beginning of it. I guess they had a whole marriage of issues to work through—not that they gave me details, and that's fine.

They're heading off to Mauritius on Friday to spend some quality time together. Nothing work-related was allowed into their suitcases—a revolutionary concept for them. It sounds like they've still got issues to work through, but I think this holiday will be really good for them. Until then, they're staying in this Waterfront hotel, and, apparently, so am I. I'll be driving through way too much traffic every morning to get to campus, and in the evening I'll be dining in style at the Waterfront while bonding with my parents—also a revolutionary concept. (I'm glad it's only five days. I think we may run out of things to talk about before then.)

They told me they've been looking for a flat in Cape Town, and they think they've found the perfect one in Claremont. It's for them to stay in when they come and visit me—which they've decided they need to do more often after they spent far too much of my childhood ignoring me—but they want me to live in it until I graduate and get my own place. (Like I can even think of graduation right now. Passing first year is going to be hard enough, never mind second, third and fourth.) Good timing, I guess, since Adam's about to kick me out of the Toll Road house so his friend Hugo can move in ...

Missing you.

Seriously. Like, a LOT.

xx

P.S. Have you spoken to Adam in the past few days?

P.P.S. I messed up. I want to talk to you, but I'm too embarrassed to tell you about it because I know it's all my fault.

Being the amazing friend she is, Sarah phones me about three minutes after I click the send button on my email—even though it's almost 1 am and she probably only saw the email because she forgot to put her phone on silent. I burrow beneath my hotel duvet and tell Sarah everything. I cry a lot, and she tries to convince me that Adam *doesn't* hate me and perhaps he simply needs some time to figure out that everything I told him was true.

When we've said everything we can say, and my eyes are raw and scratchy from far too much crying, we say goodnight. I sniff into my pillow and prepare for five days of not seeing Adam AT ALL—a thought that makes my already cracked heart threaten to split open.

I sneak back into the house late on Friday evening after saying goodbye to my parents. A sliver of light shines from beneath Luke's door, but Adam's door is open, his room dark and cold. I stand in the doorway for a minute or so, my eyes traveling over the shadowy outlines of the tattered sci fi novels lined up on one side of the desk, the computer we've watched so many TV series episodes on, the shirt hanging from the cupboard, the folded music stand in the corner.

Then I close myself in my bedroom, spend some time writing a letter to Adam, leave it beside my bed, and fall asleep easily for the first time in a week.

My alarm wakes me early. I get up immediately, my heart already thudding in anticipation of Plan Steal Adam's Heart Back. I pull my heavy winter blanket off my bed and sneak past Adam's closed door to the lounge. I spread the blanket out on the floor, then arrange all the couch cushions around the edge. In the centre go all the goodies I got at the 24 Hour Woolworths last night: strawberries, blueberry muffins, mini yoghurts, fresh cherries—and baby tomatoes because Adam loves them. Finally, I add a packet of princess gums from the collection in my cupboard. Just for fun.

I hurry to the kitchen and turn on the oven for the croissants, then skip to the bathroom while the oven heats up. I brush my teeth and splash some water on my face, but I don't shower or do my hair or change out of my pyjamas. Adam thinks I'm too concerned about my appearance, and I'm determined to show him I'm not. If he wants the real Livi, that's what he's going to get—messy hair, PJs, glasses, and no make-up. This is, I realise with a smile, pretty much how I look every evening when we watch series together.

Once the croissants are heated, I have one thing left to do. I tiptoe back to my room, grab the letter I wrote last night, and stick it on Adam's door. No, wait, he probably won't see that. He'll open his door and walk out; he won't stop to examine the actual door. So I remove the letter and stick it on the outside of *my* door. I pull it closed, then stoop down to place the paper arrows I cut out in a trail pointing to the lounge. I leave the final arrow in the lounge doorway and scamper back onto the blanket.

Then I wait.

Oh! The fireplace! I forgot about that. It's been sunny all week, but the rain has arrived in time for the weekend. Others might be grumbling about the weather's bad timing, but I think it's perfect. My indoor picnic will be even cosier with a crackling fire right next to it. I just have to figure out how to get it going …

Ten minutes later, I've discovered I'm not such a girly girl after all: I can successfully light a fire! Indoors. With matches and wood and plenty of newspaper stuffed in between. Okay, so it's not exactly an impressive achievement, but I'm still fist-pumping the air because it's my very first fire.

I get up off the floor and go to the kitchen to wash my hands. I wonder how long it will be before Adam wakes up. Perhaps I should tap on his—

Wait, was that his voice? Yes. That's definitely him. He must be talking on the phone. Or—OHMYGOSH what if there's a girl in his room with him? A girl who stayed over last night? What if he—

No, don't be ridiculous, Livi. He wants you, remember?

I peek around the kitchen doorway into the passage and listen carefully. Adam's voice—a pause—Adam's voice—another pause. So he's on the phone. I think. Unless the girl in there has a really quiet—

Stop thinking that! There's no girl!

His door opens. Crap! I hold back a squeal and dash to the lounge before Adam can step out of his room and see me. I drop onto one of the cushions and instruct my thundering heart to slow down. It doesn't listen. I bring my knees up to my chest and hug them tightly. My eyes are trained on the doorway. I don't hear footsteps, but if he's wearing socks and walking slowly, then he probably wouldn't be making much—

Ohmygosh it's him. Standing in the doorway. Holding the letter up. And because I'm sitting on the floor and because of the way he's holding the letter, I can't see his face. I can't see his reaction.

My brain whizzes through the words I wrote at top speed.

Dear Adam,

You said that what I've always wanted is to be accepted by the right people. That's true. What's also true is that the right person is YOU. I made a lot of mistakes on the path to figuring this out, but now that I've realised it, I won't ever forget. You've always been the one. You were there every day at school. You were there every holiday when my parents didn't have time for me. When I was in a faraway country, you were always at the other end of an email. And this year, no matter how many times I've taken you for granted, you've been there for me.

Adam, I don't want the popular guy, the hot guy, the rich guy. I want YOU. Only you. And if you want me too … just follow the arrows.

Yours, if you'll have me,
Livi

Falling in love with Adam was something that happened slowly. I can't pinpoint the exact moment or day or week. But seeing him standing there in his boxers and hoodie with sticking-up hair, one sock pulled up to his calf, the other scrunched around his ankle, and his glasses just a tiny bit skew, my wildly beating heart falls in love with him all over again.

He slowly lowers the letter, and the moment I see that half-smile of his, relief and hope collide within me. Maybe I still have a chance. Maybe I haven't completely ruined things.

"Do you wanna, um, sit?" I ask. He crosses the room and sits on a cushion on the opposite side of the blanket. I slide my legs down and cross them. Then I pull them back up again. I fold my hands across the top of my knees. Then I sit on them. "This is so silly," I eventually blurt out, "because I've been thinking about you every second of every day this week, daydreaming of the moment when I finally get to see you again—even though it's only been a few days—and now you're sitting in front of me and … other than everything I wrote in that letter … I can't think of what to say."

Adam smiles and looks down at his lap. "I'll say something, if that's okay?"

I nod. "Please."

"I was happy to see your car here when I got home last night. Ridiculously happy, in fact." My insides begin to melt, and my breath comes out unsteadily. "I was so worried last weekend. You were gone by the time I got up on Sunday, and you didn't come back. I just … I thought I needed time to figure out if I believed you, and I thought you needed time to figure out if you actually meant everything you said. And then you didn't come back, and I realised I didn't need any time at all. Not knowing whether you wanted me or not didn't for one second change the fact that I wanted you. So I decided that even if you hadn't meant all the things you said to me outside Jazzy Beanbag, I was willing to beg you to mean them. To give me a chance to show you I could be enough for you."

"You are," I say, my voice coming out as a wobbly whisper. My legs slide away from my chest, and I crawl across the cushions towards him. I sit as close to him as I dare and slowly reach for his hand. He laces his fingers between mine, and shivers course up my arm.

"So it's kind of funny, I guess," he continues, "that while you were planning this—" he gestures to the picnic "—I was planning something else."

Now I'm really struggling to breathe normally. "Y—you were?"

He nods, then rolls his eyes. "It's the cheesiest cliché ever, but …"

"I don't care. I like cheesy."

"I kind of … wrote a song. For you."

He wrote a song. FOR ME.

"It's, um, not really finished, but …" He stands up and hurries from the room. When he returns, he's holding Hugo's Dad's guitar. He sits, crosses his legs, and places the guitar in front of him. I'm about to hyperventilate because this—the guitar, the socks, his concentration as he slides his hand up the neck of the guitar—is one of the sexiest things I've ever seen. "Okay," he says. "Hang on. I need more sugar so I don't pass out from sheer nervousness." He leans forward, grabs two strawberries, and pops one in his mouth.

A breathy laugh escapes me. "Don't be nervous. It's just me."

He chews and swallows. "Exactly," he says, and his face is flushed as he looks up and adds, "It's you."

I hug my knees again and bite my lip. Adam puts the second strawberry in his mouth, then repositions the guitar. He finishes chewing and takes a deep breath. "I'm not nervous, I'm not nervous," he mutters.

"You're not nervous," I whisper to him, hoping it'll help.

His right hand hovers above the strings for a moment, and then he begins. I close my eyes and breathe in the music, not only hearing it, but feeling it. Notes tumble over each other. I open my eyes so I can watch his hands, watch his fingers dancing across the strings.

He takes another breath and starts singing. His voice sends shivers down my arms, and now I can't look any-where but at his lips. Then I can't think of anything but kissing them. And I know I should be concentrating on the words—"... *all the smiles and all the tears ...*"—but I'm lost in his voice—"... *all the trials and all the years ...*" Then he dares to look up at me as he continues singing, and his eyes—his beautiful, bright, luminous eyes—capture me. I can't tear my gaze away. Heat climbs up my neck and towards my cheeks—

And then he stops. "It's … yeah, I know it's not perfect." He places the guitar on the floor beside the blanket. "But I was just trying to take everything you make me feel and put it all into one—"

The moment the guitar's out of the way, I launch across the cushions and pin him down. I kiss his lips and his chin and his nose and, after only about a second of surprise, he starts kissing me back. "Please …" I manage to get out between kisses "… don't ever … sing songs to anyone but me."

"I never have," he says before dragging his lips along my neck. He rolls us until somehow I'm underneath and he's above me, pressing his lips to my forehead. "The song at Jazzy Beanbag?" Another kiss on my nose. "It was for you." His lips find mine. His tongue, my tongue. Strawberries and toothpaste. It's an odd combination, but I don't care. All I want is more. "And all the cheesy pick-up lines," he says against my mouth. "They were for you too."

I laugh. "I know." I kiss his bottom lip. "I loved them." His top lip. "Especially the one about perfect fourths and fifths. Although," I add, pulling my head back slightly so I can look at him, "that one would only make sense to someone who speaks music jargon."

He gently pulls my left hand away from where it's wrapped in his hair and kisses each of my fingertips on the pads of rough skin produced by years of violin-playing. "Good thing I used it on my favourite musician girl then."

We're wrapped in each other's arms again, tumbling across cushions, and then I squeal because I just rolled onto a tub of something. "What did I squish?" I ask, leaning to the side and laughing.

"Yum," Adam says, looking at the back of my pyjama top. "Squashed tomatoes."

"Ew."

"You might just have to lose this article of clothing," he adds with a sly smile, his hands snaking beneath my top and around my waist. It's deliciously ticklish.

"Look at you," I say through my giggles, "casually mentioning getting naked without even a hint of a blush."

That turns the tips of his ears red, and then he's burying his head in my neck and saying, "Ugh, I'm terrible at this stuff."

"No! You are *so* not terrible, trust me. However, if you'd like to learn from the master—or, in this case, mistress …" I pause and frown. "No, 'mistress' definitely isn't right either. Let's go with expert. If you want to learn from the *expert*—" I lean around him and grab a cherry "—here's how to do it." I tilt my head back and hold the cherry over my mouth. I part my lips, then slowly lower the cherry. I grip it between my teeth, intending to seductively pluck it from the stalk. But it slips from my teeth and out of my fingers, rolls down my chin, bounces off my chest, and lands in the squished tub of tomatoes.

We both burst out laughing, and Adam covers my face in kisses. "You're right," he says. "You're also terrible at this stuff."

"Seems to be working on you, though," I point out. "So I must be doing something right."

"Definitely." His eyes soften as he stares into mine. He takes my right hand and presses his lips gently against the inside of my wrist. It's a kiss that gives me goosebumps and starts my heart racing all over again. "Everything about you is just right, my clumsy princess. I love you the way you are, and you don't need to change anything about yourself."

My heart skids to a halt, then races even faster. "Did you just say you love me?"

"Um …" Adam looks startled. "I guess I did."

My smile is practically taking over my whole face. "So smooth the way you just snuck that in there," I tease.

His ears are red, but he's laughing. "That's me. I've got all the smooth moves."

"I know." I pull him closer and skim my lips along his neck until I reach his ear. "I love you too."

VISIT

WWW.TROUBLESERIES.COM

FOR BONUS MATERIAL BASED ON
THE TROUBLE WITH FLIRTING

AND DON'T MISS OUT ON THE REST OF
THE TROUBLE SERIES!

THE TROUBLE WITH flying
ROCHELLE MORGAN

THE TROUBLE WITH flirting
ROCHELLE MORGAN

THE TROUBLE WITH faking
ROCHELLE MORGAN

THE TROUBLE WITH falling
ROCHELLE MORGAN

ACKNOWLEDGEMENTS

Here I am, trying to find the words to thank God for getting me to the end of another story, and all I can hear in my head are the words of *The Butterfly Song*. So thank you, Father, for making me *me*!

Thank you to the following people who helped make *The Trouble with Flirting* the story it is:

Mariska, for letting me use your gap year abroad as inspiration for Livi's backstory.

Rashmi, for reminding me how to play a violin.

Jasper, for the Afrikaans band names (*that* was fun!).

Tim, Nicola, Gavin, and Marcio, for the pick-up lines (that was even *more* fun!).

And Kyle, for being the inspiration for every happy ending I write.

Lastly, thank you to *you*, dear reader. I had so much fun writing Livi's story, and I hope you had fun reading it.

Rochelle Morgan is the contemporary romance
pen name of author Rachel Morgan.

Rachel spent a good deal of her childhood living in a
fantasy land of her own making, crafting endless stories of
make-believe and occasionally writing some of them down.
After completing a degree in genetics and discovering
she still wasn't grown-up enough for a 'real' job, she decided
to return to those story worlds still spinning around her
imagination. These days she spends much of her time
immersed in fantasy land once more, writing fiction
for young adults and those young at heart.

Rachel lives in Cape Town with her husband and
three miniature dachshunds.

www.rochellemorganbooks.com